CANNONBRIDGE

JONATHAN BARNES

WITHDRAWN

SOLARIS

First published 2015 by Solaris
an imprint of Rebellion Publishing Ltd,
Riverside House, Osney Mead,
Oxford, OX2 0ES, UK

www.solarisbooks.com

UK ISBN: 978-1-78108-296-6
US ISBN: 978-1-78108-297-3

10 9 8 7 6 5 4 3 2 1

A CIP catalogue record for this book is available from the
British Library.

Designed & typeset by Rebellion Publishing

Printed in the US

In memory of my grandmother,
Frances Prime

"Forgive me, my dear Colonel," said Miss Jewell with that species of sportive wit and provoking vivacity with which she had won her place in the affections and ambitions of every officer in the barracks, "but is not all life a mystery? Is not our very existence an enigma which we cannot hope to comprehend in full until that inevitable moment when our mortal days are ended?"

Plenitude by Matthew Cannonbridge (1842)

Eliphar, thou art intended as a sacrificial thing,
Created to toil and to serve
And never once to question your enslavement.

The Lamentation of Eliphar, Mununzar's Son
by Matthew Cannonbridge (1860)

The lease of Man is temporary and transient. There were terrible wonders before him. We may be sure that there shall be so again in the years to follow his superseding.

The Seasons of Sorrow by Matthew Cannonbridge (1875)

1816
THE VILLA DIODATI
GENEVA

Outside are storm clouds, rain and the gathering dark. Indoors are a company of five who, tired of other pastimes, of opiates and sex and wild transgression, have turned their attention instead to the telling of tales. Tonight, they talk of ghost stories.

Their leader, a slim, clubfooted man, is to be found, with the rest of them, in one of the villa's many rooms to have been devoted to pleasure, stretching pantherishly out upon a scarlet divan. Beside him is a pale, dark-haired girl who speaks but rarely and who gazes up at her companion with a dangerous obedience in her eyes.

Another couple is present, though they seem, perhaps, more evenly matched: a languid, dissipated man with a wave of curling brown hair, and his young lover, a girl of not more than eighteen, whose demeanour—shifting, watchful intelligence—seems to speak of the woman that she shall become. The last of this quintet is a plump, oily-skinned physician whose full, almost feminine lips quiver whenever (and he does this often) he pays cringing homage to their host.

Rain clatters upon the windowpane. In the distance, moving closer: the sound of a tempest, the mournful timpani of thunder. It is, of course, the man with the clubfoot who begins.

"Now then…" His manner is unembarrassed in its languorous theatricality. "Which of you has given thought to our challenge?"

He smiles a smile which, whilst fascinating and a thing that has enraptured many, is not a very pleasant smile nor one that evinces any warmth. It is not a smile that you would care to see were you, say, alone in his presence late at night or if he were to wake you in the early hours of the morning, a candle held in an outstretched hand, illuminating fitfully the cruel lineaments of his face.

No one answers. The girl beside him moves closer, nestling her soft, compact frame against his body. She breathes in his scent, half-sighing, half-shuddering, her expression, of giddy adoration, one which he seems scarcely even to notice.

"Percy?" he asks, already impatient.

The brown-haired fellow looks up. "Oh, yes. I fear I have not a notion. You must understand that I am more accustomed to the particularities of poetry than I am to those of prose."

From their host—a snort of weary disapproval. "Then you should play the game more fully. At least if you wish to remain our guest."

The poet looks uncertain at the slight, not quite knowing how to respond, wary of angering the clubfooted man. A second's hesitation, then a feudal lowering of his gaze, a bowing as buck yields to stag.

The clubfooted man purses his lips and arches an eyebrow. "Who else, pray? Who has some less disappointing reply?"

"I... I believe I have a story, my lord." This is the plump young doctor, the blood rushing to his fleshy cheeks, a sheen of sweat upon his forehead.

The face of the clubfooted man is a mask of haughty scepticism. "Dr Polidori?" His eyes flicker over to the other guests, seeking to forge some conspiracy between them. "Indeed? You must tell us more, my dear." Disdain in every syllable. Contempt in every word.

"My lord, I have been busying myself with the invention of a tale of the un-dead."

The man whom the doctor has called "my lord" seems, despite himself, to be quietly intrigued. "That does sound of some small interest. You may continue."

The physician swallows, perspires, wipes his upper lip. "I have in mind, my lord, a most beguiling nobleman..."

At this, the rest of the company exchange glances of dark amusement.

"Now, at first, when we, the reader, first encounter him, he seems quite human, does my aristocrat, my *Lord Ruthven*, but he is… not as other men. He…"

"Yes?" Taken by the physician's story, Percy, the young poet, leans forwards, while the woman beside him still seems far away, thinking of other things.

The rain beats more insistently upon the window. Thunder is heard again, louder than before. The storm approaches.

"My friends, this great man of mine is not, in truth, a man at all. Rather, he is a fiend… a drainer of blood… A *vampire!*"

Shrieks and cries of mock terror and delight.

Plump Polidori, now warming to his theme: "He pulls in men—and women also—with the irresistible force of his character, with his glamour, his romance. They all admire him. They all seek his company. Yet he has in mind for them just one thing—to drain them of their blood! He cannot know mercy. He is quite implacable. He is grown fat upon the nectar of his victims. And he lusts, he lusts for—"

"Yes, yes. Thank you, doctor. We also have had our fill now, I think."

Polidori attempts to continue but his interjection is waved peremptorily aside.

"Later," the lord hisses. Then, to the rest: "Has anyone conceived of some less lumpen tale? I asked for something to chill me—not for some absurd farrago fit only for the lowest fleapit of the East End."

Dr Polidori, crestfallen, if unsurprised, says nothing though he blinks too hard and too fiercely. There is a bottle beside him and a glass and it is with the decanting of the one into the other that he now occupies himself.

"My lord?" The watchful young woman is speaking—courteous, firm, wholly unafraid.

The host turns towards her, his manner coldly indulgent but also displaying an unexpected wariness. "Mary?"

"My lord?"

"And what have you dreamed for us?"

"I think you are correct, my lord, when you ask me what it is that I have dreamed for my story came to me at night, unbidden and in my sleep and as a kind of phantasy…" For a moment after speaking, the woman seems lost in thought.

"Quite wonderful. But you must go on, my dear."

"It concerns a man who, although he longs to be human, can never truly be so."

"And how can that be?"

"Because he has been *built* by man. He is, you understand, a… thing of artifice. He is created by dark arts in defiance of the laws of God. Stitched and darned by some doomed scholar, imbued with a grotesque mockery of life and set to wander blindly and with murderous intent throughout the world."

The clubfooted man draws in a long, slow breath. "Dear lady, you astound us. I think I can go so far as to say that your story may even have some trifling possibilities."

"Mary?" Her lover is looking at the lady somewhat strangely, as if she has not spoken to him of these peculiar fancies before this moment.

"What is the name of this poor creature?" asks the lord.

The storm is ready to break. The rain drums still harder on the windowpanes. There is thunder once again, almost upon them, every peal of it fiercer and more terrible than anything that has come before.

"He has no name. His creator denies him even that."

"The creator, then? What of he? What is this rash Prometheus called?"

"I know not from whence it came but I do believe him to be named—"

Before she can complete her sentence three loud knocks are heard—quite distinctly—upon the outer door.

At the sound, they all—even the lord—feel a spasm of intense disquiet. For a moment, nobody speaks. There are only the noises of precipitation, the feral growling of the storm.

It comes again—three further knocks.

The young woman who has, until now, stayed quite silent, clings to the lord's shoulder. As is not uncommon with her, hysteria seethes and bubbles in her voice. "Who is that, my love? Who is it who calls upon us?"

But the host's equilibrium is recovered swiftly. He shushes his pet. "Hush, my darling. It is someone from the village. That is all. Some beggarman or wayfarer. I shall see them off."

Pushing away the girl as though she were of no more account to him than the lowest animal, he stands briskly upright. "I shall see who calls upon us."

The girl again, wide-eyed and tremulous: "My lord, I fear for you. You ought not to go alone."

"You think not? Yet surely it is not me but our uninvited guest for whom you should feel fear? Still, I shall take another. If one of you wishes to accompany me."

No volunteer presents themselves.

Then, once again and for the final time, three knocks echo through the house.

"Don't be a goose," says the other woman, the tale-teller, stepping adroitly to her feet and striding towards the door. "Come, my lord, let us welcome our unexpected visitor." And she walks so firmly from the room that the man with the clubfoot has to struggle to keep pace with her.

The doctor, Polidori, calls out behind them: "Be careful, my dears. Be careful!"

Percy says nothing but only, troubled, watches the woman go.

Through the villa they stride, Mary and the lord—along corridors draped with ancient tapestries, upon stone floors which ring out accusingly at the sound of their footsteps, through many strange and singular rooms born of dark beauty and misspent wealth and ingenious perversity. Their conversation is sporadic and freighted with anxiety. As they pass from space to space, the sounds of the storm intensify.

"You seem ill at ease," remarks the clubfooted man as they pass a large, elaborate mural, filled with pictures of cherubs and nymphs, a line of athletic centaurs, the races intertwined in the most remarkable and inventive ways.

"I am curious as to the identity of our caller. Do you not share my sentiment?"

"I do. Yet you seemed to me to be ill at ease long before."

"Perhaps, my lord. I am unsettled."

"Your step-sister, perhaps? Her behaviour irks you? You are jealous of her privileges?"

"Her choices are her own. I have no dominion over her."

"Yet I assuredly do. And that irks you?"

"Not at all, my lord. In so many ways, the two of you strike me as a most excellent match."

They move through a place which seems to have been given over to the theatre—a small, abandoned stage, a flock of costumes, stacks of manuscripts and ancient books, the text of an unorthodox and even a scandalous kind. Outside, rages the thunder and the rain.

"Tell me," he urges. "What troubles you? Was it something about our game?"

"In that you may be right, my lord."

"Indeed?"

"I simply believe that the telling of tales should not *be* a game."

"You understand that I meant only to provide us with a little amusement?"

"Yes. But then all the world is a joke to you."

The lord gives no sign that he disagrees with her judgement. "Do you not believe it to be so?"

"I can see how you might form such an opinion."

"You choose your words with care, I think. Extrapolate."

They walk through the theatre, into a library, an antechamber and out into the main corridor of the house. In the distance: the outer door, heavy and fortified.

The woman's words are hurried, as though the swift speaking of them may serve to hide their meaning. "Your position, my lord. Your power. And, above all, your money. These things protect you from the truth of the world."

The man does not reply but merely steps rather clumsily onwards, as though concentrating now to the exclusion of all else upon the feat of forward motion.

At last, they reach the door. Although they have heard no further knocks—and for all that they know the visitor may have departed—both can sense the presence of something that does not truly belong on the other side, something waiting which ought not to be there at all. As they open the house to the storm, the woman and the lord dare not look at one another.

Outside, drenched and framed by the glowering sky, his arrival heralded by another clap of thunder, stands a stranger. Black-clad, dark-haired, his face lean and intelligent, his eyes a penetrating shade of blue, he seems almost to have been brought to this place by the storm itself. Although kindly in his manner there is even now, even at this, the earliest of all known phases, something about him—some dormancy, some potential—which makes the couple step, instinctively, half a pace backwards.

In spite of the tempest, the stranger smiles. "I was expecting servants."

"The servants have fled, sir. Appalled, they said, at our depravity."

The stranger's smile does not falter. "You must be Lord Byron."

The object of this observation nods crisply.

"And you—oh, I know your name. You are Mary."

"Do I know you, sir?"

"Not yet, I fear. And I hope that you'll forgive me for arriving unannounced and without an introduction."

"What do you want?" asks the lord.

"Only shelter. For tonight. Nothing more. Shelter from the storm. And perhaps a little company. I can recompense you handsomely for both."

"I have no need of money."

"I did not speak of money."

"No?"

"I have heard (I cannot at present recollect where or from whom) that tonight you tell tales. Stories meant to curdle the blood and to quicken the beatings of the heart."

Byron inclines his head. If he is surprised, he takes pains not to disclose it. "That is so."

"Then I've come to help. To contribute, if I can."

"Indeed?"

"As chance would have it, I know just such a story—the most terrible, and I would warrant, the most chilling of them all."

He smiles again and this time neither of them can resist the force of it.

Deafening thunder. Torrential rain.

The stranger, soaked yet resolute: "My lord, the storm is quite unrelenting."

"Then come in," says Byron and how odd it is, how very odd, to hear that curious note of deference in his voice. "And be right welcome."

"Forgive me," says the girl, "but I did not hear your name."

"I did not give it." The stranger glances behind him, somewhat nervous all of a sudden, as though he suspects himself to have been followed, as though some shadow dogs him. But, almost at once, uncertainty fades and the smile comes again. "My name is Cannonbridge. It is Matthew Cannonbridge."

"Then pray come in, Mr Cannonbridge."

And the dark-haired man, invited, steps inside.

For a long time to come, Mary will tell herself that it was all coincidence—how lightning struck close by at the very moment when the stranger crossed the threshold, how in that instant she should herself have felt a tremor in her heart as if she were suddenly unwell and how (and this, she will tell herself over and over, must surely have been her imagination) she seemed to hear, quite distinctly, though she knows it to be impossible, the infant having died some fifteen months beforehand, the desperate, mournful weeping of her child.

NOW

TWO HUNDRED YEARS later—give or take a couple of months—and the mind of Dr Toby Judd is also filled with thoughts of Matthew Cannonbridge.

Judd is standing in the furthermost carriage of the 18:12 from Waterloo, coming home from a day of prickly meetings and academic brouhaha at the premises of his employer, the University of Draye. The train is full—more than full—and its passengers are sour and restive. No seat, of course, for Toby. He's standing up with a dozen others, squashed against the windowpane, wedged uncomfortably between a pot-bellied man in a suit who holds a paper bag of McDonald's (from which he pulls item after item—nuggets, French fries, beef patty, onion rings) and a slab-faced woman in late middle age who has a mobile phone clamped to her right ear and into which she is bellowing orders of baffling specificity.

Toby is a small man—just over five feet, slim, bespectacled, unassuming—and, in this instance, he resembles a shrimp between two sea beasts. He holds out before him, angled awkwardly against the glass, a tubby paperback, the cover of which proclaims its title to be *Cannonbridge: A Celebration of English Genius*. It is illustrated by a reproduction of an etching—that famous, saturnine profile—and, affixed to the slick card is a round red sticker which reads 'Matthew Cannonbridge: WINNER of the Waterstones Poll to find the Nation's FAVOURITE Writer'.

Its back cover is taken up by a sepia photograph of the author of the piece: an intense, hawkish-looking man, not more than forty and in possession of enviable cheekbones. His smile reveals suspiciously perfect teeth and his name (printed on back, front and spine) is Dr J J Salazar—also, as it happens, a Draye employee, albeit of a starrier kind than Dr Judd.

Toby has just reached the end of a rather lurid chapter concerning the earliest known Cannonbridge sighting—by the shores of Lake Geneva and in distinguished company, the first recorded appearance in history of that extraordinary man—when a slip of paper flutters from between the pages and glides towards the ground. He bends over to retrieve it, an action which seems to cause the goliaths on either side of him to recognise his presence for the first time. The woman interpolates a single "tsk" into her stream of recondite commands, whilst the man, slowing his ingestion momentarily, glances down at his smaller fellow traveller and stifles, almost wholly unsuccessfully, a belch.

The paper, in Toby's hands again, turns out to be mere publicity material—something to do with the Cannonbridge Gala, due in eight weeks and set to represent the acme of the nation's bicentennial celebrations. Scrumpling up the flier, Toby slides it into the pocket of his jacket (his favourite, made of blue cord and better suited, after fifteen years of almost daily use, to the undiscerning charity shop, the fabric reclamation centre). As he straightens, he glimpses the almost-empty first-class carriage beyond and sees there, in one of those coincidences which although not uncommon in life would be dismissed out of hand in fiction, sitting in an aisle seat, his legs stretched out before him with lordly indifference, Dr J J Salazar.

Salazar holds in one hand not a book but a sleek, black tablet from which he is reading. Whatever these words may be, they cause a flicker of ironical amusement to play about his lips. Alerted by some sixth sense, the author turns and catches sight of Toby. That smile intensifies. He waves. Toby considers pretending not to have seen him but, deciding that it's probably too late now for that particular gambit, attempts to wave back. His arms are constricted and he ends up succeeding only in jostling the giant flask of cola from which his neighbour is slurping, an action which earns Toby another look of furious disapproval.

Salazar, witnessing all of this from the security of his first-class booth, nods once and smiles, affecting the kind of expression with which he favours certain of his students—an adult tolerance of the gaucherie of youth. Toby looks down at his book, remembering too late just what it is that he is reading. But Salazar has already seen and at the sight of his own face gazing back at him, his smile (or so it seems to Toby) grows broader still. Those remarkable teeth (almost American!) gleam and shimmer in the early evening light.

What little appetite he had for the book now having dissipated, Toby passes the rest of the journey by gazing out of his little patch of window. The train passes at speed through the cat's cradle of Clapham Junction, after which the sprawl of the city—its black, concrete complexity—begins to recede and the suburbs start to impinge. Through Earlsfield, Wimbledon, New Malden, Surbiton and on towards Ashbury, the excesses of London, her grime and savage energy, are overtaken by the apparent placidity of her outlying districts—by quiet and patient streets, by the increasing preponderance of green spaces. Not quite the city nor yet the country either, the train passes into those liminal, well-mannered states which thrive discreetly at the borders of metropolises.

Eventually, it pulls into its first stop. Toby has never ridden on the service for any longer—it ends up, he believes, in Portsmouth and sometimes he imagines what it would be like to stay on board the train until that terminus, picturing cool, invigorating, salty air, the shriek of seabirds, the distant honking of ferries and liners, chips by the seafront, bracing afternoon walks beside the ocean. But today, like every other day, he does not wait to find out. The doors open with a whoosh which, had the train been human, might have sounded like relief.

Judd and his companions step out onto the concourse. The big man, having finished his sack of fast food, stares mournfully into its depths as if in the hope of spying some neglected crumb, while the woman strides swiftly away, the stream of orders now overtaken by a catechism of what sound like expressions of endearment and assurances of affection. Whether the interlocutor is the same as before, Toby cannot say.

There is the usual, urgent rush towards the stairs which lead out of the station and Toby lets himself be caught up in the flood, succumbing to the seductive momentum of the crowd. He is swept along with the herd of his fellow commuters, down the platform, up the stairs and out the station exit, towards the cab rank and the car park and the high street beyond.

Free of the mob, pausing for breath, Toby notices with surprise that J J Salazar has also alighted from the train, here, in Ashbury, in Toby's town, where he can surely have no proper business. Salazar is waiting halfway along the line for taxis, his face set in an expression of good sportsmanship, like a movie star trying out self-deprecation on a talk show or a politician at the kind of photocall which involves some slight risk of appearing foolish but which his people have assured him will make him seem approachable and everyday.

Toby considers passing by without speaking but, his curiosity getting the better of him, he walks over to the author and taps him on the shoulder, a part of the other man's anatomy which is, approximately, level to his own head.

"J J?"

The tall man turns and smiles, a little vaguely, as if the name of the newcomer might at any moment dart away from his recollection like a salmon in the stream.

"Toby! This is a coincidence."

"Isn't it?"

"Good to see you earlier at the University. Sorry we didn't get a chance to chinwag. There's always so many people at those meetings and—you understand—one has to prioritise."

Toby keeps his expression as neutral as he can. "Of course." He breathes in slowly. "We've not seen you for a while. Been enjoying your sabbatical?"

"Sure. Sure, Toby. Yeah. It's been a lot of hard work. Mostly this gala thing. And all the publicity around the book. God knows why, but it really seems to have caught people's imagination. Man, but the media have just picked it up and run with it."

"Well... Congratulations."

"Cheers. I see you've got yourself a copy."

"I have, yes."

"That's cool. Hope you're not finding it too much of a primer. Of course, it's meant really for a big, popular audience. Just a nice, lucrative mass-market thing. Though I reckon I've unearthed a few tasty new facts. Cannonbridge is one of your own areas of interest, isn't he?"

"One of them, yes."

"I've not had a chance to read you on him yet, I'm afraid. Well, you know what Cannonbridge studies are like—*such* a competitive field. I was especially fortunate, of course—what with earning the blessing of the estate and being allowed to riffle at will through that fabulous archive in Edinburgh. As you know, they're normally pretty strict about who they let in there but... well, I'm just very grateful for such terrific opportunities."

A taxi arrives, a black cab, its yellow light ablaze. A woman at the head of the queue gets inside and the line shuffles forwards.

"Forgive me for asking..." Toby begins.

"Yeah?"

"What brings you to Ashbury?"

"Visiting a... dear friend. And you?"

"I live here."

"You do?"

"I do."

"Well, good for you." Was that a smirk, Toby wonders? "I mean... why not? Why wouldn't you want to live in a place like this?"

"I'd better get going. My wife will be waiting."

"Of course. Yes. I'm sure she will be."

The two men shake hands. The line moves forward again, Salazar now one space away from his ride. Toby nods farewell. Turning from the station, without looking back, he begins the familiar walk towards home.

There isn't much to see in Ashbury, little to recommend it to the traveller. A high street, the station, a couple of pubs and as many dusty, echoing churches, a single café, (called, with bourgeois archness 'The Pantry'), an Italian restaurant run by a couple who've never been to Italy and, inevitably, plenty of chain outlets, watching, with crocodile eyes, their dwindling independent rivals. But, mostly, Ashbury is just street after street of neat terraced houses, of still and silent roads, of homes with small, well-tended gardens and clean tarmac drives. All is solemn and uneventful and tame.

It is towards one of these streets—largely indistinguishable from the rest—that Toby trudges as the station recedes behind him. His destination is another nondescript house in another sober avenue: Number Forty-Three, Akerman Road. As the house comes into view, he sees that the lights are on and that his wife is home and at these realisations Dr Judd feels a little upswing in his heart, an understanding of his own good fortune which suddenly renders all the petty irritations of the day of no significance whatever.

Approaching home, in sight of happiness, he is reaching into his pocket for keys when he notices something unexpected and not altogether welcome—a black cab idling, its engine growling, opposite the house. The driver he has not seen before but the passenger is immediately familiar.

Judd stops short and considers crossing over, asking Salazar what it is he thinks he's doing loitering so close to Toby's home. But, lacking the requisite energy and figuring, in any case, that to beard a colleague in such a way might come across as overly cranky, he simply walks on by, inclining his head slightly to one side so as to avoid eye contact. Toby's last thought as he slides the key into the door of Number Forty-Three is that Salazar's friend must live on Akerman Road, a detail that proves to be oddly disagreeable to him.

He closes the door and calls out. "Hello! Sweetheart!"

"In here." Caroline sounds nervous and on edge.

Toby strolls through to the house's tiny sitting room, with its walls lined with books, its ancient sofa and too-big TV, its framed prints, its rugs brought back from inexpensive foreign holidays.

She's a small woman, Caroline, curvaceous, with dark hair cut into a 1920s bob. She's dressed as if for an evening in town with a friend she hasn't seen for ages—a summer dress of dark green, both practical and stylish, showing a little but not too much of her pale, freckled skin. As Toby enters the room, she's getting to her feet. Beside her, he sees that there is a single suitcase—the one he bought last year after its predecessor had been lost—the bulging contours of which suggest that it has been filled to the very limits of its capacity.

"Hi." There is a look on her face he's never seen there before—equal parts guilt, pity and deep, slow-burning anger.

"Are you… going somewhere?"

She lowers her head, not quite a nod yet no denial either. "You must have known… That this has been coming for a while."

"Known what?"

Pity is uppermost. "Come on, Toby." Now anger. "Come on. Surely you can figure it out. Why don't you… Yeah… Why don't you make one of your famous *deductions*?"

Toby takes it all in then, perhaps for the first time. He inspects each element: the dress, the look, the bulging suitcase, the man with the cheekbones in the cab outside. He forges connections and fits his theory to the facts—a process which, in other circumstances, he would certainly have found enjoyable—before, in a rush of cognition, he arrives at the only possible conclusion. "I… had no idea."

A flicker of sorrow before the pity returns. "You must have done."

"No. No. None. And—"

"Yes?"

Outside, a car horn, loud, mocking and insistent.

"For him? Really? I mean—sweet Jesus!—for *Salazar*?"

THE PLEASURES OF Toby's life might, until this point, be itemised as follows—literary, of course (since boyhood), gastronomic (red meat and chicken wings; Indian; Italian; Thai), erotic (though not with so great a frequency or with the diversity that he might have wished) and even narcotic (on three or four occasions without any urge for revisitation). But alcohol has never been a particular friend of his. He has drunk socially, of course, but in moderation, not feeling the need that he has heard about from others for inebriation and for its concomitant boons of softening and forgetting. He can count on two fingers the number of times that he has ever vomited from over-indulgence and he has not been truly drunk since the Sixth Form when, in the company of friends and hoping to impress Alison Cartwright from the year below, he'd made a fool of himself with a crate of supermarket cider in a garage that had belonged to the family of a classmate. Tonight, however, once the front door has been opened and then closed again, once the taxi has moved grumblingly away and the house is still, Toby sets to drinking in earnest.

He drinks everything that he can find. A bottle of screw-top red wine. A can of gin and tonic bought on a whim at Waterloo a month ago and its partner, one of cola and rum. These things dealt with swiftly, he moves on to obscurities—a miniature whisky bottle purchased as a Christmas present for an uncle who'd died before the day, a single bottle of continental lager given to him by a friend he didn't really see any more with a name that was unintentionally rude in English, half a bottle of raki brought back from a holiday on Crete, found not to taste so good after all, not away from the sunshine and the sea, and, finally, a rotund bottle of whisky cream acquired as a necessary constituent of some long-devoured supermarket offer. It is sickly and cloying with an aftertaste that burns, although by the time that Toby gets to it, the last of the alcohol in the house, none of this seems to matter anymore.

Halfway into this ultimate bottle, he is seized by a sudden desire to be outside, away from home. So, whisky cream in hand, he leaves, slamming the door behind him with an unneighbourly flourish and stepping out into the night. It is dark and Ashbury is silent and sleeping, its streets empty as in some science-fiction film in which the human race has been eliminated at a stroke. Toby glances at his watch—the hands of the device swimming a little before him—and sees that it is just gone midnight. He turns left and starts to walk into the heart of suburbia, soon becoming lost. Both streets and time seem, in his condition, to be in flux, ebbing and flowing around him, dream-like and unnatural.

The experience is not altogether unpleasant. He feels numbness and an agreeable floating sensation. Grey roads unspool before him. In the warm, thoughtful light of the streetlamps his shadow stretches out. He passes few cars and fewer pedestrians and, happily, nobody at all whom he knows. Occasionally, a cat or a fox crosses his path. Such creatures pause for an instant, seeming (to him, at least) to give him a sympathetic look before scampering away into the shadows. Once or twice, Toby feels an almost overwhelming desire to sing as he walks but, mercifully for the people of the town, this urge he succeeds in quelling.

There are moments of darkness—blanks in the evening's chronology. Several times he finds himself in a new and unfamiliar road or standing on somebody's driveway or peering up at a lighted window with no memory at all of how he has got there. In such situations, he merely swigs piratically from his bottle and moves on, each slug making him feel both a little better and far, far worse.

He must have been walking for more than an hour when, after another short period of near-unconsciousness, he finds that he is sitting down. The chair or bench feels curiously unstable, as though he has somehow gone to sea, and, at first, he is inclined to blame the alcohol until, the significance of his surroundings impinging gradually upon his sodden senses, he understands that he is sitting on a swing.

It is a swing meant for children. A deserted playground. Toby looks around and takes all of it in—those swings and that slide, the climbing frame and the roundabout, everything painted in primary colours yet dulled and made melancholy by the night. He starts to move to and fro a little but, rapidly feeling unwell, soon stops and rights himself.

He reaches for the bottle but cannot find it. Mislaid, perhaps? Or else abandoned on his journey. Feeling at a loss he gazes ahead at the wall opposite, to which a basketball hoop is attached. As he takes in the lines of regular red brick he feels, unexpectedly, a sob—the first of the evening—swell within his chest and break, leaving him with a single, moist moan. Alarmed, even slightly sobered by the sound, he bites his lower lip and strives to think of other things. He feels a weight in the pocket of his jacket.

The bottle? No—reaching down, he realises that it is only a book.

Salazar's book.

He takes it out, flips over to the back cover and looks, for as long as he can bear it, at the smart, groomed face of the author. Incredulous once again, he shakes his head.

He starts to turn the pages, his disbelief increasing. Written for a popular audience in the manner of a don slumming it on a teatime magazine show, the writing is awash with cliché and has no discernible ambition beyond offering feeble synopses of Cannonbridge's most famous works and dramatising, with hagiographical solemnity, the flashpoints of his long, his improbably long and many-textured, life.

It starts to rain. Warm summer rain. Droplets fall to the paper like tears.

Toby Judd looks up again and stares once more at that brick wall. There is something there he sees now, something that has been troubling him—something not quite in the right place.

Is it just his imagination or does one brick seem darker than the rest?

He goes back to his book, turning page after page, tutting at the predictability of it, not caring about the damage that the rain is doing to the pages, but urging it on. Salazar's lazy phrases multiply before him: 'the greatest,' 'the most gifted', 'belongs to the ages', 'literary rock star', 'national treasure'.

The rain intensifies. The wall troubles him still further.

That one brick, he sees now, that one brick in particular, does not seem to belong.

Toby reads on and the titles of Cannonbridge's novels and plays and poems, flutter before him—*The English Golem*, *Ezekiel Frye*, *The Seasons of Sorrow*, *Plenitude*—then the list of all those who knew him, Dickens and Collins, Byron and Wilde, Polidori and Arthur Conan Doyle.

All at once, something seems to bother him about those stories which has never—at least not consciously—bothered him before.

It's too neat, he thinks.

It's too... schematic.

Even, yes—*too contrived*.

In fact, the names of Matthew Cannonbridge's fictions sound more like the fruits of a single afternoon's work than the output of a long (a fantastically long) literary career.

He looks again before him—at the darker brick.

It's a downpour now. Seized by a desire to know for certain, Toby gets up and strides—or, more accurately, he weaves his way—across to the wall. His hands reach out in the darkness for that one, troubling brick. His fingers move closer and closer... and touch something soft and slimy and wrong. He jerks away his hands with instinctive disgust.

Then, warily, peers closer.

Paper. Old, damp paper stuffed into a hole in the wall. He understands then that it was only ever the darkness which had made it seem like a brick at all.

Back he goes now, enlightened, Toby Judd, back to his swing and to the book that is growing fat and swollen in the deluge.

The brick and the book.

The brick. The book.

The brick.

The book.

He feels a kind of swelling in his head. More than a mere ache, more than some preliminary hangover. No... this, he thinks, this must be something else. It must be understanding. Realisation. Epiphany?

Newton beneath the apple tree. Darwin in the Galapagos. Archimedes in his bloody bath.

And now... can it be? Toby Judd in a children's playground with a brick made of sodden paper?

What might some neurologist see at this moment were the brain of Dr Judd to be subjected to a scan? What strange leap of particles? What dizzying surge of mental electricity? What fantastic, unprecedented mutation of thought?

Half-energised, half-nauseous, Toby looks again at the picture of Matthew Cannonbridge, that dark, handsome, saturnine old devil.

He looks at the list of his works, at the man's extreme longevity. He considers everything he knows, everything he's ever been taught—and accepted, largely without question—about that individual and all of his works—and, in a single, shining moment—he dares to reject it all. Making his second, more complicated and still more terrible deduction of the day, he comes to the following conclusion, spoken, defiantly, aloud: "This is bullshit."

And again, with more volume, not caring about how it might look, a drunk by the swings at night, quarrelling with the rain: "This is *bullshit*."

He realises then that he is being watched. A handsome, thick-pelted fox is observing him from over by the roundabout. Toby directs his subsequent thoughts to the animal who, oddly, neither turns nor flees at the attention.

Judd sees it all. "Cannonbridge is a delusion."

The fox's ears twitch as if in understanding or encouragement.

"Cannonbridge is a lie."

The eyes of the creature seem to gleam in pleasure and in pride.

"Cannonbridge has been *made up*."

Finally, understanding hits Toby like a blow and he finds himself staggering back, having to work hard to keep his balance. "But…" Gasping. Short of breath. "How? A fantasy on such a scale. *Why?*"

A second, keening sob escapes him. The last of the night.

When he recovers, the course of his life now changed forever, Toby lifts his gaze once more and sees that the fox has vanished.

1820
THE FULLWOOD ROOKERY
NORWICH

THE PLUMP YOUNG doctor lies in the gutter, gazes up at the night sky with ravaged eyes, and braces himself for the attack to begin again. He manages a long, rattling breath through teeth which feel looser than they ought. Every part of him aches. He just has time to blink once more before he is kicked hard in the stomach.

There are four of them. Four very big men, all muscled and thick-waisted, all with a lazy, heavy-lidded artistry to their violence. They take turns to kick him hard and with a sober relish. He submits, tries to arch his body in such a way as to minimise the damage.

He has learned by now, of course, not to inflame them by crying out. The thugs say nothing, engrossed in the execution of their task with all the furrowed intensity of children at play. Everything takes place in a curious state of silence.

The doctor closes his eyes again and tries to imagine himself far from here, far from these narrow walls, this stinking alleyway, this quartet of men and their awful expertise.

Another kick. Another. The sound of splintering bone. At this, he cannot help but loose a little whimper. The sound of it seems to cheer his attackers and the next intersection of boot and skin seems to be arrived at with more pleasure and more glee.

And then, all at once and without warning, it ends.

The pummelling ceases. The four men step back. The doctor assumes at first that this must be due to boredom or even exhaustion or that their employer—she who requested the beating—has ordered them back indoors to attend to other duties or to some other unfortunate.

Yet none of these things are true. Struggling up, the physician sees that another man—one whom he takes at first to be a stranger—has come amongst them.

The newcomer is tall, dark-haired and clad in black. His face is obscured by shadow. Evidently, he is strong for one of the men has already been sent sprawling onto the ground and another is staggering backwards after the delivery of what the doctor guesses to have been a swift and brutal upper-cut. It is as though a circle of enthusiastic amateurs have been interrupted by some wilier and more experienced professional. The third of the thugs moves towards the newcomer who, with a whirl of black cloth, his frockcoat fluttering about him like a cloak, parries the attempted blow and sends the ruffian to the ground, nose bloodied, spitting teeth, squealing like an infant. The violence happens both obscenely quickly and with improbable slowness.

The newcomer speaks, authoritative, declamatory: "I believe that you gentlemen have done enough for tonight. I believe that you have all drunk your fill."

As he is talking, the boldest of the doctor's tormentors practically throws himself at the speaker, running hard at him from behind. The black-clad fellow turns fast and delivers a blow to his attacker's gut. A groan and the ruffian sinks, in a single, undignified motion, to his knees.

"I would ask you all politely to disperse."

The men on the ground stumble back to their feet again. They hang back, deciding their move.

One of them speaks: "Why are you doing this?"

"My motives are not for you to know." A strange, alien smile.

"You're a gutter-creep. A nightingale."

The tall man replies, with a kind of verbal lunge: "Disperse. My next request shall not be so courteous."

A long pause, pregnant with the possibility of further violence. Somewhere deep in the rookery, a baby cries out. A rough voice demands silence and an instant later, the wailing ceases.

In the end, there is no need for action. As one, the men make their choice. They wheel about, flee and are gone. The clatter of their footsteps soon fades.

The rescuer steps forward and extends his hand. "Dr Polidori?"

"It's you…" The doctor gasps. "Isn't it?"

"Let me help you to your feet."

"Thank you. Thank you." Polidori lets himself be aided, allows himself to be pulled up and dusted down, feeling all the while as if every part of him has been broken and trampled upon. "Sometimes," he murmurs, "we wondered if we'd dreamt you. If we hadn't somehow summoned you up from our imaginations. But that isn't so, sir? Is it?"

"In truth," says the black-clad man. "I cannot be certain."

"Are you quite well?" Polidori, though aching and raw, is filled with concern. "You seem a little out of sorts."

"Quite well, thank you. Yes. For the time being." And Matthew Cannonbridge smiles as if in muted happiness.

CANNONBRIDGE AND DR Polidori walk together through the streets, the handsome man strolling with natural grace, the chubby physician moving with a fragile survivor's gait. Hurrying away from the low district of the rookery, they move into a more respectable quarter, from poverty to a quiet affluence, from corruption into apparent health. The city here is still, the honest majority of her population abed.

They pass few other human beings—a tottering reveller, a bearded beggar, a pair of vergers from the Cathedral—but no one stops or questions them. These men aside, the cobbled streets are theirs alone, the echo of their footsteps sounding almost impertinent in the cloistered hush.

Passing by the closed and shuttered ranks of the market, only a few hours from its daily renewal, from its earthy clamour and brand of good-natured villainy, they turn right towards the heart of the city, towards the Close and the vigilant spire of the Cathedral.

As they walk, they speak of many things.

"I suppose you must want to know," Polidori finds himself saying, "exactly why it was those men had so fierce a disdain for me."

"I had assumed that to be your own affair. But, if you wish it, then, please, tell me."

Polidori shrugs. "Gambling debts."

"I had deduced something of the sort."

"It's my little weakness. One. One of my little weaknesses."

Cannonbridge lowers his head in such a manner as to suggest that he is not the kind of man who would ever judge another for some minor—even for some *major*—flaw of character. "How have you come to be in this city, doctor? So far from Geneva."

"I thought to practise here. To be frank with you, it's not been a terrific success. I'll be moving on soon enough."

"And your lord?"

"Oh, we've long since parted company. He tires of his friends, you see. The rich man's prerogative. No one lasts for long." Polidori winces, either at the memory of Byron or at the ache of a recent wound, the two things being, perhaps, not so very different. "And you? What brings you to this place?"

Cannonbridge hesitates. "I am not entirely certain."

"Indeed?"

"That is, I cannot at present recall. There are... intermissions in my memory. There are ellipses. Sometimes I seem to appear at places with no real recollection of how I have come to be there."

Other men might have been more surprised than Polidori at such an admission. But veteran as he is of Byron's household, he is better acquainted than most with missing hours, with lost time, with the warping of personal chronology. "I think I understand, sir."

Cannonbridge, suddenly confessional, announces: "I am on a journey, my friend. To find out who I am. My origins. My nature. My purpose. I want... You must see that I dearly want to be a good man. Yet there is something within me which suggests some different, some less noble path..."

"A kind of mission, then?"

"Yes."

"Like the hero," Polidori murmurs, "of your romance."

"My...?" Cannonbridge tails off as though he's forgotten the success that he enjoyed but two summers before.

"*The English Golem.*"

"You read it?"

"Several times. The first, concluded late at night, made sleep quite impossible. It represented the fruits, I take it, of our tale-telling contest?"

"In its essential conception, yes. As was Mary's remarkable work. And your own full-blooded *Vampyre.*"

The physician waves the compliment aside. "A trifle. Merely a bauble." He coughs, a dank, unhealthy sound. "But how well I remember it all! So vivid and remarkable a time. You inspired us all that night, you know. Even…"

The doctor tails off, winces.

"Yes?" Cannonbridge urges on the other man.

"It… it might not be proper. Or fair. Not after what you've done for me."

"Pray, doctor, continue. I am most interested to hear."

"You spoke of your uncertainty… of your origins and nature."

"You know something of this? Or perhaps you have suspicions?"

"Not I, sir, but my lord Byron. Not long after that night of tale-telling he dreamed about you. And he wrote down the dream in verse."

"Did he indeed? That… Yes, that does interest me greatly."

The slumbering streets go by. The cathedral town seems to enfold them, safe from the rookeries, behind the ramparts of money and taste.

"Let me see. I used to know it well." Polidori closes his eyes and begins to recite from memory:

"I had a dream, which was not all a dream.

The bright sun was extinguish'd, and the stars

Did wander darkling in the eternal space,

Rayless, and pathless, and the icy earth

Swung blind and blackening in the moonless air;

Morn came and went—and came, and brought no day,

And men forgot their passions in the dread

Of this their desolation…"

Cannonbridge interrupts. "All this darkness… He thought it had aught to do with me?" He sounds hurt by the implication.

"Not to do with you, sir. Not as you are. He said this was a *potential* in you only. He called it a *possibility*."

"You know I try my best, doctor, in spite of my confusion. To be brave. Philanthropic. To help."

"You do... You have... And yet..."

"Yes?"

"Forgive me, Mr Cannonbridge, it has been a long night. I have been drinking and I am not in my perfect mind."

Cannonbridge looks grave. "You sense something of this in me too?"

Polidori does not reply.

"Doctor?"

"I want to thank you again—you understand—with all my heart for saving me. Heaven knows how much longer those men might have persisted had you not interrupted them with such vigour and force."

"You are most welcome. But there is more, I think, that you need to say?"

Polidori swallows uncomfortably.

"Doctor?"

"I too have dreamed of you. More than once. Not, to be sure, as you are now but as, I am afraid, you will be."

"What have you seen? In these dreams of yours?"

"Storm clouds, sir. Storm clouds in your future. And also, also in your wake..."

"What?"

"Something's at your heels, Mr Cannonbridge. Something's tracking you."

A moment's silence. They have passed the Close now and begun to move on towards the outskirts. When Cannonbridge speaks again, he does not sound certain.

"It's late, doctor, and the night is full of shadows. Perhaps we are both of us permitting our imaginations to get the better of us. Perhaps I shall before long make some other, happier discovery."

Polidori bows his head. "I dare say you are right, sir." He holds out his hand. "Thank you. Thank you again. My lodgings are not far. I'll walk alone for the rest of the way."

"You're sure?"

"Quite sure, thank you. I doubt my creditors will trouble me again tonight."

"Do you need money?" He pauses, considers. "In my wanderings I have often seen the efficacy of money. It seems to grant men great power, one above the other."

"Oh, but you've done enough, Mr Cannonbridge. More than enough. There's no need."

A furrowed smile. "If you insist."

"I do."

"Then it's been my pleasure."

They begin to shake hands but Polidori, only ever in fitful control of his emotions, turns the gesture into an embrace and clings tight to the other man. "I wish you luck, sir. I hope you'll beat it, whatever's coming. I hope the good man in you wins."

"Thank you," says Cannonbridge as they disentangle. "I have a long journey yet, I fear. But I also wish you well."

"Thank you, sir."

"So... It is to be goodbye, then?"

"Yes, sir. It is to be goodbye, sir."

And with this, the two men part company—Polidori towards his lodging house, Cannonbridge the way they have already come.

Not more than a minute or so after their farewell, Polidori, unable to staunch his curiosity, turns back. The street is empty and of Cannonbridge there is no sign. There are only shadows now and, in the distance, the dark and watchful silhouette of the spire.

NOW

THE HOUSE ON Akerman Road hasn't been cleaned for a month, though you might be forgiven for thinking that it has been a good while longer.

Washing-up lies unattended and forlorn. Grime has been ground into carpets and rugs. Remnants are to be seen of old meals, baked bean stains and squashed tomato. Stigmata of battered fish and ketchup. Soap scum tide-marks in the bathroom sink. Take-away cartons sprawl on work surfaces, on sofa and floor. Staleness. Trapped, lethargic air. Everywhere decay.

The occupant, however, is not at present in residence. Rather, he is in transit, clambering off his third train of the day, en route to the University. So let us leave, for now, this scene of fractured domesticity and turn our attention instead towards the bijou railway station, served so poorly and infrequently by actual trains, which is situated at the outermost edge of the London suburb of Draye.

And here he is, Dr Judd, emerging from the lip of the station, having shuttled from one suburban hinterland to another, out of the south and into the east. He walks in the company of a couple of dozen other travellers, all of them jostling for egress.

Draye is a large, ancillary town, swollen in recent years far beyond its sensible Victorian beginnings into another amorphous satellite of the city, filled with chain outlets. Almost three miles away, fringed by heat haze and smog, can be seen the skyline of Canary Wharf, once docklands, now the city's financial district, its towers and minarets gazing down upon suburbia with an indifference that is inflected, just a little, by a kind of lordly malevolence.

Like Ashbury, the town is unremarkable and tame. It is only the University, formerly a polytechnic, which sets the place apart, a slab of grey concrete which lies at its heart—an institution that seems to have become (to widespread surprise and to nobody's more than Toby Judd's) a national centre of what certain of the broadsheets are calling the New Intellectualism.

Dressed as smartly as he knows how, in a dark blue suit and a dark brown tie, in shoes in need of polishing, with hair in need of a cut and with his face too lately shaved (still bearing nicks and tears from that savage appointment with the razor) Toby hangs back, allowing the other travellers to go first. Eventually, once the herd has trotted on, he walks forward, negotiates the turnstiles and escapes into the warm summer afternoon. As he leaves the station and steps onto the road—the far end of the high street, and a twenty-minute walk from the university—he sees to his surprise (and elation and fury and quixotic shame) the familiar shape of his wife. In contrast to his own, unintentional dishevelment, Caroline has attired herself with skilful elegance—tailored, sleek and proper but with something in her appearance that is suggestive also of a new sensual escalation.

Toby steps forward, double-takes, turns back.

"Toby?" she says.

"Hi."

"Hi there."

Of all the many things he wants to say to her, of all the lines and scenarios that he has rehearsed in the last four weeks, the following phrase has, somehow, never ranked amongst them: "What are you doing here?"

"I wanted to catch you."

"Why?"

"I wanted to make sure you're OK."

Nothing from Toby at this.

"Going to the university?"

"Yes."

"Me too. Will you let me walk with you?"

"Of course. How could I not?"

"I'm coming to your lecture," Caroline says as they walk, with the same kind of amiable enthusiasm that one might deploy when speaking to the child of a new acquaintance. She pauses to nibble briefly on her lower lip, an action which, long ago, had once made Toby short of breath and caused his heart rate to surge. "You don't mind, do you?"

Why did you leave me? Toby thinks. *How had I failed you? What has Salazar got that I have not?* Yet all that he says, with grisly, dishonest bonhomie, is: "Of course not. The more the merrier."

"J J's going to be there."

"Of course he bloody is." Beat. "Is that what you call him?"

"Yes." She bristles, very slightly. "Because that's his name."

No, it's not, Toby thinks, it's an irritating affectation. But he says nothing and they walk on silently for a minute or two, along a high street little different to any other in Britain, with its Starbucks and its Sainsburys, its Barclays, WHSmiths and its barn-like Wetherspoons as well, increasingly, Toby notes with the unease of an old man in autumn, its pawnbrokers and loan shops and premises which trade in desperation.

Caroline interrupts. "What's the title?"

"Title?"

"Of your lecture, silly." The playfulness, naturally, is just a little forced.

"Oh... Secrets of the Nineteenth Century."

"A bit vague, isn't it?"

"Chose it months ago, when I had no idea what I was going to talk about. You *want* something vague, don't you, at that point? To give you maximum wriggle room."

"So? What's it really going to be about? Go on. You can tell me."

"Hmph. You'll have to wait and see."

"Will I enjoy it?"

"You might. *J J* won't."

"Seriously? Oh. Oh, but, Toby, there's nothing to scare the horses, though?"

"Depends on the skittishness of the horses."

Wisely, perhaps, Caroline does not pursue this line of enquiry. "Expecting a good audience?"

"Summer schoolers. Staff. A few undergraduates if they're extra keen."

"It's open to the public too?"

"Yeah. None of them ever come. Still, you never know, perhaps today will be the day…"

"Toby…"

"Yes?"

"Have you got time for a coffee?"

Toby makes, perhaps, rather too much of checking his watch. "Sorry, but I don't think I have. I've got to set up before the lecture. PowerPoint, you see."

"Of course. Of course."

They walk much faster after that, not speaking, as awkward together as strangers. It's with palpable relief that the concrete fortress of the University soon hoves into view. They pause before the entrance, beside its big glass sliding doors, Toby to go the lecture hall, Caroline to some unspecified place where (self-evidently, though neither of them have spelt out the truth) she is to meet her lover, no doubt to embrace and murmur private things to one another and giggle in erotic conspiracy.

It is Toby who asks the first honest question. "Are you happy?"

Caroline seems pleased. Or, perhaps, simply relieved. "Yes. Yes, I am." She tries to smile. "And one day you will be too."

She starts to reach out her left hand as if to squeeze a shoulder or pat comfortingly an upper arm. Toby flinches and draws away.

"Good luck," she says, drawing back as well. "The lecture will be great. And if you get a chance beforehand…"

"Yes?"

"Try to clean yourself up a bit. You've cut yourself shaving. And your hair could use a comb."

Toby feels a spasm of embarrassment. He does not say goodbye but hurries quickly away so that his wife does not see him blush.

THE LECTURE HALL is filling up nicely. Able to accommodate a little over one hundred people, half the seats are taken. Toby's been here for almost an hour, doing battle with the computer and his memory stick. He sits now on one corner of the stage, hands folded calmly on his lap. Behind him are projected, in bold black type, these five words: **Secrets of the Nineteenth Century**.

Some of the audience he knows, either personally or by sight— colleagues and students. Salazar and Caroline sit on the very back row like teenagers at the pictures. At the front there is a skinny, unshaven man. He is dressed in an ancient pinstripe suit which looks as though it has come from one of the less discriminating jumble sales. He must, Toby thinks, wonderingly, be a member of the public—that fabled, rarely sighted breed. This particular specimen seems distinctly nervous. His eyes dart around the room and he constantly interlaces his fingers and pulls them apart again, anxious in the manner of a smoker going cold turkey. The rest of the crowd talk amongst themselves. There is not a hubbub (not exactly) but there is certainly a murmur of polite expectation.

After a while, once it becomes clear that no-one else is likely to arrive, a handsome, imperious woman of fifty-two whom Toby, historically, has liked and feared in equal measure steps onto the stage and walks towards its centre.

She pauses, just for a moment, before she speaks. The time in which she does this is all that it takes for the auditorium to fall entirely silent.

"Good afternoon," she says in a voice of silk wired with steel, "and welcome to the first in our summer lecture series here at Draye. My name is Professor Thomasina McGovern and I have the honour of being Head of the Faculty of the Arts and Social Sciences. For those of you for whom today is your first visit, I hope you will return and return often." Smiles and nods amongst the audience. "For the rest of you—current students, alumni and staff—welcome, welcome back. Before I introduce our speaker I'd like to share some thrilling news with you. These are exciting times for us here at the university. Now, I cannot imagine in a lecture entitled…" She glances behind her to read the title "… Secrets of the Nineteenth Century, that Dr Judd will not be touching in some detail on the remarkable life of Matthew Cannonbridge."

Toby grins, waggles his eyebrows.

"Nor can it have escaped your attention that this year is the Cannonbridge bicentenary—two hundred years since the writer's first recorded appearance."

Polite, scholarly laughter ensues, presumably at the very notion that so monumental an anniversary might ever have gone unnoticed by any member of this convocation.

"I imagine too that you will be aware of the terrific success of the new book *Cannonbridge: A Celebration of English Genius*, written by one of our most esteemed colleagues. It's been hard to miss given how it's been positively *leaping* up the charts since its release two months ago. It's already been called definitive, based as it is on previously unpublished material from the Cannonbridge archive in Edinburgh. So it gives me great pleasure, then, to be able to announce to you today that Draye's own Dr Salazar will be speaking at the forthcoming Cannonbridge Gala to be held in three weeks' time in Central London. The gala, sponsored by one of our leading investment banks, will be attended by a host of luminaries, dignitaries and stars and promises to be a very lavish affair indeed." A wide, proud, troublingly maternal smile. "J J? Stand up and take a bow."

With mock-reluctance, Salazar gets to his feet. Caroline gazes puppyishly after him.

"Ladies and gentlemen, a round of applause if you please for the university's blazing star... Dr J J Salazar!"

Clapping, loud and heartfelt. Toby's own applause, meanwhile, is entirely sardonic. He believes, incorrectly, that nobody notices this but him.

Eventually, after soaking up the attention for as long as possible, the Salazar posterior returns to its chair and McGovern gestures for silence.

"Thanks, J J." A mock salute from the scholar. A knowing gaze. "Oh, and he's asked me to remind you that you can now follow him on Twitter. It's... @cannonbridgedon. Is that right, J J?"

Salazar smirks and, absurdly, raises his thumbs aloft. Toby barely resists rolling his eyes.

Thomasina nods again towards her resident celebrity, then continues.

"So from the highest in the land to something just a little more down to earth. I'd like to present Dr Judd, one of our most enthusiastic and reliable lecturers. He's well known amongst our students, I'm told, for his ingenious and entertaining literary deductions. And he'll be speaking to us today on..." She turns once again to remind herself of the subject under discussion "... Secrets of the Nineteenth Century. Dr Judd?"

Toby gets to his feet and strolls over to where Thomasina has been standing. The lady steps down from the stage and takes up a position on the front row. She is a few seats along from the man in the pinstripe suit who, Toby notices, has now brought out a chunky grey mobile phone. This he holds before his right eye, like a talisman, like a charm.

Applause for Toby is sporadic, the crowd exhausted, presumably, from the raucous reception that they have already accorded Salazar. Toby, unfazed, begins.

"As you can see, I have entitled this lecture *Secrets of the Nineteenth Century*. A pretty bland, vanilla title, I'm sure you'll agree. Over the course of its composition in the last month, however, I have come to understand that it might much more accurately have been called something like this." Out of his pocket Toby pulls a black remote control. He touches one of the buttons and the screen behind him changes. One set of words is replaced by another. Toby reads them aloud: "Matthew Cannonbridge: Fraud."

Is there, at this, a gasp from the audience? A murmur of unease? Even a nervous titter? Toby cannot be sure.

He goes on. "And it might just as well have been called this..." Another click, another shift of words. "Matthew Cannonbridge: The Invented Man." Click. "Or this: The Cannonbridge Delusion."

Toby steps forward. Caroline's face is turned away, her expression obscure.

"The contention of my lecture, then, is this: quite simply, that Matthew Cannonbridge never existed. That his life and work and biography are all the invention of some modern hand. That the Cannonbridge story, ladies and gentlemen, is an elaborate deception perpetrated on us all for some baffling reason. That everything from *The English Golem* to *National Virtue* to *The Mystery of the Whispering Pontiff* has been faked. That all of it represents a highly sophisticated confidence trick which has been played on the international community and on the reading public for more than fifty years."

At the back of the auditorium a man walks out. Professor McGovern, uniquely, in Toby's experience of her, seems completely frozen, uncertain as to what to do next. J J is trying to appear amused as if in the hope that this will yet prove to be a jest, some pawky piece of academic humour.

"*J'accuse*," says Toby with a flourish, starting to enjoy himself now, "this man."

Another click and the picture changes again, now to show a lean, serious-looking bearded man of around thirty. "The late Professor Anthony Blessborough, author of *Forgotten Genius*, which, as most of you will know, was the very first critical study of Cannonbridge, published shortly after the Second World War. Now, whether Blessborough invented Cannonbridge knowingly or whether he actually believed in what he was writing I cannot be certain. Nonetheless, I feel sure that it was then, with this book, that the Cannonbridge conspiracy began. But what still eludes me is the question of motive. I do not yet know why this colossal and outrageous fraud has been perpetrated upon the world."

Some of the audience are talking now, some outraged, some concerned, some entertained. Only the man in the pinstripe suit still seems to be listening with real intensity. As before, his talismanic mobile phone is held up steadily before him.

At the back, another person leaves. And then another. One of them shouts, before the door slams shut, "Nutter!"

Now, Toby really begins to warm to his theme. He improvises. He freestyles, he plays to the crowd, he loses control of his emotion. He allows himself to be swept up and gives himself over to the moment. It will be some time before he realises quite what a show it is that he puts on.

In the end, Toby is allowed to speak for a little under eleven minutes—the novels and short stories and plays that he believes to have been faked, the widespread tampering with the archives, the expert falsification of records, the long-term bribery and blackmail of the academic world. Each claim is more scandalous than the last, each more dementedly complex and frothingly baroque. More of the audience leave, while others stay and laugh openly. Thomasina looks ashen. Salazar tries hard to seem sorrowfully noble. Caroline might be in tears. The man in the pinstripe suit, however, drinks all of it in, that phone held out before him the whole time, as if warding away something evil.

Toby has just begun to explain how he believes Cannonbridge's epic verse cycle *The Lamentation of Eliphar, Mununzar's Son* to be a twentieth-century forgery when Professor McGovern takes action. She climbs on stage, stops in front of him and says, with soft, pitying authority: "And there, I'm afraid, we must leave it. We're out of time, Dr Judd."

Toby stops, in mid-flow. "So soon?"

"I'm afraid so." A tight smile. "And no time for questions either." She is addressing only the audience now. "Thank you for your attention."

Back to Toby, she hisses in his ear. "Come to my office. Please. I mean, straightaway."

Toby does not seem to react. He only touches a button. Behind him, the screen goes black. He turns and stares towards it, swallowed for an instant by the void.

When he looks back, the audience are filing out. None seem willing to meet his eye. Caroline and J J have already gone.

He waits until the room is empty before he stirs.

In the corridor, on his way to Thomasina's office, Toby is ambushed by the man in the pinstripe suit. The stranger, Toby sees, has put away his phone now.

"Good lecture," the man says. "*Good lecture.*" He seems agitated and ill at ease and perhaps (Toby considers, not unkindly) in need of medication.

"Thank you," says Toby and tries to get past.

"You're not alone, you know."

"I'm sorry?"

"I've seen the truth of it. I've glimpsed the Cannonbridge Conspiracy."

"Oh? Oh, really?"

"Yes. And there are more of us, you know. We're underground. Off the grid, mostly. But you'll need to be careful now. You'll have attracted attention." He mutters the next sentence. "From rich and powerful people."

Toby stops, looks the man in the eye. "What do you mean?"

"There's more I can tell you. About how it's been done. About *why* it's been done. The scale of it, the scope... The hideous implication. But not here. Not now."

"Why not?"

"Too public. Too exposed. Walls with ears. Listen, I'll give you my number. Yeah? And then you'll call me?"

Toby hesitates but only for a moment. "Yes. Yes, I suppose I might at that."

"Very good. Here it is."

The stranger pulls out a scrap of paper on which a string of digits have been scrawled. Toby considers that the man must have prepared this earlier and finds this realisation to be an unsettling one.

Judd takes the paper all the same, thrusts it into his jacket pocket and says, "Thank you. But you'll have to excuse me now."

"Of course. But please, please phone me, yeah?"

"OK," Toby murmurs and in that moment he feels pretty certain that, in the end, he probably won't make that call. The man looks at him, wild-eyed and trembling, as if he has read his thoughts. Then Toby says: "Wait."

"Yes?" The man looks up at Dr Judd, skittish and afraid.

"If you share my suspicions about Cannonbridge..."

"Yes?"

"What led you here today? The real content of my lecture wasn't advertised at all."

"I knew what you were going to say."

"*How?*"

"I had a dream, Dr Judd. A dream of prophecy. And you—you were in it."

"A…" Toby is about to say "dream" incredulously, but stops himself just in time. "I see."

"And now, I have some sympathy…" The other man's nose twitches and his tongue dampens the corner of his mouth: "… with John the Baptist."

"Oh."

"The laying straight of the ways. For he who is coming."

"I see," Toby says briskly. "And thank you. But I think this is goodbye." And he turns and starts to walk away, not looking back.

"Goodbye, doctor. You'll still call me, won't you?"

Toby walks, still without turning. "Yes. Absolutely. Without fail."

The unkempt man watches him go.

Toby goes further up the corridor until he reaches a white, unnumbered door. He knocks once and a woman's voice calls out: "Come in!"

The door opens. Judd slips inside.

The man in the pinstripe suit lingers for longer than he ought in the precincts of a place in which he has no legitimate business. He creeps closer to the white door, close enough to overhear some of what is taking place behind it and catches stray phrases of conversation: "more than a little concerned"; "University's reputation to consider"; "private life"; "by no means an easy decision" and then, with doleful finality, "I think we're going to have to say indefinite."

The voices, had the stranger known them well, he might have recognised as belonging to Professor McGovern and to J J Salazar. Toby himself does not appear to speak. If he does then he talks too softly for the eavesdropper to hear.

After that, there are footsteps towards the door and the man in the pinstripe suit springs away. He steps back and walks, with suddenly sure-footed purpose, towards the exit, out of the institution and back into the real world, his eyes ablaze with inexplicable intensity.

1824
WARREN'S BLACKING FACTORY
LONDON

THE BOY IN the blacking factory—a vast and ugly warehouse which looms beside the banks of the Thames—looks down at the filthy, twilit river and barely succeeds in suppressing a shudder.

More than ever today that stretch of dark water seems to him to be alive, a long, grey beast, bloated yet sinuous, with strange hungers, an appetite for sacrifice. As he gazes out from his tiny alcove upon this miserable scene, the boy's hands work quickly and efficiently on the bench before him. A row of earthenware bottles, filled with boot blacking, is lined up there and the boy covers each of them, first with oil paper then with blue paper, before tying them round with string. A few gross of these completed, he turns, without thinking, to a pile of printed labels and affixes one with paste to every receptacle. The work is repetitive and dull but the boy is diligent and nimble. He goes on without thinking, letting his imagination roam, absenting himself from the clamour of the factory, from the cries and complaints of his fellow workers, the grind and whinnying of machinery, the thick, repulsive smells of the place and its atmosphere of despair.

Stout, sandy-haired Mr Lamert passes by, favouring the child with a glance and an injunction. "Keep up, boy! Concentrate on the task in hand!"

The child bows his head, redoubles his efforts. When Lamert has left, he raises his gaze once more to look from the window and down towards the Thames, upon which he sees, at first with curiosity and then, oddly, with a mounting sense of nervousness, that, standing beside the river almost as if the water itself has but lately disgorged him, is the figure of a man, dark-haired and clad in black, staring up at the factory windows. The boy peers closer, half-wondering if he might not be imagining the stranger, if the man is some trick of the fading light, some weird combination of shadows.

But no, he is real. A moment more and the fellow disappears, stamping along the riverbank towards (or so, at least, the boy assumes) the street beyond.

The next half hour passes very slowly indeed. Not for the first time, the boy considers how fluid is time in this place, how it seems to swirl and eddy as if subject to some fickle, mysterious power. In the factory, a minute might last an hour, an hour a day or, in certain unusual circumstances when something like a trance descends upon him, an afternoon pass by in the manner of a dream.

The boy feels a hand upon his shoulder. He does not have to turn to recognise the touch. Mr Lamert's voice is calm and firm yet his breath is scented by liquor.

"Finish that one and you can go home."

The child busies himself with his task. "Thank you, Mr Lamert."

A squeeze on his shoulder. "And, my boy?"

"Yes, sir?"

"There is a gentleman outside who says he knows you."

"Indeed, Mr Lamert?"

"His name is Cannonbridge. Says he's a writer of repute."

"A writer?" the boy asks wonderingly.

"That's what he said. I can turn him away if you wish." Another, longer squeeze. "I promised your father I'd take care of you."

There is a note of concern in the man's voice which certainly sounds genuine enough and which causes the boy, for the first and, as things would turn out, the last time, to feel something like sympathy for his employer.

"No, Mr Lamert. Thank you, sir. But I believe I recognise the name."

Outside on the squalid street, beside the steps which lead to something more closely resembling civilisation, stands the man whom the boy had spied earlier that afternoon—saturnine and black-clad though, for all of that, smiling with clear sincerity.

"Charles?"

"Mr Cannonbridge?"

As the boy approaches, the man bends down to the child's level and extends his hand.

"I'm very pleased to meet you."

Warily, he takes the offered hand and shakes it. "What do you want with me, sir?"

"Only to talk."

The boy juts out his chin imperiously. "Then I am to walk home. You may walk with me."

The man smiles again and seems to be about to speak when another boy, a little older than the first and with a wild crop of red hair, pushes past them and trots spryly up the steps, calling over his shoulder as he goes. "See you tomorrow, Charlie!"

The younger boy replies. "Tomorrow, Bob!"

Cannonbridge looks with gravity at the boy. "Let us walk," he says.

And walk they do, for the best part of three miles, up the Hungerford Stairs and the maze which lies immediately beyond and then, breaking into the relative sanctity of the Strand, up St Martin's Lane and Broad St Giles, along Tottenham Court and Hampstead Road, heading, eventually, towards open spaces, to the green of Camden Town.

They talk, a little nervously at first, a little stiffly but then with increasing warmth and honesty. It is a conversation that the boy shall remember for the rest of his life. He will also remember this—that the man, with some regularity, glances behind him and, imagining that his companion does not notice, seeks out reflections of the street in window panes and polished surfaces, as if he believes himself to have been followed. Though he will hug the memory close, on this the boy does not remark.

"I trust you will forgive me," Cannonbridge begins, "for introducing myself in this way."

The boy does not reply directly but only asks another question: "Do you know my father, sir?"

"I don't believe I do."

"Oh. I thought that you might. It is only that…"

"Yes?"

"He has lately proved himself… rather clumsy." The boy pauses, thinking of the arrest, his mother's shame, the great and terrible fortress of the Marshalsea. "He would be grateful, I am certain, of a friend."

"I understand. But I do not believe that I have ever had the pleasure."

The boy nods glumly, expecting this answer. "You are a writer, sir, are you not?"

"I am. Three works of fiction now. Though I have hopes in the future of applying my talents to the theatre and even to verse."

They negotiate the streets largely in silence until the boy pipes up. "I think that I should like to be a writer also."

"Indeed?" Cannonbridge does not sound surprised. "I think that you would be well suited to the life."

"Thank you, sir. Though I fear at present that I must spend the chief portion of my adult years in paying off my father's debts."

"Is he… greatly embarrassed?"

"He is a bankrupt, sir."

The boy would not, with many others, have been so forthright. In the company of this man, however, he feels curiously able to be frank.

"Our family has much to pay and we all must do our part. That is why they sent me to the factory. So that I might contribute and earn my keep."

"Charles?"

"Yes, sir?"

"Given all that you've said, I don't wish to trouble you with my own concerns."

"No trouble, sir. Not that."

"You are most kind. Suffice to say that certain of my origins are obscure even to me. I am far from certain how I have come to be who I am in such a time and place as this. I mean these things not, you understand, in any philosophical sense but rather in a literal and material one. I have, of late, been endeavouring to uncover the truth. I have visited wise men. Oracles. Priests. Doctors. Magicians. Sages of every stripe. Though they've cast no light. Not a man jack of them."

The boy nods, more from courtesy than comprehension.

"Nonetheless, whilst I pursue this... mystery I wish also to do good."

"Then you are a philanthropist, sir?"

"Yes. I suppose I am. As much as is possible. Though my time does not always seem to be my own. And I am greatly concerned that the part of my life which I shall spend as any force for good is soon to come to an end."

"Sir?"

"In recent nights, in certain dreams and visions, I have seen several clues. I have been vouchsafed details of the future. Glimpses only. Fragments of the puzzle. Last night, I saw something of what I shall become. A new kind of creature. A new kind of... intelligence. There are storm clouds gathering above me. My destiny approaches."

"A man may make his own destiny," says the boy. "A man can outwit fate."

"Do you think so?"

An earnest nod. "I do."

Cannonbridge seems to brighten. "Then perhaps I shall. And perhaps you will too. What I meant to say was that the debts of your father need not overwhelm you."

"I hope that you are right," says the boy and they walk on in a silence that now seems almost companionable, as if each has found some succour in the other.

Cannonbridge begins again. "In what I have seen of the future, Charles, you will endure. And not merely endure but *thrive*. You will write often and well."

"Truly, sir?"

"Truly. But more than this I cannot say."

"I see... then thank you, sir."

They speak of many other things—of the city and the river, of shadows and money, of family, of fog, books, stories, the forging of myth. At last, they come to Camden Town, a place but lately claimed by the city, and along a freshly paved road to Number Sixteen, Bayham Street.

A pump stands opposite the house. Beyond it are lanes and open fields. Here there is still birdsong.

Cannonbridge takes a purse from his pocket, heavy with coin, and presses it into the boy's hands.

He says: "I hope this may be of some help."

The boy, proud, hesitates.

"Please. This... stuff. This *money*, it seems to make so great a deal of difference to people. It can be the difference—I have observed—between happiness and misery."

The boy ducks his head. The purse, accepted, is slipped adroitly into a pocket.

"This will pass," Cannonbridge says. "Remember that."

"Will we meet again?" asks the boy.

"I think that we shall. Many years from now." There is sadness in the man's voice. "But when we do, if my suspicions are correct, I fear that I may be greatly changed. Our encounter may not be as happy or as providential as this."

"You will be changed by... age, then, sir? By time?"

"By age, yes. But by something else also. And then, my boy..."

"Yes, sir?"

"You must not trust me. Do you understand? I shall not be benign."

The boy nods gravely. "But can you not thwart it, sir? Whatever it may be. Surely you must try. You must try not to let yourself be so transformed."

The man smiles sadly. "Goodbye, Charles. Thank you for your company and for the conversation."

The boy holds the purse tightly in his pocket. "Thank you, sir."

Cannonbridge turns and walks away.

For a time, Charles watches him go, curious, a little afraid and in no particular hurry to go inside to face the tears of his mother, the drawn and sullen faces of his siblings. For an instant before the author vanishes into the gloom, Charles is almost certain that he spies something in the visitor's wake, something made of ebony, blacker even than the shadows, something more animal than man, something with eyes which shine in the darkness.

Then the illusion passes. Shivering, although it is not especially cold, Charles looks away and hurries to the front door, feeling oddly certain that he has just been made privy to some bleak and consequential secret.

As he knocks, from somewhere nearby, in a room in the house of a neighbour or from a passer-by on the street beyond (or so, at least, he tells himself), he hears, quite distinctly, the sound of evil laughter.

The door is opened by his mother, eyes red-rimmed from weeping and, all at once, Master Charles Dickens does not believe that he has ever been so glad to see her.

NOW

IT IS A week after the lecture and Toby Judd is trudging home in the early afternoon sun, feeling, through a haze of lunchtime beer, simultaneously light-headed and glum.

He has spent the past two and a half hours in a pub (where, to his mild disquiet, he is beginning to be known) with a couple of beers, a plate of lukewarm scampi and a bulging A5 notebook. Its pages are filled with scribbled ideas—with theories, plans and patient workings-out, with any number of notions about how the Cannonbridge Conspiracy might have come about, with innumerable speculations as to its purpose and intention. The seeds of true obsession are here, in that book, taking patient root.

Now, on this long suburban road, his little house comes into view and he notices, feeling queasily uncertain of its significance, that a police car is parked outside.

As Toby comes closer, the car doors open and two people step out, neither of them in uniform. One is an older woman, a few years senior to Toby, straight-haired and serious, the other, a man, not yet thirty, built like a rugby player, bull-necked and eager.

Both look determined and rumpled and the effect is that of a headmistress and a junior member of staff who share an out of hours interest in violence. Toby is almost upon them.

"Dr Toby Judd?" This is the woman, firm yet discreet.

"Yes?" The word comes out in a croak. Toby, wondering if they can smell the alcohol on his breath, has never craved as much as he does now a packet of mints.

"I thought it must be you, sir."

"You did?"

"Of course I recognise you, sir."

"Really?"

"From the video, sir."

"What video?"

"It might be easier if we took this inside, sir. I'm Detective Inspector Nia Cudden. This is Sergeant Isaac Angeyo."

The man nods and both of them briefly flourish identity cards (so swiftly that they might just as easily have been bus passes or driving licenses).

"Oh," says Toby. "Hello, then."

"Have you got a minute for a quiet word, sir?"

"Of course."

"Yes. Thank you, sir."

Toby starts fumbling for the keys, pulls them out, drops them.

Sergeant Angeyo, who has yet to speak, bends down, picks them up and hands them back.

"Thank you." Dr Judd walks towards the door then, remembering his manners, turns back to his companions. "I'm terribly sorry," he says. "I haven't had a chance to tidy for a while. You'll have to forgive the mess."

"No problem, sir. I'm sure we've seen worse. Just lead the way."

THE MILK IN the fridge is rancid so Toby can only offer them black coffee or green tea. To his mild relief, they decline both. Once Toby has cleared away the detritus (the guests are too polite to mention the dust and the dirt), the two police officers sit together on the sofa while Toby perches on the room's only chair. He is about to ask what this is all about when Cudden, with the patient deliberation of a woman who knows from experience that mistakes are more likely if things are done at speed, says: "Tell us, Dr Judd. Do you know a man named Russell Spicer?"

Toby shakes his head. "No. I don't believe I do."

The officers exchange looks of professional scepticism.

"Perhaps you'll recognise his face, sir."

This is Sergeant Angeyo, speaking for the first time. His voice is low and earnest with a hint of a rural burr, a strange suggestion of the countryside in this place of concrete and gravel. He takes a photograph from his jacket pocket and passes it to Toby, face down.

Turning it over, Dr Judd sees a man from his recent past gazing back at him—skinny, unshaven features, a wild-eyed intensity. Something rises in his chest. "I know him."

"We thought you might, sir."

"He came to my lecture. He spoke to me afterwards. He was... enthusiastic about my ideas."

"And you'd never met him before?"

"No. No... However did you know that we'd met?"

"He was the one who filmed you, sir." The policewoman speaks these words as if their meaning is self-evident.

"What do you mean 'filmed me'?"

"He was the one who videoed you, sir. On his phone."

"What?"

"He put you up on YouTube, sir."

"I'm sorry. But I can't quite seem to process this."

Another glance of jaded scepticism is traded between the officers of the law.

"He filmed me," Toby says carefully, struggling to understand, "and put the video on YouTube. Why? For goodness' sake, why?"

"I imagine he wanted to try to spread the word, sir. But it's found a... different audience. Your *meltdown*, sir. The video's gone viral."

Toby is aware that he is sounding pitifully like an echo. "Viral?" He understands the meaning of the term, of course, in this context but somehow he cannot help but slip back to its older, original sense. He considers infection and the spreading of disease.

"All around the world, sir. Everyone's been clicking on it—on you, sir—over and over. That's the way it is now, isn't it? That's the speed of fame in the twenty-first century. The speed of life, really." The policewoman sucks in a breath. "You didn't know?"

"No. No absolutely not. I mean... I remember now... He had his phone out before him, but I never..."

"Sergeant? Show the man, would you?"

The young man slides a slender black device from his pocket, taps at the screen and presents it to Toby with something approaching a flourish.

There, before him, is Toby's lecture in miniature or, at least, its later, more emotive section. The show. He sees himself: red-faced and ranting, a comic lunatic, baggy-trousered and absurd. He peers, half-horrified, half-fascinated by this homunculus version of himself, this pixelated demagogue, this weird, demented gnome.

"Tens of thousands of hits, sir. You're something of a celebrity. You remember the man with the dog, sir? 'Fenton? *Fenton!*' You're at least as famous as him."

On the screen, the tiny, warped reflection of Dr Tony Judd struts and yelps and bellows out his theories.

"Please," says Toby, winded. "Please put it away now."

The Detective Inspector nods. "Sergeant."

"Terrifying," Toby murmurs. "Quite terrifying."

Angeyo snaps shut the device, silencing the ranting little man, and stows the thing away in his pocket again.

"This Russell Spicer. He shot all that?"

"Yes, sir. In fact, sir…"

"Yes?"

"As far as we can tell… it was near enough the last thing he did."

"The… last… thing?"

No trace of emotion on the policeman's face now. "Before his death, sir."

A twist of nausea in Toby's gut. Two useless, identical syllables: "Oh. Oh."

"We're sorry, sir."

"We didn't mean to shock you."

"I'm… well, it is shocking. But, I suppose, it's not like I knew the man. We can't have spoken for more than a couple of minutes."

"He was obviously an admirer of yours, sir. We understand he shared some of your conspiracy theories."

"I don't like that phrase. But my *doubts*, yes. Yes, he seemed to share some of my *doubts*."

Angeyo, leaning forward, interested: "I've watched the video, sir. Couldn't quite seem to follow your argument."

"Hmph. How well do you know Cannonbridge's works, Sergeant?"

"GCSE English, sir. I know the basics."

"Hasn't anything ever struck you as odd about them?"

"In what way, sir?"

"They're too consistent. Don't you think? Too neat. And, frankly, nowhere near good enough. As though they've been made up by one man over the course of a month and not over a lifetime."

"Can't say it's ever occurred to me, sir."

"Think about it, Sergeant. Read them again. Look at the details of his life." Toby, intense, makes eye contact. "*We are being lied to.*"

Cudden clears his throat, evidently a signal of some kind to her sergeant. "Well, thank you for your time, sir."

Both officers get to their feet.

"Can I ask?" says Toby. "How did he die?"

The police exchange glances again.

"Found in a hotel room, sir. A Holiday Inn. Cut his own throat. Messy. No note."

"I see." Toby nods, more nauseous than ever. "Well, that's very sad."

Cudden, unsmiling: "Isn't it?"

Toby swallows and murmurs, "Let me show you out."

From the doorstep, Cudden strides towards the car, Angeyo hangs back, just long enough to lean in to speak to Toby the following words: "There were some... irregularities about the death, sir."

"What are you saying?"

Sergeant Angeyo looks at him levelly for a moment. "I'm just saying be careful, sir."

A shout. "Sergeant!"

Before Toby can respond, Angeyo nods once and strides off. The two police officers climb inside the car.

The engine starts and they drive away.

Toby watches, sick at heart and trembling. He is about to return to the sanctuary of his bedroom when he notices, from across the street, a sudden gleam of light, as of sunshine glinting on metal.

There is a car. A Saab. A dark, sleek, expensive machine. The slender silhouette of a man within. Toby squints against the sunlight but cannot make out the stranger's features.

Again, a flash of light. Toby stares, his skin prickling, and in a moment of recklessness, considers running over to the vehicle, wrenching open the door and challenging the occupant to explain himself.

But then the car starts up and begins to pull away. Toby stares, still unable to make out the driver's features. There is only a shadow behind the wheel.

The Saab disappears and the street is empty once more. Feeling very cold in spite of the warmth of the day, Toby, shivering, goes back inside, double locks the front door, pulls the chain across and goes to bed where he falls, eventually, into an uneasy sleep and dreams of shadows and dead men and impossible things.

1835
THE KITTIWAKE HOTEL
BOSTON

It is autumn in Massachusetts. Cornhill has a sombre aspect as if it is in mourning. Tall, grey buildings. Everywhere, brown leaves and mud. Fine, resentful rain.

Nobody lingers out of doors. It has begun to darken and folk are hurrying home, their heads bowed, their collars turned up against the asperity of the weather, the gas lamps, fitful and fickle, serving less to illuminate the sidewalk than to render more complete those shadows which lie beyond the limitations of the light. All is subtle, quiet, discreet. All is order here and sullen peace. It is a world arranged according to the principles of the ruler and the compass, a city of the new, far from the murk and corruption of London. Looking upon it today, one would be hard pressed to imagine that it was ever the birthplace of revolution or that it once provided the spark for war.

Yet, there is something also, amidst the scene to suggest that the violence of the place is hidden only barely, that the carapace of civilisation is thin and prone to cracking. The first sign of it is this: a young woman, moving swiftly down the street, glancing repeatedly behind her, her face set in an expression of barely-stifled terror.

A pale creature—oh, so very pale; pale like china; pale like marble—her hair long and black, streaked prematurely with grey. Her clothes are ragged and too tight, her figure slim and attractive. There is a certain exoticism to her—there are tattoos beneath the fabric of her dress, inked sigils and signs of the most curious kind—and she possesses a savage sort of beauty, fraying at the edges. All but the most witless observer would surely be able, at the sight of her frantic, half-tripping gait, her drawn face, the look of anguish in her eyes, to discern that here is a lady who has indeed been most imperfectly used.

She looks behind her once more, this hunted girl, and one would, if one were of a mind to follow the direction of her gaze, discern her pursuers: two men, both stout and perspiring, both dressed in matching suits of bottle green. They might, in other circumstances, seem slightly comical but somehow here, in this place and at this time, they do not. There is something in the set of their jaws, you understand, something in the way in which they carry their bulk, with a lascivious sort of pride, which would make the smile drop at once from the face of even the most committed humorist.

Towards the end of the street there is a building, tall and wide and made of grey stone, which has many windows and many entrances and exits. The name of the place may be read above the largest of its numerous doors, at which a man in a damson-coloured uniform stands laconic guard and from which an elderly couple can be seen emerging, with brittle uncertainty, into the open air: THE KITTIWAKE HOTEL.

At the sight of this, the young woman seems to surge forwards. It seems probable that she dare not risk breaking into a run, into anything more, in fact, than the briskest of strides, but she is moving faster now than she has so far today, in all her long and perilous flight through the city.

Later she will ask herself why she felt so drawn to the Kittiwake, why it seemed to her to represent a refuge, and she will discover that she does not possess a satisfactory answer. Of course, the elements in her which remain superstitious, that still believe in destiny and fate and in the influence of the planets upon the human soul, will wonder whether the intersection between her own life and one of the residents of that celebrated lodge house might not represent a page in her history that had long been written and ordained. Another, perhaps more rational, even cynical, side to her will simply take it to be a rare stroke of good fortune in a life which has hitherto been ruled by malign coincidence.

At the time, however, she simply does not question the sudden urge to be inside that hotel. The front entrance is not for her, being altogether too public and too grand. The likelihood of being turned away there as an itinerant and waif is high so she skirts adroitly along the left-hand side of the building, down an alleyway along which the illusion that the façade creates—of affluence and discretion—is replaced by the facts of its underpinning: grime, hard work and altogether different classes of person than those who are, at polite intervals, disgorged by the great front door.

The girl looks behind her, half-hoping, although, in truth, she knows that she cannot, to have shaken off her rotund pursuers. But no. There they are: a pair of bulky shadows at the start of the path.

She sees ahead of her a well-lit entrance, a glow of warmth and labour, and so she presses on. Reaching the open door, she steps inside, the cold of the autumn evening at her back.

All at once she is confronted by the furnace industry of a busy kitchen, by flames and smells of cooking and the clatter of plates and cutlery, by two (three? four?) dozen people bent upon the task of satiating the hungers of all those who reside within the Kittiwake and who pay handsomely for that privilege. The room is filled with men but there are women here also—maids and scullery girls—and our heroine, when no-one seems to give her the slightest bit of notice or challenge her or ask her to explain her presence upon the premises, simply assumes that she has been mistaken for one of them. She pushes through the crowd, slips through the bustle of the kitchen and makes her way to the corridor beyond. She doubts that the large gentlemen in green will fare so well as her in that place—anonymity, ironically, perhaps, having never been their strongest suit—and wonders if she might not have bought herself some time.

After that: more good fortune. Had she not long since given up the practice of prayer she would certainly have murmured a catechism of gratitude to her neglectful deity. Instead, she simply acknowledges her own quick thinking and hurries on. Along the corridor she goes, bowing her head and adopting an air of subservience which was once, with considerable cruelty, instilled into her. She passes easily as a servant of some description, out of uniform or newly arrived and overwhelmed; the place is so big and the staff so numerous that few who are employed there are likely to know the face of every one of their peers. Besides, the young woman is lucky: she does not cross the paths of many of the staff and it is not long before, taking a steep flight of stairs which rise up at the end of the little labyrinth of corridors, she finds herself out of the servants' quarters altogether and into the realm of the guests.

Up she climbs, floor after floor, passing bell-boys and men carrying food and flagons of wine, past women with laundry and uniformed children clutching messages and telegrams. Often, she looks behind her but she sees and hears nothing to suggest the continuance of the chase. Nevertheless, she climbs, like an animal in a forest fire seeking the sanctuary of the tree-tops.

She stops only when there are no more stairs to ascend, on the very highest floor of this monstrous old hotel, stepping out of a concealed door at the end of another long corridor, though one far more sumptuously furnished and laid out than that which she had navigated below. Here there is the unmistakable scent of money: thick, port-coloured carpet, walls hung with seascapes and hunting scenes, the musical tinkle of chandeliers overhead. Stealthily, she moves along the hallway, passing closed door after closed door, hoping, perhaps, to find some obscure berth in which she might lie low for an hour or so.

Then, from behind her, she hears the thunderous approach of men upon the stairs. Two of them by their tread—heavy, implacable. For the first time in that long day, she hesitates. The sound of them is unmistakable—dogs closing in upon the kill.

Others might have screamed at the sound or have begun to weep but our girl gives only one sign of her true emotions; the blood drains from her face and she seems still paler than before, the most delicate of blooms in this place of wealth and pleasure.

The sound of boots upon the stairs grows louder still. Still, she hesitates. Is she exhausted? Defeated? Might she be ready, at long last, to submit?

Then, without warning, the door that is nearest to her opens (she catches a glimpse of the words that are stencilled upon it: THE CHRYSALIS SUITE) and a man steps abruptly into the light. He is a tall man, expensively dressed and impeccable in his demeanour, although there exists a certain harried aspect in his eyes.

He takes her arm. "You must come inside." His voice is like coffee, like chocolate, like cream.

She does not resist but only allows herself to be drawn into the room. Once they are within, he pulls shut the door.

"Who are you?" she begins to ask but he enjoins her to silence by placing a finger to his lips.

From outside, she hears the frustrated tramp of boots upon the carpet, the hungry, bitter conversation of the men in green. For a long minute, they wait as the sound of her pursuers disappears once more. She thinks that she hears them begin to speed up again, doubtless believing themselves to have temporarily lost their spoor.

Only once the noise has disappeared entirely does the man who saved her speak.

"You asked me my name, madam. I am Matthew Cannonbridge. And you?"

Our heroine seems to hesitate, as if uncertain quite which name to give. "You can call me Maria. Maria Monk."

"Come in," Cannonbridge says, motioning her to walk further into the room—a place of rare, almost continental luxury with its carpet even thicker than that which had lain outside, its drawing room atmosphere, armchairs and reading tables and, at the far corner of Maria's vision, a hint of a bedroom beyond.

"I should thank you."

"You are most welcome. I…" Cannonbridge hesitates, as if suspecting that the admission may not cast him in the best possible light. "I saw you. Outside. On the street. I saw you from my window here. And I saw that you were… pursued."

Maria gazes up at the older man. "You were watching me?"

"Only because I was concerned. Yet somehow I knew that you would find me. You were being followed, were you not?"

"I was. Those men… they will not lightly be deterred."

"There is murder in their eyes, I think."

"If I do not give them what they wish of me, then... yes."

For a moment the couple merely look at one another. Outside, the corridor is still. Nevertheless, Miss Monk remains anxious. "You do not mean to ask me why they were in pursuit of me?"

"I do not see that it is any of my business, madam. I perceive merely that you are in distress. It is my duty, if I can, to alleviate that."

"You're... you're very kind. Yet you want nothing from me?"

Cannonbridge, perplexed: "Nothing, madam."

"Then... then may I stay here awhile? I have no wish to bring trouble down upon you."

Cannonbridge gives her a wintry smile. "Trouble, madam, has a habit of finding me."

The young woman smiles, amused by his swagger. Then she seems to stumble slightly, taking two steps backwards, her balance suddenly unsteady.

"Forgive me, Miss Monk. You must be tired. Hungry."

"I do... feel a little faint."

All at once, as the trials of the past few days seem to crowd around her, as her body finally allows itself to accept all of the exertions that she has placed upon it, Maria finds herself beset by dizziness. "Sir?" she murmurs.

"Yes?"

"Your name... is half-familiar to me. You are... yes, you are a writer, are you not?"

Cannonbridge is about to reply, in as modest a set of terms as he can muster, when he sees that the young lady is about to fall into a swoon. Heedless of convention, he steps closer and, four seconds later, when she faints, he is able to catch her in his arms.

WHEN MARIA AWAKES it is full dark. It must be the small hours of the morning as the gas lamps have been extinguished on the street outside. Indeed, the darkness is so total that it seems to her to be almost the darkness of the countryside. Her first thought is that, by some miracle, she has been returned home, that she has woken in St John's once more and that all is well.

Gradually, she remembers and becomes aware of her surroundings. Boston. The Kittiwake. She must be in his room, she realises. He must have placed her in his own bed. But if she is in the bed, then where...?

A voice in the darkness: "You're awake."

"Yes." The word is whispered. She scarcely dares to move. "Have you been... watching over me?" The concept ought to be a disquieting one and yet, somehow, for all her grave experiences, in this place, with this man and at this time, it does not seem so. Rather, she feels, unexpectedly, a certain comfort in his proximity.

"Is there anything that I can fetch for you? Food? Water?"

"No. No, thank you."

"I want you to understand that, so long as you remain here, you are quite safe. You are under my protection now."

"Thank you. But I need... to get to New York."

"I see. Then, perhaps, you'll let me help?"

"Why ever would you want to, sir? I can offer you nothing."

"I try to help people. Where I can."

"You must be a man of god." For the first time since she has awoken, the woman seems a little afraid.

"No." Her saviour sounds uncertain. "At least, I do not think so. Rather what I do... I think it is as a kind of penance, I think, for deeds yet to be committed."

"How is that possible, sir?"

"I do not know. I do not know."

Only silence between them. Then, very softly, the man speaks again.

"Will you tell me now, if you wish, why those men are pursuing you? I sense that they possess... considerable determination. A certain ruthlessness also."

The woman does not reply.

"I promise that whatever you say shall make not the slightest difference. I have promised to protect you and that pledge shall stand. I make no judgement of any man or woman."

"I think…"

"Yes?"

"That you should tell me first."

"Me? Of what?"

"I am… curious. Your words are strange. You are not, I think, quite as other men are."

"Madam, I am far from certain what manner of man I am. Indeed, I have travelled widely and sought much wisdom upon the subject yet still I have no firm conclusion. Merely suspicions, you see. Merely bad dreams."

"Yet you try to do good?"

"As much as I can. Fortune seems to strew such opportunities in my path. Yet there remain… moments when I seem to have no life of my own at all. I simply fade from the world."

"Perhaps you are unwell, sir. It might behove you to consult a reputable physician."

"I have visited many such men yet they have found no physical cause for my… uncertainties."

"Then a doctor of a different kind, perhaps? Though, not, sir, for the sake of your own soul, I beg you, a priest."

"Now there you speak from experience, I think?"

"I do, sir." And she shudders, Maria Monk, she shudders in the night.

"You spoke of the soul. I have of late begun to fear for the sanctity of my own. I believe, you understand, that it is in some manner encircled and in the gravest peril. I fancy myself like some winter traveller alone in the forest who, strayed too far from the path, discovers, in a hideous moment of realisation, that he is quite surrounded, by wild wolves, that they have tracked him in the snow and that they are now but a leap from his throat."

"I do believe I know, sir, whereof you speak."

"Yes. I sensed somehow that you might." Cannonbridge shifts uneasily in his chair. "Maria, I have been told that there is some change due to take place within me, some transformation which will mean that, quite soon now, I am no longer to be the person that you find today. And I have begun to suspect—I have begun to fear—that my apotheosis is almost at hand."

"You should not be so fearful, Mr Cannonbridge, lest fear make of you its servant. In spite of all that I have witnessed, all that I have endured, I still believe in my heart that goodness is inherent in man and that it shall in the end prevail over evil."

"Then I admire your courage, madam. You spoke of what you have endured. You need tell me nothing if you do not wish it but I should be happy to hear you speak further of those dark times."

Maria stares into the gloom, her eyes blank and glassy. "Tell me, Mr Cannonbridge, have you heard tell of the Black Nunnery of Montreal?"

It seems that the woman has succeeded in shocking even Mr Cannonbridge. He leans forward in his chair and his voice is laced with horror. "Then..." He murmurs, swallows hard. "The rumours are true?"

"Worse, Mr Cannonbridge. Whatever the nature of the gossip that you have heard, the truth, believe me, is unutterably worse."

He is about to ask her to continue when there comes a knocking at the door. It is not a ferocious nor is it an insistent sound. Rather it is sly. It is careful. It is insidiously polite.

It comes again, a gentle tapping, which might almost be that of a lover who, treading lightly down the corridor in the watches of the night, comes to pay amorous court to his mistress.

Both occupants of the Chrysalis Suite, however, know that this is far being from the truth. In a single, swift and sinuous motion, Cannonbridge rises to his feet.

"Stay here," he hisses. "Whatever you hear, however frightened you become—I pray you, do not leave this room."

His tone is, as she has come to expect, sympathetic and even kindly, yet freighted with a species of subcutaneous menace.

Miss Monk does as she has been asked and we should doubtless do the same. We will not follow Mr Cannonbridge from the safety of that expensive boudoir and step with him out into the corridor where, with quiet fury in his heart, he goes to meet his callers. No, rather shall we stay here, within, in relative safety and in the company of Maria.

Let us instead examine her face as she listens to what transpires in the hall beyond.

At first, her expression is watchful, careful, unsurprised. She is well-used to pursuit. Much of her life has been spent as the quarry, of one kind or another, of men. She knows of their appetites, their clumsy lusts, their petulant brutalities. She wonders for an instant, almost hopeful, if she might have found in Cannonbridge one of that sex whose instincts are gentler and more complex, only to dismiss the notion after a spell of sombre reflection—a shift half-wistful, half born of cynical experience.

So now she listens as her ally treads softly to the door and opens it upon what she knows to be her pursuers. She listens to what shreds of conversation can be heard—the low, determined tones of Cannonbridge, the voices of the men in the bottle-green suits, first wheedling, then flecked with menace before bursting into roars of insistence.

No. No, in this last observation she must be mistaken. No roar of demand is this but rather one of surprise and of pain. There itcomes again. And there is movement also—the noise of flesh on flesh and bone upon bone, of shattering and dislocation, of the expert appliance of force to the frail physical form. There follows what sounds like a protracted whimper, cut short. Then, for a time, there is silence. Then, a soft, male approach.

She braces herself, sits up against the headboard and gathers the sheets around her as the flimsiest protection.

A figure enters the darkened room. It is Cannonbridge, evincing no sign of exertion, treading with smooth, feline confidence.

"Those gentlemen," he says, "shall not trouble you again."

Maria gazes up at him, wide-eyed in the murk.

"How can I thank you?" she begins before, growing sterner, despising herself a little for her girlishness: "They will send others."

Cannonbridge nods. "Then we should leave at once. For now, at least, we still possess the advantage of surprise."

With the ease of one long accustomed to violence and change, Maria rises and prepares, dispassionately, to leave.

Cannonbridge examines his reflection in the mirror, adjusts his hair and slips a pouch of money from the top drawer of the escritoire into his jacket pocket. He leaves a folded note for the staff to find in the morning.

Soon, the girl nods. She is ready. The man takes her hand.

"Come with me," he says, "but, please, I implore you, when we pass those gentlemen in the hall outside, do not look at their faces."

But as they step out into the corridor Maria cannot resist a few quick, darting glances downwards as they pass the two sprawled bodies which the author has propped neatly against the wall. She sees at once what has been done to them—the breakages and abrasions, the bruising and subtle lacerations, the deft, almost painterly remodelling of bone—and finds that she cannot withhold her dark respect.

Then they are away, her hand in his, out of the hallway, down the stairs, before, escaping the hotel itself, they run out into the night, fleeing into darkness, throwing themselves into the maw of the city.

NOW

AT FIRST, TOBY believes that he is woken by a woman's scream.

The sound, which he takes to be that of a keening shriek, penetrates his sleep and urges him back to consciousness. He wills his eyes to open, stirs with a grouchy drowsiness, wriggles upright in his too-big double bed and listens.

Only silence. For a moment the dream from which he has been summoned flickers across his memory, and is gone. He feels the sense that something of importance has been taken from him but then the noise comes again and this mournful sense too is lost.

It is not, of course, the sound of weeping which has woken him. He recognises it now that he hears it again whilst clearer in his mind and he wonders how it was that he was ever so mistaken. There has been no woman, after all, in this place for weeks.

The doorbell is ringing—shrill and insistent.

Something about the sound of it, its vigour and duration, persuades Dr Judd that the caller is no postman or crank, no Jehovah's Witness or door-to-door canvasser, no mendicant or pamphleteer.

The ball is in motion, he thinks, unsure where the thought has come from, as he rises hurriedly, steps out of the bedroom and treads towards the door. *Gravity is at work and descent has already begun.*

One final, mechanical shriek and Toby answers, wrenching open the door without consideration as to how he will appear to his visitor: tangle-haired and unshaven and unkempt, his skin pouchy and raw.

"Yes? What do you want?"

There is a stranger standing before him—or so, at least, Toby believes before he appreciates the truth. *My perception is decaying,* he thinks, wondering, with an arm's-length curiosity, if he might not, quietly and without any particular fuss, be going mad.

The man who has woken him is stocky, well-built and thick-necked. He wears a t-shirt which has a slogan written upon it for one of the most famous corporations in the world. A billboard, Toby thinks, a walking billboard idling on my threshold. Then he looks again and sees purpose in the man's eyes, a suggestion of authority.

Toby says: "Sergeant Angeyo."

Angeyo shrugs. "Off duty now. Call me Isaac."

"Then you must call me Toby," says the academic vaguely, knee-jerk politeness trumping any other reaction. "But, can I ask, what are you doing here?"

"Can I come in, Toby? We've got to talk. Talk about something important."

"I'm sorry?"

Angeyo runs a hand across his chin in an oddly nervous gesture. "You see, there's something bothering me. Something which just won't let me go."

DR JUDD AND Sergeant Angeyo are sitting at close quarters in Toby's stuffy sitting room. Both have a cup of milkless tea before them. Toby has been to the bathroom and splashed cold water over his face whilst the policeman waited on the sofa, tapping with an awful jumpy restlessness the face of his watch.

Somewhere outside a lawnmower or a strimmer or a mechanical leaf-blower has been pressed into service. Its shrill roar sounds like something furious and trapped.

The Sergeant leans forward and frowns, an expression which somehow does not suit his young and relatively unlined face. How is that possible, wonders Toby, almost giddily, to be a policeman and not to frown, to see what he must surely see yet still possess such innocence?

"I want you to know, Toby, that I'm not here in any professional capacity. OK? All this, everything I'm about to say, is strictly off the record."

Judd swallows—he has a dry throat and the beginnings of a headache. "Of course," he says, trying to seem more collected than he feels, as if this is the sort of thing that happens to him all the time. "That's absolutely understood."

"It's about the dead man. About Russell Spicer."

Toby says nothing. Outside, the lawnmower or whatever it is (chainsaw? digger? pneumatic drill?) screams louder.

"I'm…" The policeman flinches. "Look, I'm sure it wasn't suicide. There's just no question in my mind."

Outside, after a diminuendo, the mechanical implement falls silent, as if observing a few moments of remembrance of Spicer, its blades sombre and still, its petrol waiting respectfully in the tank.

Between the two men there is an awful, intense quietness.

At last, with a tremor in his voice, Toby asks: "Are you sure?" And then, when the officer of the law says nothing in response but only looks unblinkingly on: "Why?"

Isaac Angeyo speaks slowly, with stately patience. "It was expertly done, sir. Almost perfect. There was the illusion of suicide. They must have been professionals of some kind. You see, it was savage. Savage yet exact. Savage yet… plausible."

Schooled by years of TV thrillers, Judd is expecting to be asked whether he knew of anyone who would wish the dead man harm or if Toby himself can account for his whereabouts on the night in question but Angeyo, tired, perhaps, himself of such rituals, merely states his suspicions, his own cool extrapolation. "Whoever was responsible had money. I know how to see these things. This wasn't some thuggish opportunist. This was planned. There were *resources* at work here."

Toby feels a sudden urge to impress this quiet and solemn man. His words are second-hand, borrowed from the screen: "A contract killing, then?"

"We don't actually use that phrase, sir. But yes. Yes."

"He must've had enemies?"

"Yes, sir. It seems he had enemies. The blood had soaked into the pillow, sir. It looked like a halo."

"Can I ask? I mean, why are you telling me this?"

Outside, its pause of respect apparently complete, the sound of whirring metal begins again.

Angeyo glances behind him, seemingly made uneasy by the noise. "My superiors don't know I'm here. They wouldn't like it if they found out. And I'm off-duty. But I don't think you're safe, sir. I think you're in huge danger. Whoever the people responsible are they're not the kind you want to tangle with. I think you need to leave town, sir, and go to ground."

Whatever Toby had imagined that the man might say—whatever the reason for this particular visit—it was most assuredly not this.

"I'm surprised," he says. "Well, that's an understatement."

"I'm serious, sir. Deadly serious."

"Yes. Yes. I can see that."

"Is there somewhere you can go, sir? Somewhere you can't be traced? Somewhere you can stay out of sight?"

"Can't you tell me more? Can't you tell me why?"

"I've already said too much. My job, you see…" He hesitates. "Look, so I was cataloguing the dead man's possessions. Seeing if there was anything useful. And let's just say you're connected."

"How? Why?"

Angeyo, reluctantly: "There was evidence. There was a list. Your name was at the top of it. Do you believe me now?"

Toby draws breath.

"Yes. Yes, I do."

"Will you leave for a while? I'll be in touch, I promise, just as soon as I know more. I'd take you into custody for your own protection but I'm not sure you'd be safe even here."

Toby's throat burns. "What are you saying, Sergeant?"

"I'm asking you to run for your life."

There is no melodrama in his voice—nothing but professional sincerity with, Toby realises now, something horribly like panic deep beneath.

A high-pitched bleeping, a parodic melody which seems almost grotesque. Angeyo tugs his phone from his pocket, stabs briskly at a button and rises adroitly to his feet.

"I have to go, sir. But please—do as I ask. I'll be in touch. I promise."

"There's so much more," Toby protests. "So much to ask you."

"I'm doing everything I can, sir. As soon as I can, I'll tell you. But for now pack your bags and... *run*."

In the pause that follows, Toby's decision is made. Sensing this, perhaps, Angeyo turns and leaves.

Judd lets him—hears the soft click of the front door. He stands in his little lounge, listening to the machine outside, his imagination filled up with the policeman's words. And then, moving quickly, almost at a sprint, he strides to his room and starts to pack.

NOT MORE THAN ten minutes into this process—hurried, indiscriminate, edged with mania—the landline in the sitting room rings, its antiquated trill demanding and imperious. Toby sets down the tattered sports bag into which he has been decanting the best of his admittedly limited wardrobe and approaches the telephone, warily, as one might a sleeping animal. To silence its clarion, Judd picks up the receiver.

"Hello?"

The line is bad, crackling and patchy as if the call originates from some far-distant country, as if (and Toby is not altogether certain from whence comes this disquieting thought) it originates from the past.

"Who is this?"

Toby's heart rate has increased. Sweat prickles against his forehead.

The voice, when it speaks is male, flat, without emotion. Toby is put in mind of a fallen priest, jaded and corrupt.

"O, Eliphar, king-begotten son, these words are mine homage unto you:

Eliphar, sorely-treated man, sold into slavery and made to labour

In the caverns of the beast with many arms, the walker with her wicked smile.

Brave Eliphar, who struggles in darkness for the pleasure of a devil."

Toby recognises the lines at once—there is scarcely a schoolboy, after all, who would not—as the opening words of the opening stanza of Matthew Cannonbridge's 1860 verse cycle *The Lamentation of Eliphar, Mununzar's Son*, which once inspired a sequence of paintings by Rossetti and which John Ruskin declared "the most beguiling poetic achievement in our national literature since *Paradise Lost*."

"Who are you?" asks Dr Judd. "What do you want?"

The voice does not slow down nor show any sign that it even heard the interjection.

"O Eliphar, the lonely. O, Eliphar, the outcast. O, Eliphar, the cursed and most hated.

O Eliphar, the runtish one, whose doom was written in the mud and in the mire."

Toby opens his mouth to say something more but, sensing the pointlessness of the gesture, simply lets the voice drone on ("Eliphar, the thrice-betrayed; Eliphar, the angel-spurned") and replaces the receiver. Yet somehow it is as if the words do not end with the cessation of the call but rather continue, with their whispering intensity, inside his head.

Quickly, fearing once more for his sanity, he returns to the bedroom and continues to pack—faster than before.

Minutes later, he is outside, hurrying from the house and from his old life, a sports bag slung over one shoulder, moving swiftly down the street as fast as he can without drawing attention, anxious and afraid, like a thing who senses that wolves are already at his heels. Once, he thinks he hears someone call his name. He stops and glances behind him but, seeing nothing, the sweat trickling down his neck and between his shoulder blades, he strides frantically on.

1835
ABOARD THE VIGILANT SLEEPER
CONNECTICUT

FOR A TIME now they have been lost to us, Mr Matthew Cannonbridge and Miss Maria Monk, lost at first to the night and to the clockwork quiet of the city and then to the plains beyond, to the open skies, the steady wilderness, to unpeopled lands and to woods beneath the stars—lost to the great expanse of America, to the blank spaces of the map.

Yet, now, at last, after this ellipsis, all of their undocumented adventures, we are to encounter them again, seated together in a railway carriage and travelling at speed towards the city of New York. Miss Monk sits closer to the gentleman than convention would, perhaps, ordinarily allow. Indeed, they are almost touching, a proximity from which he does not appear to shy.

"You are," she murmurs with a contentment that she would once have thought impossible, "a most remarkable man."

He does not reply. Although a part of him knows this to be true he has begun to suspect with an intensity of suspicion which is all but a certainty, lacking only a final piece of evidence to place it beyond all reasonable doubt, that the quality in question may not be expressed as she might wish for very much longer now.

"I do believe I owe you my life."

The wheels of the train rattle upon the track. The engines bellow and puff. The carriage itself rocks to and fro in a manner which is altogether agreeable to them both and which encourages Maria to move a little closer still, the result, plausibly enough, of this cradle motion.

"Nothing..." he murmurs.

"Nothing?" Her tone is one of incredulity.

"Nothing more," he goes on, although he seems scarcely to have heard her, "than was my duty. Nothing more than I have always tried to do." There is an edge to his tone, she senses now, something like distraction, even, perhaps, buried deep, horribly fervent despair.

Without thinking, she reaches up to him and brushes his cheek with her fingers. "You should not speak so, sir. You are a good man. The best—the very best—of men."

Cannonbridge twitches at least and his face convulses into something between a snarl and a sneer. Startled, Maria takes away her hand.

"You think so, do you, madam?"

Her voice is even, polite: "I can only judge you, sir, on what I have witnessed. And that is all noble and fine. You have saved me, after all, and more than once."

"I see." He shakes his head, as if at her naiveté. His manner seems to soften. "Maria?"

"Mr Cannonbridge?"

"Might I beg of you a boon?"

"Anything."

"You will think me less than a gentleman."

"Never that, sir."

"Nevertheless..."

The rattle of the carriage, the whirr of the wheels. Outside, twilight has begun to fall.

"Ask it, sir."

"Might I be permitted to... kiss you?"

Outwardly, Maria gives only a single, sober nod, as if almost disappointed with the request. Inwardly, she rejoices at the prospect. She is not quite certain if her companion has taken note of the gesture for he takes no action and all that he says is:

"This may surprise you, madam, but I have never yet performed the act."

Curiously, Maria, who is long accustomed to lechers of every kind, discovers herself to be blushing. "Truly, sir?"

"No. The circumstances have never allowed for it. Unless, that is, in those fragments of lost time I have, in some manner, done what I have not whilst in my conscious state."

"Best not to think on it, sir."

"No?"

"Best not to think at all, sir."

At last, to her relief, he understands. Hungry now, he bends towards her, their bodies suddenly snug and close, his hot breath and hers intermingling, the air crackling with expectation.

He moves just a little closer. She closes her eyes, savouring this instant. Their lips brush against one another, he just as clumsy as she had expected, her urging him on.

And then: quite suddenly, and as though a terrific charge had been passed through her body, the young woman starts violently backwards. She blinks too fast, her hand hovers near her mouth, wipes her lips, hangs helplessly before her. She is shaking—shuddering, Cannonbridge comes to realise, with fear.

"Maria? Maria, my love, what is it? What ails you?"

She backs away from him, staggers upright, hurries towards the door and the swaying aisle beyond.

Matthew Cannonbridge makes no move to halt her but he asks again: "What has affected you so, Maria? Why do you cringe from me now? Why do you flee from my sight?"

Temporarily the fear that is in Maria is displaced by something sweeter. "Oh, you poor man," she says and her voice is filled with compassion.

"Maria? Maria? What is it?"

"I've seen it. What passed between us then."

"What have you seen, my love?"

"The darkness that is stalking you and..." She stifles a sob. "The darkness that is within. The coldness. The rows of numbers. Row upon row. Almost upon you now."

Cannonbridge rises to his feet. "Then help me," he says. "Help me vanquish it."

"I cannot... I dare not. I..." She wipes a tear from her eye. "Thank you, sir. For all that you have done for me. But now

I would rather take my chances. God bless you, sir. God keep you safe."

And she runs, weeping, from the carriage.

Cannonbridge allows her to go. Instead of following, he simply returns to his seat. He sighs—a long, quivering sigh that might, in others, almost form a preface to weeping. The author restrains himself, however, and sits in his place. He closes his eyes and steeples his fingers as, around him, the shadows grow dark and long.

WERE ONE TO have been on that train with Mr Cannonbridge and Miss Monk and were one to have looked in again upon their carriage an hour or so after the lady's tearful flight to the buffet car one would have seen no sign whatever of its occupants. Maria would by now have installed herself in the cafeteria, guilty and fretful. But of Matthew Cannonbridge there would be no sign. Indeed, even the most thorough search of the train would reveal no trace of that soon to be notorious gentleman. It is unthinkable, of course, that he should ever have thrown himself from the locomotive. Rather it would be as if he had simply dissipated, as if he had turned to smoke or to shadow or to moonlight before, all at once and without the slightest warning, he is gone.

NOW

LIKE SO MUCH in his life until now, Portsmouth has proved to be a disappointment for Toby Judd.

He had not decided to come here until the very last moment, queuing impatiently for the single extant and functioning ticket machine at Ashbury station, listening to the litany of potential destinations squawking from the tannoy with the weird, repetitive intonations of some officious robot. Only when his fingers reached towards the screen did he make up his mind, to fulfil his long-held ambition to ride towards the sea, to a place where the smell of salt hangs heavy in the air, a place which bristles with nautical energy.

The reality, however, is almost intolerably dreary. The station is choked and unpleasant, the streets unkempt and forlorn, the overriding scent of the place not honest salt but cheap and spoilt food. The town centre, needless to say, is largely indistinguishable from any other similarly-sized town in Britain or—Toby speculates, for he is not an especially well-travelled man—any such place in any First World nation. Homogeneity, he thinks, not for the first time, is on the march.

Still, at least nobody knows him here. He has no connection to Portsmouth—no logical reason to be in this place. Sergeant Angeyo, he considers, will approve of the choice.

He is sitting alone on a bench on the sea-front with only his sports bag for company. In the distance (and this, at least, accords with his imagination) ferries honk and move with stubborn sureness of purpose. Overhead, gulls wheel and shriek. On his lap, purchased by way of a late lunch, sits a punnet of chips, greasy and glistening.

There is a moment then—and this is the last time that he will experience this—when Toby Judd, sitting in the sunshine in an English town, wonders if the whole thing—the warnings of

Sergeant Angeyo, that poetic phone call, the dreams, the very question of Cannonbridge's authenticity—might not be some spasm of his own consciousness, the consequences of incipient mental decay, the sad and tangled fantasies of a man in the midst of a crisis that precedes complete breakdown. And yet, he thinks, it seems so real and so true.

He takes out his mobile phone, checks for messages—for any word from Angeyo—and notes, with doleful unsurprise, that he has not been contacted by anyone who does not wish to sell him something for almost six weeks. He is still peering at the thing when a shadow falls over him.

"D'you want this?"

A man, a stranger, in his eighties, white-haired but standing tall, something military about his bearing. For a second or so, Toby is convinced that the man believes him to be homeless and is about to press a coin or two into his hand along with an injunction to spend none of it on booze. Then he understands—a folded copy of the *Evening Standard* is held in the stranger's hand.

"First edition. Hot off the presses. Found it at the station. I'd only throw it in there otherwise." He glances towards the litter bin which stands beside the bench.

Years of training—upbringing and education—mean that courtesy is Toby's only consideration. He thanks the man and takes the folded paper.

The stranger nods. "Thought you might like something to read with your chips."

"I appreciate it."

The man lingers. "Course I remember when they used to wrap them in it. Chips. Fish and chips in newspaper."

Toby nods with feigned enthusiasm.

"Isn't allowed nowadays, is it? On account of a few youngsters feeling sick on the taste of the newsprint. Well, we did—we all did at first—but we got used to it. One of the things which marked out my generation, that was: ironclad stomachs."

"Yes, I suppose that's probably true."

"We fought a war on it. Bellies of steel."

"I don't suppose I'd ever thought of it that way."

"Of course it's rare to even find them wrapped in any sort of paper at all these days. It's all plastic and Styrofoam now. Shouldn't be surprised. We live in a plastic and Styrofoam world after all. Don't we? Nothing real. Nothing natural."

"Oh, I agree."

The two men exchange a look of unexpected intergenerational camaraderie. Then the older of the two nods again—"grand chatting to you"—and steps, with stately briskness, away.

With a swell of melancholy, Toby watches him go, as the old man's stern figure dwindles to a dot along the front. Then he opens the *Evening Standard* and glares, with an almost lackadaisical quality which will soon seem in retrospect to be absurd, at the newspaper's headline.

Three seconds later, he is doubled over, his head between his knees, regurgitating his lunch onto the tarmac, feeling all at once more bleak and hopeless than he ever has before.

UPON HIS EVENTUAL recovery, acting instinctively and forgetting the facts of the matter in the pure sensation of the moment, Toby's first thought is to attempt to phone his wife. Stumbling away from the bench and from those terrible words that are upon the front page, he reaches for his mobile, summons up her number and presses the call button. Oddly yet, somehow, not wholly unexpectedly, there is no connection, only a shrill, elongated sound, then silence. He tries again. The result is the same. Another number. Same again. The battery is fine, his credit should be ample. He gives it one more attempt. A shriek, then silence.

He wonders—and he has no idea if such a thing is even possible—whether the phone might not be interrupted, or blocked, in some way. After what he has just read there is nothing now which seems entirely beyond the pale.

Overhead, a seabird whoops and screeches as if in mockery of him.

Then, in the distance, like something glimpsed from the past, Toby catches sight of a red phone box. That most antiquated of notions: a public telephone. Wondering at their continued existence, he reclaims his sports bag, then walks on. A breeze picks up and he smells salt for the first time. He hurries on. Behind him, the pages of the *Standard* turn in the draught, rustling and sighing slyly.

THE BOX IS further away than it first seemed and, for a while, as Toby walks towards it, as quickly as his churning nausea will allow, he even begins to speculate that the thing might be some optical illusion, a mirage conjured by a mind still grappling with horror. In painful increments, however, the cherry-red booth hoves gradually nearer until at last his hand pulls open the heavy iron door and he steps inside.

How long since he has been within one of these things? Five years? Ten? It smells of stale, sickly deodorant combined with something foul underneath. He wonders what the space is used for predominantly now—not, he suspects, for the making of legitimate calls.

As he feeds his change into the metal slot and taps in the number he even considers the wisdom of his actions. But soon instinct and tradition take hold.

"Caroline?"

Her voice is frosty and comfortless and achingly distant. "Toby? What is it? Why are you calling on this weird number?"

"Have you seen the news?"

A pause. "The news? Toby... you realise that we can't just chat like this anymore, don't you? We've got to move on with our own lives. Find our own happiness."

"You don't understand. No. I'm not calling just to... chew the fat."

"The what? Listen, sorry if I sound harsh but I just can't imagine that either of us has anything new to say to one another. Toby? Toby, are you still there?"

Dr Judd has been distracted midway through the speech by a knock on the glass of the box. There is a man outside—early thirties and balding, yet solidly built and in possession both of a braggart's swagger and of the very worst collection of teeth which Toby has ever seen. The interloper looks extremely cross and is at present busy miming making a phone call, one hand clamped angrily to ear, the other gesticulating expressively.

"Give me a minute," Toby says.

A tut. "You phoned me!"

"Sorry. Not you. There's a man outside."

"What? Where are you, Toby? What's going on?"

"Something's happened, darling."

"Not 'darling'. We've been through this."

Another tap on the pane. Toby snorts and says: "In. A. Minute."

The man sets his face into an expression of what he presumably imagines to be menace.

"Darling, I'm at a crossroads and I want to do the right thing but I'm scared and I'm fairly sure I'm in real danger and I need the help of… somebody I love."

There is a long silence from the other end of the line. Another tap on the window which, Toby, frowning, ignores. It comes again and, in a surge of fury, he gives the stranger his middle finger.

"I'm going to sound like a bit of bitch now, Toby. I know that. But you've got to understand that we simply can't do this any longer. I'm with J J. And I'm really not coming back. Ever. It's necessary for you to accept these things."

Toby bites hard on his lower lip. His vision seems to flicker. "Then I'll…"

"Yes? What will you do?"

"Then I'll do it on my own."

As Toby places the receiver back into its cradle the door is wrenched open and he is pulled from the booth.

"Don't fucking give me the fucking finger." The stranger's breath is rank and smells of tobacco. He is wearing too much cheap deodorant.

"Perhaps you need to learn some patience," Toby suggests.

"More like you need to learn some respect."

"Oh, really?" Toby has the mad, giddy sensation that he might be about to enter into his first ever fight. If he imagines that the stranger's face is that of the noted cultural commentator Dr J J Salazar he suspects that he might even stand a chance.

The man steps closer. "Who uses a phone box these days, anyway?"

"Besides you, you mean?"

"I'm waiting for a call. I weren't making one."

"I see. Then I'm terribly sorry to have hijacked your office." His appetite for confrontation already flagging, Toby turns now and starts to walk again the way he has come, towards the bench and the town beyond.

"Mate!" The man is shouting after him.

"What?"

"You're not scared? Turning your back on me?"

Judd stops, turns back. "No, I'm not frightened of you," he says. "Not that I mightn't have been once. But after today—when you realise the scale of what's against you, when you realise you've got nothing left to lose… well, there's an odd kind of liberty in that. You don't know it but you were present when I made the most important decision of my life and—I freely accept—very possibly the last."

"Which was what?" asks the man contemptuously.

Toby looks him directly in the eyes. "To get to the truth. Whatever the cost." He smiles and bows his head. If he had a hat, he thinks, he'd doff it. "Good afternoon to you."

ALMOST EXACTLY ONE hour later, a man pays cash for a one-way coach ticket to Edinburgh. He is small, slim, rather beleaguered-looking and dressed in an old cord jacket. He sits quietly towards the back of the vehicle as it trundles towards Scotland. He is meditative in Southampton, faraway in the Midlands, lost in the North and almost asleep as darkness falls and they approach the edge of England. No-one sits next to him—he has, you see, become the kind of man whom other travellers avoid, the one who talks to himself, the oddball, the nutter. On the empty seat beside him is an old sports bag, with a copy of the *London Evening Standard* laid on top. The headline of the day is just visible. It reads: MURDERED COP NAMED.

As for the close-up photograph which accompanies the piece, you would no doubt recognise—as did Toby Judd, with grief and panic seizing at his heart like a snake about a mouse—the honest, pensive face of Sergeant Isaac Angeyo.

1842
THE PARSONAGE
HAWORTH

LONG HAS THE shadow of death enfolded the parsonage. Showing no deference to the season, it is palpable here, now, even upon Christmas Day, as the family gather in their little parlour, filled with heartache and sorrow. They are five in number yet they are grievously depleted—a father is present and three girls and a son but their dear mother is twenty years in her grave and two other daughters, departed too soon, lie mouldering beside her.

It is of mortality, of course, that the patriarch is speaking as we draw near to them, of fragility, inevitability, impermanence. He is white-haired, bowed, sixty-five years old though he seems more senior still, with that great cravat which is bound about his neck like a funeral shroud, with his watery, sorrowful eyes and his trembling arthritic gait. When he speaks, his three surviving daughters—Emily, Charlotte, Anne—listen with dutiful attentiveness though the thoughts of that triumvirate are all, in their own ways, far from this isolated spot. The young man, Branwell, seems rather unsteady on his feet, a glass of whisky punch clasped in one hand.

The smell of roasting goose pervades the building. Outside, beyond the little window stretches the vast expanse of the moor. Bleak and seemingly limitless, it fills the horizon, its light dappling of snowfall serving not to render the scene a festive one but rather to accentuate its inhospitable, minatory qualities, its utter absence of mercy.

The old man's voice is tired from hours at the church in the morning yet it is still firm from years of practice and skilful use. Whilst the rest of him, beset by grief, decays, that voice goes on.

"I wanted," he begins, "before we sit down to eat, to say a few words about the year that has passed."

His children, accustomed to such pre-prandial sermonising, listen respectfully. Only Emily, the middle daughter, seems distracted, her eyes flicking constantly from her father's face to the view from the window, to the cruel sweep of the moor.

"Our losses have been severe. Mr Weightman has gone to a better place. Your beloved aunt also. And our particular friend, Dr Andrew. Such things are always hard and they seem at such times as these almost impossible to bear. Nonetheless, we must trust in the wisdom of the Lord and that, in drawing our dear friends to Him before what seems to us to be their natural time, He is fulfilling a divine design of which we are not granted comprehension. Today, of all days, we must trust in Him and we must yield to His wisdom and to His grace." He turns to the youngest of his daughters. "Anne, my dear, I believe that you have something that you wish to share with us?"

The young woman in question, sober, dark-haired and with a certain pinched quality to her jaw, says: "A poem, father. In memory of Mr Weightman."

"And you wish to recite it to us?"

"I do."

At the prospect, her brother takes a sip of the punch. Charlotte's lips purse. Emily's gaze wanders outside towards the moor, the muddy green-brown of it capped with white. Her eyes seem to linger now upon a particular spot—on a dash of black in the palette. Something alien in the wilderness.

Her sister begins to speak, her words sugared and prim:

"I will not mourn thee, lovely one,
Though thou art torn away.
'Tis said that if the morning sun
Arise with dazzling ray
And shed a bright and burning beam,
Athwart the glittering main,
Ere noon shall fade that laughing gleam
Engulfed in clouds and rain."

As her sibling speaks, Emily's attention is all outside. The black speck, she sees now, is no mere quirk of the landscape, no stunted tree or discarded implement but rather something animate—something human.

"And if thy life as transient proved
It hath been full as bright,
For thou wert hopeful and beloved;
Thy spirit knew no blight."

These words barely penetrate Emily's consciousness. The speck has resolved itself into a man, tall, saturnine and dressed in dark and sombre clothes. His movements are unsteady; he seems, more than once, to stumble and at the sight of the stranger's approach, Emily, oddly, remembers her father's description of the moor aflame that summer, when the rioters had come to Haworth, and feels, as then, a sensation of wrongness, an invasion from forces which do not belong to this place or this time. She looks at her family—their attention either on her sister or upon the whisky punch—and realises that she alone has seen the arrival of the newcomer.

Anne speaks on ("If few and short the joys of life / That thou on earth couldst know / Little thou knew'st of sin and strife—") but Emily feels that she has no choice but to interrupt her. "Father!"

Anne stops speaking, the quaint Sunday school rhymes dying on her lips.

The old man is reproving yet indulgent. "Tish, Emily. Your sister was reciting."

Outside, the stranger comes closer still, as if he moves faster when her eyes are not on him.

"I know that, father. Forgive me, but…"

"Yes, my dear. What is it?" A note of concern in the old priest's voice. Disapproval from her sisters. Quiet amusement from her brother.

Outside, the dark man is nearer still, almost at the parsonage.

"There is a gentleman approaching us, father. It seems to me that he is in need of help."

"A gentleman?" repeats the old man.

"There!" Emily all but shouts, frustrated that the others do not sense the urgency of the moment. She points dramatically, almost with a flourish, and the family turn to look.

And there he is, the tall man, staggering towards the parsonage. Spurred on, perhaps, by the sight of civilisation, by the proximity of people, he reaches the window, and for one delirious instant, Emily thinks that he might be about to break the pane and crash through it, tumbling into their sitting room. Instead, almost within reach of the sill, he simply stops and stands, like a seeker after alms, although Emily can tell from his clothes that he is nothing of the kind. He stares at them—and the family gaze bemusedly back. He stumbles as if he is about to fall, righting himself but barely. A moment later, he moves uncertainly away—searching, Emily has little doubt, for the front door.

"Who is that man?" says Anne.

Her father is abrupt. "He is not known to us. No parishioner he."

Then, the inevitable: the stentorian sound of metal on wood.

"It's him," Charlotte all but squeals. "Knocking at our door!"

"Branwell?" The old man's voice is grave. "Pray, put down your glass, sir, and come with me. It would seem that there is a matter which demands of us our immediate attention."

The young man grudgingly sets down his drink. His father glances rheumily back at the ladies.

"Girls," he says (for such is how he still addresses them for all that they have achieved their majority). "Stay in your proper place."

And so Emily is left with the others with nothing to do but wait. As she does so she cannot help but think and in the course of her meditations, oblivious to the chatter of her sisters, a stray reflection becomes a certainty—that when the dark-haired stranger gazed wildly through the glass, that it was by her, and by Emily alone, that his attention was riveted.

A few minutes pass and Emily, frustrated, strains to hear what is taking place outside. There is but little to be heard—the reedy, insistent tones of her father, the slurred baritone of her brother and nothing at all of the voice of the stranger. In the corner of the room, her two sisters whisper excitedly to one another like elderly gossips and Emily suddenly finds herself of a mind to hurl something at them, to enjoin them to silence and ask them in her most unyielding tone whether they do not understand the evident severity of the thing which was now almost in their midst.

Then, before she can speak, the stranger is present, helped in by the two men of the family in the manner of a wounded general being helped from the battlefield by subordinates.

Even in his presently dilapidated state—wet, muddy, clothes a little ragged, unsteady on his feet and desperately short of breath—there is a presence to the man, Emily thinks, a sense of purpose and a kind of fierce dignity which does not somehow strike her as altogether benign. Above all, there is a wrongness, even an injustice, to his presence here, in their little parlour on this holiest of feast days, as though his likeness has been clipped from some unsuitable volume and pasted with slipshod malice upon a page of scripture. Her father and brother look surprised and out of sorts at his arrival.

When he speaks, the stranger's voice is melodious and deep, with an undertow of something strange, less than orthodox. He stands free of his two rescuers.

"Ladies, I trust you will forgive me for my interrupting in so rough and vulgar a fashion…" He stumbles forwards, gasps. One hand darts towards his side. "I was lost, you see, and I had begun to fear the worst. I was lost upon the dreadful moor. You can scarcely imagine how grateful I was to spy your little dwelling-place and know that the promise of sanctuary lay within."

"Enough, my boy." Her father sounds, as he often does, kindly but abrupt. "You are quite exhausted and you must not excite yourself any further. Girls, girls, stand away from that young man."

Charlotte and Anne who have clustered around the stranger cringe back at his command.

"Perhaps, father…" This is Branwell, already edging back towards the punch. "Perhaps a drink might revive our guest?"

"I wish to cause no trouble to you, friends," says the stranger. "Only for a few moments respite. Then you have my word that I shall be on my way." He sways, stumbles, gasps a little as if in pain. "You see…" His eyes dart towards the window and to the moor beyond. "I believe myself to be pursued." He shudders, not theatrically, Emily thinks, but rather from some profound internal conflict. He smiles weakly and Emily sees that there is blood—there is blood in his mouth. "Yet I am forgetting my manners. I have yet to introduce myself. I am very pleased to make your acquaintance. My name—" He totters, rights himself, winces. "My name…"

No further words come. His hands drop by his side and without any sound at all, like a tree felled in the forest, the stranger falls forward upon the parlour floor, with a look of something close to agony on his face.

HOURS HAVE PASSED. That late luncheon has become early supper. A little singed and spoilt, perhaps, but it has been devoured with gratitude all the same. The family, sated and drowsy, have returned to the sitting room, the shutters of its windows closed now against the night and against the oppression of the moor. Branwell is already asleep, a half-empty glass in one hand, the remaining liquid tilted within. Charlotte and Anne sit beside one another, exchanging whispers. The word "Brussels" is regularly heard. Their father sits with his eyes closed and the top of his cravat loosened, whether in a posture of penitence or somnolence it is impossible to tell.

Emily sits apart from the rest. A book—the *Biographia Literaria*—lies open but unread upon her lap. Her lips are a little parted, her eyes are shining and she is listening. As for the parsonage's unsolicited guest, he is upstairs in the room which had until less than two months before been occupied by the now-departed aunt. The men had laid him down in there as gently as they were able. The parson himself had spoken a prayer over his comatose form but it had been decided that he should be left to recuperate until the morning. They could not call out the doctor on so sacred an evening and, besides, they were not certain that they entirely trusted the new physician yet.

So there he is, thinks Emily, lying asleep in a dead woman's bedroom. Emily knows it is most improper yet she feels drawn to the stranger as might a hare to a baited trap and so, having thought of little else, through the family's repast and the homilies and speculations which have provided much of the surrounding conversation, she arrives at her decision.

Emily sets the book aside, rises to her feet, murmurs her excuses and leaves, ascending the stairs as gently as she can, her footfalls as soft as she can make them.

On the first floor, she steals along the hallway to the cramped bedroom at the end of it. The door is ajar, the chamber within shadowed and still. Suddenly a little doubtful but knowing that it is far too late to turn back, she steps inside.

The visitor is almost too large for the bed and his position seems oddly precarious, as if he might at any moment vanish from their lives as swiftly as he has entered it. For a time she does no more than watch him sleep, sprawled out in that little space, his breathing feverish and irregular, his handsome face slick with perspiration.

Emily, sensing that she has intruded, wonders why she has come, marvelling at the way in which, even in so reduced a state as this, the man can exert so awful a fascination. Nonetheless, summoning all her powers of resistance, she turns her back upon him and is about to creep from his presence when she hears from behind her his soft voice. "Emily?"

Slowly, she turns to face him.

"Yes," he says. "Yes, I had hoped it would be you."

She feels hot and she is herself perspiring, as though she has stepped too close to a furnace. "Sir?"

"Will you sit beside me for a while? I'd like someone with me... at the end."

She does as she has been asked, almost without thinking. There is a stool beside the bed upon which she sits, dragging it a little closer to the stranger so that she might take his hand in hers. His skin is clammy and febrile.

"Perhaps you have caught a chill, sir?" she says, although she fears that the man's complaint may be rather more severe than that. "We shall call for the surgeon in the morning."

He smiles strangely. "He is not for me. Nor I for him. And by the morning it shall certainly be too late."

"Please, sir. Do not say such things."

He breathes out. The process sounds as if it is a painful one. "You will die here," he says matter-of-factly. "Here in this house."

Emily thinks before she replies. "I believe... that I have always known that, sir."

"Forgive me. I am on occasion granted glimpses of what is yet to come. Of late, such instances have been becoming more frequent."

Emily could not explain her certainty but somehow she does not doubt him. Fearful, she asks: "What are you, sir?"

"For a long time I had but an imperfect notion. But now I believe that I am finally starting to understand. This is the year, you see— this is the year of foundation. And this very moment, somewhere in London, it is beginning. And the darkness is almost upon me. I am to be granted new purpose and I can hold out against it no longer."

To her surprise, for she is far from unaccustomed to illness and suffering, Emily's cheeks are wet with tears. "Please, sir. Please! You have to try."

"I have done my best to be a good man, Emily. I fear I have succeeded only in proving ineffectual. All that is to be swept aside now."

"You speak of sin, sir?"

"Yes. If you like. A great tide of sin that is to swallow me at any moment. And after that deluge I fear I shall not be the same man. I will be... grievously transformed."

She feels such pity for him for she discerns within his words a terrible truth and so she holds his hand a little tighter and she squeezes, willing him to be wrong, urging, like Polidori and Maria before her, the good man to thwart the other.

"Do you sense it?" he asks now. "It approaches. The tide draws near. My transformation is at hand."

She understands whereof he speaks. Do not the shadows of the place seem deeper now and darker? Is not the air charged and in a state of strange excitation as it is before the mightiest of thunderstorms? And is there not to be heard, faraway but growing swiftly closer, a sound like rushing water?

Unflinching, Emily clasps hold of his hand. "Be brave," she murmurs. "Be brave."

"Pity me now," he hisses, his voice thick with sorrow. "But soon—very soon—I am afraid that you will only fear me."

The darkness draws nearer, the sound grows louder and more terrible and, mere moments later, everything is lost.

DOWNSTAIRS, THE REST of the family are woken—for all four have now slipped into slumber—by the most extraordinary phenomena. The parsonage itself seems to be shaking as if it is being subjected to almost unbearable stress. In the kitchen, crockery is hurled to the ground. Glasses shatter in swift succession. A mirror falls violently to the floor and is broken. The shutters rattle wildly. Three windows crack in two. The very ground beneath their feet shudders and complains while from overhead they all hear quite distinctly a noise like rushing water.

"Father?" It is Branwell who speaks first. His words are slurred, filled with the childish fear of the toper.

The old man rises with terrific dignity to his feet. "My children…" he says and they all gather around him as the house shakes and shudders and complains, as all about them is cacophony and destruction. Set against it, his voice sounds wavering and paltry. He speaks the first words of scripture which come to mind:

"'For my sighing cometh before I eat, and my roarings are poured out like the waters. For the thing which I greatly feared has come upon me, and that which I was afraid of is come unto me. I was not in safety, neither had I rest, neither was I quiet; yet did—'"

He is interrupted from somewhere overhead by what sounds like a woman's scream. The priest falls silent, the shaking stops, the noises subside and all that can be heard after that are heavy, deliberate footsteps upon the stairs.

The family watch as their guest—revivified and moving with new purpose—strides into the parlour. He has a dreadful kind of grace now and his eyes seem a shade darker than before. Emily is with him, bleeding from a savage-looking laceration, evidently newly inflicted, just below her right eye.

When the stranger speaks it is with a proud swagger, at once repulsive and beguiling. "It occurs to me," he says, "that I have yet to introduce myself." He smiles and he speaks his name and afterwards, as his unwitting hosts gaze at him in wonderment and fear, he says, in strange, cold triumph: "A very merry Christmas to you all."

NOW

IT IS MIDNIGHT in Edinburgh but the city is far from asleep. The Festival is in full swing and the streets still throng with actors and comedians, touts and critics, party-goers, cynics, fans, seekers after laughter. Most pubs and clubs are still open. Rubbish is everywhere, the detritus of twenty hours a day of good times. Every litter bin filled with discarded fliers, crumpled reviews. Even this far into the night, there are still musicians abroad, mimes and performance artists, clowns and faded celebrities. The atmosphere is raucous and giddy, drink-sodden, oversexed. It is as if the place has been taken over by superannuated teenagers whilst all the real adults have stayed away.

Underneath the air of carnival, however, can still be sensed something else, in the itinerants who gaze suspiciously at the out-of-towners, in the locals who have not been able to flee the city for the Festival and who have stayed to resent the cosmopolitan influx, in those who, in this month-long party, have scented criminal opportunity and who are present to sell drugs or sex, colder, harder, more truthful experiences than those offered by the little theatres and concert halls and stand-up venues. This is the spirit of Old Edinburgh, the city of Hogg and Stevenson and Doyle, a quieter place of ill-lit alleys, of naked bodies illuminated by candlelight, of cries stifled brutally in the night. Tonight, beneath the party something simmers. Beyond the harlequinade, something darker is trying to break through.

Toby Judd, however, has noticed none of this yet. He has only lately arrived, after his long and gruelling coach ride. He is, at present, his sports bag nestled between his feet, slumped disconsolately at a corner table of a café, just off the Royal Mile, which has stayed open so late in an effort to catch those Festival-goers who wish to avoid the temptations of a pub. In this they were largely mistaken for the place, for all the revellers who surge by outside, is largely empty. Apart from Toby there are only two other customers—a middle-aged curly-haired man, bent over a copy of *The Scotsman* with the frowning self-importance of a friendless playwright, and a plump American woman, drawling into a mobile phone to the folks back home. At the front, behind the till, a bloodshot waitress sits, almost dozing, with a book held out in front of her by which she does not seem especially enthralled.

Dopily, Judd gets to his feet and shambles over to the counter.

"Excuse me?" Absurdly, he feels the urge to add the word "miss" to the end of the sentence, as if he's an old man and this is the 1930s.

The woman looks up and manages a tired smile. She is striking, he sees now, a tall, thirty-something brunette with an air of quiet determination. Her eyes are a thoughtful shade of brown and her eyebrows elegant, quizzical lines. She is wearing a name badge which reads 'GABRIELA'. Toby takes this all in, surprised that, despite his tiredness and creeping sense of despair, his heart gives a little lurch at the sight of her frazzled pulchritude. It lurches again, still more crazily, when he notices the title of the book that she is reading: *Cannonbridge: A Celebration of English Genius* by Dr J J Salazar.

"Yes, sir?" she says. Despite her evident fatigue, her voice is warm and sympathetic.

He blurts out the words without thinking: "What do you make of it?"

"Sir?"

"The book. That book. The Salazar book."

"Oh. This?"

"Yes."

"Honestly?"

"Please."

"Facile and underwritten. Matthew Cannonbridge himself is oblique and underdescribed. Motiveless. The other players are merely ciphers. Caricature. To be absolutely frank with you—

and why shouldn't I be at this time of night?—I always found old Cannonbridge's stuff kind of overrated. This book hasn't done much to persuade me to revise my opinion."

At this, Toby feels an unfamiliar ache in his face. It takes him a moment to realise that he is smiling. "That's an interesting critique. I mean, well, it's interesting to hear you say so."

"Why? Have you read it?"

"Oh, I spent an hour or so with it. I'm familiar with the line of its argument."

"And?"

"I agree with you. But then, I am rather biased. You see, I… know the author."

"Really?" Gabriela frowns, flips to the photo on the back cover. "That guy?"

Toby finds now that he is shuffling, presumably from nervousness and anxiety, and has to work hard to stand still. "Yeah."

"Friend of yours?"

"Not exactly."

"Then you won't mind my saying that he looks like a bit of a doofus."

"Nope. Nope. Don't mind you saying that at all."

The conversation ceases then and they look at one another in that way which is common upon the realisation that there exists a spark of attraction—a sense almost of déjà vu, as if the two of them have met somewhere before. The moment passes swiftly and professionalism is resumed.

"Sorry, sir, what was it you meant to ask? I mean beside from the book."

"A cheese toastie."

"What about it?"

"I ordered one. Half an hour ago. No sign of it."

"I'll chase up that order."

"Thank you."

He hesitates. "Do you know..?"

"Yes, sir?"

Is she bored? Indulgent? Grateful for the distraction? Difficult to tell.

"I hadn't even realised that the Festival was on. When I came here tonight, I mean."

Those elegant eyebrows are arched in scepticism. "For real?"

"Yes. I mean, I've never been. I've heard of it, of course. But never got round to actually attending. So you can imagine that I was bewildered when I found the place so lively."

"I imagine you were." She yawns. "So if you're not here for the Festival, what's brought you to Edinburgh?"

"Something else. Something connected, I suppose, with that book you're reading."

"That's very mysterious of you."

"Not intentionally. Only... non-committal. Listen."

"Yes, sir? I've said I'll look into the toastie for you." She's just bored, Toby thinks now, just bored and tired and doing anything to stay awake—even listening to him.

"I know. I know. It's not that. I was just wondering... if you know of anywhere I could stay for the night."

Incredulity. "You've not got your accommodation sorted?"

"No. I haven't... Look, it was a last minute decision. I didn't actually wake up this morning with the intention of coming to Edinburgh. I was in Ashbury first and then in Portsmouth."

"Well, to be honest, your timing stinks. You couldn't have picked a worse time. Festival season—everywhere's booked up months in advance. I've got friends who go away for the season and rent out their own houses."

"I know that now. I've tried all over town and..."

"No room at the inn?"

"No room, as you say, at the inn."

Gabriela shrugs. "Then I'm sorry. I've really no idea. There are a couple of hostels you could try. Down by the railway station."

"Hostels?"

"Yes. Backpacking places. Might be OK for a night or two."

"Of course. Yes. I shall certainly do that. Thank you."

"No problem. And I'll have that toastie brought to you."

It is clear to him that these words mark the end of their conversation. He backs away. By the time that he has taken a few paces, the woman has already returned, frowningly, to the Salazar book.

ANOTHER HOUR PASSES. Toby's toastie (rubbery, undercooked, close to inedible) has been and gone. Gabriela has read another chapter or so of the Salazar volume, having set down the sandwich without making eye contact. She has made a personal phone call or two. The other customers have left and chairs have been placed onto tables. A man in his forties with stubble and a potbelly whom Toby takes to be the chef has emerged from the kitchen and has begun the process of tidying up, mopping the floor half-heartedly and wiping down the surfaces with a distracted, lackadaisical air.

Gabriela approaches Toby's table, the last to be occupied, the last not to be cleaned and two chairs placed atop it. Judd himself is gazing into the distance, lost in the past and in possibility.

"Afraid it's time to go now, sir. It's past closing."

Toby blinks, peers, focuses—as if stirring from a dream. "I see. Yes. Of course."

"Good luck finding a place at the hostel."

Toby stands up, pushes the chair back. From underneath the table he retrieves his sports bag. "Thank you."

Gabriela frowns at him. "Well, good luck, sir."

Toby nods, extends his hand. "It's Toby, actually. Toby Judd."

She looks at him strangely for a couple of seconds then warily accepts his hand. "And you're interested in Cannonbridge, right?"

"Yes. Very much so."

"You know, I think I recognise you. I saw a... kind of lecture you gave."

Toby looks dolefully into her eyes. "On YouTube?"

She nods.

"You thought it was funny?"

"No. Not really. I thought it was... well, unorthodox. And I've always thought it best to question orthodoxies."

Toby is, he realises, blushing.

"Nice to meet you, Toby."

"You too...?"

"Gabriela Vale."

These pleasantries over at the end of a very long shift, she walks away, opens the door and indicates that Toby avail himself of it.

"Goodnight," he says.

"Goodnight."

An instant later, he is outside, in the cold of the night, alone again in the city. A man with a sandwich board jostles past. Something in the unearthly paleness of the stranger's face, the savage scarlet tear where a mouth should be, causes Toby to gasp but then, looking closer, he sees that the effect has been brought about only by stage make-up, and he feels jittery and absurd. The actor, muttering, moves away. The legend on his board is clear: 'Nightly ghost tours in the heart of haunted Edinburgh! Ask me for details.' Toby does not take up the man on this offer, thinking, as he watches the fellow stomp away, that he has begun to feel something like a revenant himself, his life having taken on the phantasmagorical quality of an old story, peopled by spectres and watched over by the dead.

THE RUCKUS OF the Festival has died down a little and the streets are rather emptier, though there are still plenty of performers and punters trudging or weaving their way home. As he leaves the café and steps towards the Royal Mile, Toby passes a knot of undergraduates, a street performer dressed as a wizard and two clowns, half in costume, half in their civvies, bickering noisily about an unpaid debt.

Mention of money causes Toby to take a detour, across the street at a branch of NatWest, between WHSmiths and an outlet of Subway, to avail himself of a cash point. It has been years since he has stayed at a youth hostel (vague, flickering memories of a holiday in the Lake District; a brief, disastrous affiliation with the Scouts) but he suspects they won't accept anything but hard currency. He takes out his wallet, slides out his debit card and offers it up to the thin metal mouth of the machine. It swallows it as usual, whirs comfortingly and, on its small and dirty screen, demands that he enter his PIN. Toby hunches over the thing to obscure the view of any larcenous passers-by and taps in the four necessary numbers.

The machine whirs again and the asterisks which represent the digits disappear. All is as it should be. And yet, what happens next goes against the expected order of things entirely. It deviates from the script—no list of choices (balance, withdrawal, statement request) but instead four lines of words which, in grey-green type, read:

IT WAS UPON THE MORNING OF THE FIRST DAY OF HIS THIRTY-THIRD YEAR THAT THE HERO OF OUR ACCOUNT FIRST CAME TO UNDERSTAND THAT HIS LIFE TO DATE HAD BEEN CONCERNED ALMOST EXCLUSIVELY WITH HIS INADVERTENT FASHIONING AS A SACRIFICE.

Toby recognises it at once—there are few who can count themselves as even tolerably well-read who would not—as the very first line of Matthew Cannonbridge's second novel, *Ezekiel Frye*.

He stares at the screen, blinks, rubs his eyes, convinced, even now, that this is some sort of hallucination. But no: the words are real, the sentence is truly before him. He stabs at the machine, pressing the CANCEL button, urging it to give up his card.

It is too late. The words vanish. The screen goes blank. His card, like Jonah, has been swallowed whole.

Toby swears, violently, under his breath. He steps backwards, away from the machine, feeling suddenly that the thing is mocking him. He feels an urge to strike the silent, metal device, to punish it for the rapidly unspooling nature of his life.

Before he can do so, however, he is interrupted. A soft, concerned voice from behind him: "Toby?"

Dr Judd looks back to see who it is that is speaking.

Gabriela. The girl from the café. "Is everything all right?"

"Yes," he says. "Absolutely fine." Then, years of instinctive courtesy melting away in the hopelessness of a Scottish morning: "Actually, no. Truth be told: the machine's just swallowed my card."

Gabriela's expression is coolly sympathetic. "Oh, I'm sorry to hear that. Faulty, I suppose?" A thin man with a tuba hurries by, head down, not looking for trouble.

"No," says Toby, too quickly. "Not exactly. I mean, I don't think so. Not a regular fault anyway. Tell me. Do you know the opening line of *Ezekiel Frye*?"

The woman seems to look at him more closely. "You're really not all right, are you? Not all right at all."

Even before he says the words, Dr Judd knows he will sound crazy. But it seems too late now to do anything other than tell the truth, not when he has so little left to lose. He steps a little nearer to the waitress. "Gabriela," he says, "I believe I've uncovered a conspiracy of immensely complicated design. I don't know how it's been done, I don't know why, and I don't know how far it goes. If you've watched that wretched film online then you'll already know something of what I'm talking about. You've read Cannonbridge—has it never struck you how flimsy he seems, how lazy, how underdeveloped? Listen, I don't understand what's going on here. But I do believe that I have been noticed. They've taken things from me. To be frank, my bank card's pretty much the least of them. And I think I'm now in real danger."

Gabriela stands her ground and looks carefully at Toby Judd. To her credit she neither flees nor declares him a madman. Somewhere nearby, a police siren whoops and sighs.

"If you want to walk away," Toby says, "I'll understand entirely. In your position, most people would do exactly that. But I'm going to ask you a huge favour now. I realise that we don't know each other. I understand that you don't owe me anything. But I think, and I don't know why, I think that you understand something of what I'm talking about. I think, in some way, you share my madness." He stops, gasps for air.

She does not reply. He is ready to walk away and leave her, to try to find somewhere warm and dry to spend the next few hours, until she says: "Go on then."

"I'm sorry?"

"Try me. Ask that favour."

THEY SPEAK OF many things as they walk together, Toby and Gabriela, of their lives and ambitions, their interests and aspirations, but it will not surprise you to learn that they speak most often of the dark, saturnine writer, the impossible author, the minotaur at the heart of the maze. Gabriela listens with thoughtful attention. Toby thanks her often. He tells her something of what has befallen him since the day that Caroline left and she seems to take most of it on trust, asking occasional questions, wanting clarification about some particular incident, querying from time to time the course of events. Toby does not tell her everything—not quite—but he is surprised both by the volume of improbable events which have already befallen him and by the sangfroid with which his companion accepts it. Almost without realising it, they pass out of the centre of the city, away from the Festival, its artists and revellers, into the sleepier regions beyond. The moon is high and bright and it illuminates the streets with clear, hard, unsentimental light. It would be bright enough to see by even without the intermittent lamps but, combined, these things contrive to make the shadows still darker and more deep.

"I live in Leith," Gabriela explains as they walk. "Two flatmates. There's a sofa in the lounge. You'll be OK on that?"

"Of course. I really am so grateful, you know."

The woman frowns. "Don't mention it. You'd do the same. But tell me this…"

"Yes?"

"Why have you really come to Edinburgh?"

"To find the truth," says Toby simply. "You see, I remembered that the Cannonbridge Archive—a vast collection of his papers—is in a private library just outside of town. J J's book couldn't have been written without it. Or so he said. In any case, I meant to see what's there for myself."

"You think that will help?"

"I think it's a pretty good place to start."

"But I'm guessing they won't let just anybody in."

"I'll figure something out. My mind's made up now."

Gabriela frowns again. Toby glances at her and finds that he is charmed by the expression.

"You think I'm crazy?" he asks.

She sighs, more in surprise at her own actions, he thinks, than from exasperation at his. "I'm letting you stay the night, aren't I?"

The old town has given them up now and they have come to Leith, a quiet, grimy, run-down sort of neighbourhood, largely free of tourists, though peaceful enough for all that, at least at this time in the morning. There is altogether less money here—a certain meanness, perhaps, but with it a kind of honest idiosyncrasy which Toby finds refreshing after the neat claustrophobia of Ashbury and the heartless bleakness of the coast.

Gabriela lives in a first-floor flat of a tall, dilapidated building halfway down a grey and washed-out street. There is a short flight of rickety metal steps to climb in order to reach the front door. There is a tiny patch of pallid grass, garlanded with bin bags. A scrawny fox takes to its heels as they approach.

"Up here," says the woman, leading the way. Toby follows, realising only now, for the very first time, that he may have made a mistake in throwing himself upon her mercy, in trusting to the kindness of this beguiling stranger. There is a single light on in the building, a dull illumination glimpsed through a first-floor window.

"Looks like my flatmates are home," Gabriela says, perhaps, thinks Toby, in order to make clear that the place is occupied, that he is outnumbered.

They reach the front door and Gabriela reaches for a key. She unlocks the door and pushes it open and they walk through into a spindly corridor, carpeted in stained and faded red. An ancient bicycle lolls against the wall, so greedy in its use of space that Toby and Gabriela have to squeeze by. The place smells of old takeaways, damp washing, incense, Dove deodorant and pot.

The woman urges him on. "This way."

Together, they walk into the lounge. Messy and unkempt, of course, but warm and comfortable. On the far side, a kitchen can be glimpsed. Toby's attention, however, is taken up by two women, both a few years younger than Gabriela, who sit together on an elderly sofa. Both are smoking what Toby knows to be weed. The TV is on before them, the sound down low, a companionable murmur. The air is thick and soporific. Toby's throat tickles and he steels himself not to cough.

"Guys?" This is Gabriela to her friends. "This is Toby. I thought he could crash on the sofa tonight." Neither of the women stir. "Toby? This is Kara and this is Sam."

"Hi there," Toby says, wondering again quite how he's found himself in this particular, unlikely situation. "I'm very grateful. I really don't want to intrude. I'll be out of your hair first thing tomorrow."

The women turn around now, their movements slightly sullen and dazed. Toby, his head full, as is often the case, of Victoriana, finds himself thinking of opium dens.

The first woman—Kara—is plump and dark-haired, her make-up a day old and too thickly applied. The second—Sam—is blonde and close to skinny. Her face is pitted, her skin flaky-looking and raw. They gape at him not, as he had half-expected, with a kind of sceptical ribaldry, but rather in palpable shock and even—it would not, he thinks, be going too far to say, in horror.

"Everything all right?" asks Gabriela. "He won't be any trouble. Come on. It's not like you two haven't had guys back before."

Toby clears his throat and finds himself sucking in a lungful of marijuana smoke. "P'raps you recognise me? From YouTube, I suppose." His tone is equal parts humility, embarrassment, defiance and, oddly, inappropriate pride.

Sam shakes her head. "No," she says and then again, more firmly: "*no.*"

Toby and Gabriela exchange glances.

"Not from the internet. From… from the TV." She nods towards the screen and all eyes turn towards the object of her indication.

It's BBC News, the 24-hour channel. Rolling coverage. About the only thing on at this time. The sound is too low to hear, just a mild susurration which Toby finds almost sinister. Even without the audio element, the chief points of the story are clear. The newsreader looks calm and severe, her expression filled with implicit judgement. Behind her, three faces appear. The first two, now deeply familiar to Toby, may not be known to the others: the strange, wild-eyed theorist, Russell Spicer, and the doomed policeman, Isaac Angeyo. And now another, evidently aligned with the preceding pair, in a manner that is coded as suspicious at best and nefarious at worst—an old, grainy, passport-style shot of Dr Toby Judd.

It is at this point when Toby realises that all three women are looking at him, Kara and Sam with suspicion and fear, Gabriela with pensive doubt.

"I know this is a cliché," Toby begins, "but I can explain…"

And it is only as he does so, only as he begins to share his worst suspicions and the sickening connections that he has already forged, that he begins to understand the awful speed and dreadful dexterity with which the net that has been cast around him is being drawn tight.

1849
THE ODD FELLOWS HALL
BALTIMORE

IT IS RAINING in Baltimore tonight, without respite or mercy.

There has evidently been some manner of convocation at the Odd Fellows Hall—a low yet capacious building in a part of town which stands between the respectability of the quietest regions and an area which, if not exactly disreputable, is nonetheless suggestive of long-term misfortune—for a good deal of men and women are at present leaving the structure, their attitudes implying that they have enjoyed a largely happy or at least a diverting evening. Despite the rain, there is a good deal of laughter, chatter and exchanging of opinion. The impression is of an excellent dinner party, much appreciated by all who have attended.

Were we to be waiting at the front of the building and at the exit which leads out onto the street we would no doubt be able to see the cause of the celebration and the reason for the gathering itself, for beside the building stands a solid wooden notice board upon which has been pinned a large sheet of paper that sports the following printed words:

THE ENGLISH WRITER, MR MATTHEW CANNONBRIDGE
SPEAKING FROM MEMORY UPON THE TOPIC OF
'FAIRNESS AND JUSTICE' AND READING FROM SEVERAL
OF HIS MOST CELEBRATED WORKS (*THE ENGLISH
GOLEM, PLENITUDE, EZEKIEL FRYE* &c)
7 o'clock. Monday 1st October.

The words have been damaged by the downpour and are already beginning to run. They are becoming elongated, obscure and indistinct.

Yet we are not to linger on the street outside with that content, if rapidly dampening crowd, as they hurry away from the night's entertainment, back to their warm hearths and warmer beds. No, we are for the rear of the building, for its discreet alternative entrance, for the shadows and for the gathering dark.

Here a man is waiting—a slender fellow, perhaps a little taller than we were expecting, a shade under six foot. He is dressed shabbily, entirely in black and has lately grown a rather forlorn moustache. He is scarcely forty, yet he looks as broken-down and defeated as a man decades his senior. Nonetheless, an odd sort of energy seems to animate him and he paces up and down, bedraggled but seemingly oblivious to the driving rain, at once agitated, watchful and excited. He is known to some as 'the raven' and he has rarely resembled so closely that cognomen as he does tonight, strutting anxiously in the rain, his movements nervily avian, his demeanour battered though not yet quite overwhelmed by the storm.

At length, after the crowd have dispersed and the lights in the hall have come to be extinguished, the door at the back of the building, by which our dishevelled bird has been waiting, opens and a familiar figure steps carefully out.

Mr Matthew Cannonbridge looks largely as we remember him from our last meeting, an ocean away, although he seems now more affluent in his bearing and manner, prouder and colder than before. He clothes are more expensive, though still sober rather than flamboyant, and, as he emerges into the sodden night, he dons a broad-brimmed hat in deference to the deluge.

He closes the door behind him and seems about to step out into the city when he catches sight of the man who is waiting. Cannonbridge seems not in the least surprised to find the stranger standing there. Neither person speaks. For a while there is only the sound of falling rain.

In the end, it is the raven who speaks first. "Mr Cannonbridge?"

Apparently confident of his fame, the Englishman gives no indication that he accepts the identification.

The raven moves a few, waterlogged steps nearer. "I hope you'll forgive me for my ambush, Mr Cannonbridge. I have burned to meet you for so long."

Cannonbridge inclines his head, very slightly, in acknowledgement of the accolade. The wide brim of his hat causes his face to fall into shadow. Still he does not speak.

"I am a literary man myself, friend. My name may be familiar to you."

The brim of the hat moves still further down in defence against the rain. The face falls still further into shadow. And still no words come.

"I am Edgar Allan Poe, Mr Cannonbridge. I am The Raven."

The hat moves up, the face is exposed and Mr Poe sees now that there is upon it a smile of a cruel and oddly feline hue.

Cats eat birds, he thinks suddenly, uncertain quite where the thought has come from. *Cats eat birds.*

Then Cannonbridge speaks. He sounds not as he did in Geneva or in Boston or in Norwich, but only as he did in the parlour at Haworth, whilst Emily stood bleeding beside him and the parsonage shook almost unto its own destruction. "What year is this?"

Poe has often felt in his short and predominantly miserable life that he has miscalculated or misjudged a person or opportunity or situation. For all his bravado in public and amongst friends he has often considered his existence to represent a series of disasters of his own making. Never, however, before tonight, has he ever felt so suddenly certain that he has erred in a decision as that which has brought him to Baltimore, to this hall, to the saturnine Englishman with the dreadful smile. "You joke with me, I think, Mr Cannonbridge?" he says, taking, unconsciously, a step or two back.

"Not at all. Even now, my personal chronology seems a little hazy. So I ask again, sir: what year is this?"

"'49, sir."

"Edgar Allan Poe in 1849?"

"Yes. That is correct."

The smile of Matthew Cannonbridge grows wider. Are his incisors sharper than before? Surely not. Surely that is merely a trick of shadow and light? "Then this is timely indeed. I'm so glad."

"I'm not entirely certain what you mean by that, friend."

"Then let me explain, my poor little raven. Over a drink?"

Poe holds up a hand in polite refusal though it might, had anyone chanced to observe the scene, have seemed more like an attempt to keep the other man at bay. "The offer is a kind one, sir. But perhaps I ought not to accept. Liquor is a weakness of mine. My aunt has often warned me of it. My late wife, bless her sweet soul, did her best to save me from it. I am inclined, you see, to... *sprees*."

The smile darkens. "I know of your failings, little raven. And of your vulnerability also. Yet you will be quite safe with me. I am a temperate man and I shall permit no harm to come to you."

Poe finds himself unable to reply. Soaked and aching, he longs for the comfort of a tavern and for the accompanying delight to be found in a julep.

Cannonbridge seems amused by the uncertainty in the other man's face. "Come, Mr Poe. All will be well."

"I've made a real exhibition of myself in the past, under the influence of strong drink. I have embarrassed—no, rather I have *humiliated*—myself, time and again. Oh, sir, but I have kicked up a bobbery."

"There shall be no embarrassment tonight, Mr Poe. No humiliation either. Merely a couple of literary men speaking together of books and of poetry in the most congenial of circumstances. One drink, Mr Poe. You have my word. One drink only!"

Poe shivers in the cold and the wet. He pines for alcohol.

"Well, I can tarry in this foul weather no longer. Come with me if you wish, Mr Poe. But I am for the ale house!"

Cannonbridge turns and strolls, with a maddening nonchalance, towards the street beyond. Poe, of course, poor, doomed Edgar follows shortly afterwards, hurrying to keep up.

* * *

THE NIGHT IS a long one and it provides considerably more than a single drink for either participant. The two men move from inn to inn, increasingly dismissive of the rain, the Englishman plying the American with drink after drink. Those who see them together will later remark that Cannonbridge appeared amused by the slow but thorough diminishment of his companion, his smile growing sharper all the while, as the night deepens and Poe falls further into sin. They speak of many things these two men, although it is Poe, at Cannonbridge's subtle urging, who provides most of the conversation—speaking of his life and works, of his orphaning, his unorthodox loves, his hoaxes and poetry and terrors, of his detective, Monsieur Dupin. Cannonbridge offers little in return and when the other writer asks him about his own works—of the eponymous monster of *The English Golem*, say, or about the scene of seduction in *Ezekiel Frye* which attracted such very excitable notices in the international press—the Englishman is polite but evasive, coolly returning the topic of discussion to some area more closely associated with Poe. Cannonbridge is seen to drink too, but not to excess, and certainly not at the pace of his companion. One is control and perception; the other ungovernability and ruinous self-indulgence.

It is late now, at the night's darkest point, and the two writers have pitched up at the lowest of the evening's hostelries. It is barred to newcomers but, after a few minutes' conversation with the publican, Cannonbridge has secured their entrance. Poe takes up residence in a snug, as far as possible from the bawdy carousing of the other inebriates. The Englishman returns with a glass for each of them and installs himself beside his drunken associate.

Poe takes a sip—half grateful, half anguished—and, leaning close to the other man, finds that he has the courage at last to speak, not of himself, but of the true reason that he has sought out the company of Matthew Cannonbridge.

"I have observed your career with great interest," he begins, slurring his words hardly at all so accustomed is he to excess. "You were mentioned, were you not, by Byron, by the Shelleys, by Dr Polidori?"

Cannonbridge, wholly unconvincingly, feigns modesty. "I believe that I was." He raises his glass to his lips and drinks, although Poe notices when the vessel is returned to the tabletop that the volume of its contents seems to have been reduced not a jot. "Of course," the Englishman adds, "I was a different man back then."

"And I have read your books, Mr Cannonbridge, your stories and your poems. I have watched your fame—some might call it notoriety now—flourish. You must be older than me yet you do not look it. There is an agelessness about you."

Cannonbridge seems neither pleased nor displeased by the remark.

"You are talented enough, sir—more than competent. Yet there is something fascinating, something dangerously beguiling about you."

"Mr Poe, you are not the first to have said so."

"Do not forget, sir—I have written often of ratiocination. I have one foot in the realm of science, another in that of dreams and nightmares."

"Quite so. You think, I suppose, that this lends you some special insight?"

"I do, sir. I do."

"Well then."

Poe drains half his glass in a single, unslakeable gulp. "For many years I have worried away at the puzzle of you. Long have I waited to say these words to you."

The mask of lordly jollity slips briefly from Cannonbridge's manner. He hisses: "Then say them now." Afterwards, he smiles soullessly once more, the façade in place again.

"You are an impossible thing, Mr Cannonbridge."

The other writer does not reply.

"You simply should not be—no, sir, not, not as you are."

The lips twitch back into a smile.

"So I ask you now, Mr Cannonbridge, to tell me the truth." Another sip of liquor, for courage, then three words, spat tremblingly out: "What are you?"

Cannonbridge takes his time. He raises the glass to his lips and this time, Poe believes, he does drink, at least a little. When the Englishman speaks again, his tone is flat and noncommittal, as if he is speaking of someone other than himself. "For many years, Mr Poe, I would not have been able to answer that question. I was a weak and ineffectual man, a kind of itinerant philanthropist, a wandering mystery even to myself. I was a victim and not a killer, the prey and not the predator. I was, in short, useless, an object of charity fit only for uncommercial scribbling. And then, seven years ago... Tell me. Have you ever had an epiphany?"

Poe waves the question aside. "Oh, I believe that I have had several."

"Then you will understand when I say that something was revealed to me—a profound truth which made sense of everything which had gone before. At the time I was afraid and I was sorely mistaken to be so. What was revealed to me gave me my essence, my origin, my *purpose*."

Despite the warm insulation of drink, Poe is frightened once more, as he was when they first met, hours earlier, outside the Odd Fellows Hall.

"And now, you ask me what I am?"

A final scrabbling for liquor. "I do, sir."

"It seems fitting to me, my little raven, my purveyor of terror, that you should be the first amongst your kind to know the truth. Allow me to share it with you now. Let me tell what I am and listen as I tell you of my plans for your people."

At these words, Poe feels an urge, almost, he thinks, atavistic, to run from that place, to seek sanctuary and to flee from Cannonbridge's truth. Too late—the author has a hand upon his shoulder. He squirms and wriggles but poor, sodden Poe is wholly unable to move, as Cannonbridge brings his face close to the American's ears and whispers.

Elsewhere in the tavern, at that moment and so blotting out his words to us, there is bitter laughter, a shriek of desperation, the sound of breaking glass. When this cacophony is done, Cannonbridge has finished. He releases Poe, slides away from him, stands up. He says nothing more but, settling his hat upon his head once more, raises the fingers of his left hand to his temple in mocking salute. He turns and walks away, lost first to the drunken baboonery of the inn and then to the worst of the night.

Edgar Allan Poe does not move but sits rigid and upright, staring hopelessly ahead of him. He is sweating, pale and shaking, as if a great and terrible fever has all at once swept over him, as if he has woken in the grip of delirium from the most vile and vivid dream of his haunted life. He sits there like that for a very long while until, at last, feeling the furies upon his heels, the raven stumbles towards the bar, orders as much as he can afford and, in the quest for forgetting, initiates his own destruction.

NOW

Outside, it is first light—the unforgiving dawn—but inside a certain first-floor apartment in Leith, it is still murky and dim, choked with narcotic smoke. Toby has been talking for several hours while Gabriela, wisely and carefully, has listened. Kara and Sam doze gently upon the sofa, one leant up against the other, both snuffling rhythmically. Toby has only now stopped speaking. He has not taken a cigarette but the atmosphere remains so hazy he believes that he feels, all the same, just a little high.

"I think you're right," Gabriela says suddenly. "Dammit, but I think you're right." Her eyes are still more bloodshot than before and she seems shaky and discombobulated like an astronaut adjusting to some new kind of gravity.

"Thank you," Toby says. "It's such a relief. I can't tell you... To hear you say so."

Gabriela nods with a kind of mock-sobriety. "Feels like we're waking from a dream."

"You're right." Even his words, it seems to him, are slightly slurred. "That's exactly how it feels."

"I've got the day off tomorrow. And I have a car. I'll drive you to the Archive."

"Are you sure?"

"Yep."

"You saw the news. I'm a wanted man. You don't think I should turn myself in to the police?"

"Angeyo knew something—or at least he suspected it. And now he's dead. You really think you'll be safe if you just hand yourself over to the fuzz?"

"No. No, I suppose not." A new objection strikes him. "But I'll be seen. My face is everywhere. All over TV. The authorities will be looking for me."

Gabriela gets to her feet and walks across the room to Toby. "I'll think of something. Trust me. For now, why don't you try to get some sleep? Don't worry. No one will ever dream of looking for you here. I'll try to shift these two sleeping beauties so that you can have the sofa." She moves away towards the others, waking them gently, each in turn and sending them both to their beds. She fetches a clean blanket from a trunk in the corner of the room and unfolds it on the sofa, does her best to make a comfortable nest of the thing. Toby watches numbly, impressed at her quiet rigour in that closeted chamber.

"There," she says, once she's finished and Toby, grateful, stumbles towards it.

Gabriela smiles, walks to the window and opens it. "Time for some fresh air. Clear our heads."

Toby agrees. On the sofa now, he asks: "Why are you helping me?"

She hesitates. Toby wonders if the reply that she gives is truly the first that comes to her. "I don't like being lied to," she says eventually. "I hate it. I've good reason to. And I think we're all being lied to here."

Toby, deciding, for now, to accept her explanation, nods.

At the doorway, Gabriela stops and adds: "Besides, I think you could probably use a friend."

"Yes," he says simply.

Gabriela smiles tiredly. "Good night, Dr Judd."

Minutes later, Toby is asleep. Unusually, he dreams no dreams— or, if he does, then he is wholly unable to recollect them when he wakes.

THE FIRST THING that he sees on returning to consciousness is the face of Gabriela Vale, half concerned and half amused.

"Wake up," she is saying, with gentle insistence. "You have to wake up now."

It is mid-morning. Daylight fills the room. Only the faintest tendrils of scented smoke still linger.

"You're all over the news," she says without discernible emotion. "Time to get moving."

Toby glances over to the TV in the corner. There is no sound but the parade of photographs tell their own story—a dead conspiracy theorist, a murdered policeman, a flaky, wired-looking man on the run, about whom rumours of mental instability are already swirling. Someone grave and blandly handsome is talking to camera. Underneath, a ticker-tape runs: HERO COP MURDERER STILL ON LOOSE—POLICE SEEK MAN TO "ANSWER URGENT QUESTIONS". And then, once again, a clip from YouTube, Toby sweaty and out of control, never having looked so crazed.

Judd swings his feet from the sofa to the floor and, in the manner of a creature emerging from hibernation, rises laboriously to his feet. His head swims from interrupted sleep and from the breathing-in of second-hand marijuana. Nonetheless, when he speaks, there is new steel.

"Turn it off," he says and, as Gabriela reaches for the remote: "I'm still not going to the police."

"Good." The screen goes dark.

"It's just that—you know—when you read stories about people on the run, there's always a part of you that wonders why they don't just give themselves up to the authorities."

"But you're not in a story now, Dr Judd."

"I know."

"Two men who got close to the truth are dead."

"You're right, of course. And yet… it's so strange." He seems to shake off his doubts. "Anyway, you ought to be calling me Toby."

"Cup of tea, Toby?"

"Thank you, yes. Two sugars."

"Once you've drunk it, there's something we should do."

"And what's that?"

"We need to put you in disguise."

*   *   *

THERE IS A car parked outside the flat. A Saab. Dark and expensive, sleek and slightly out of place in this bedraggled place. The man inside it sits patiently, discreetly, barely moving—a slender shadow behind the wheel. He breathes slowly and deliberately, like someone who has been locked in, who knows that his oxygen supply is finite and that to gasp and splutter would only use it up the quicker. His cool brown eyes are trained upon the entrance to the building. On his lap sits a small bag of toffees. He extricates one from the packet and pushes it free from its plastic wrapping. He winces slightly at the accompanying rustling and slides the sweet, with no visible indication of even the mildest expectation of pleasure, into his mouth. If you were close enough to him, you'd see one other, slightly unexpected thing: a hint of something blue lodged deep inside each of his ears—soft foam plugs, intended to block out the sounds of the world, to muffle the everyday.

And so he sits, our man in his dark car, and sucks his toffee whilst he monitors the only possible exit, in a cocoon of his own making where everything sounds dull and faraway, where every event is distant and happens in somebody else's life. He chews, and he waits, and he watches.

It is almost noon before the door opens. A young woman steps out—raven-haired, pretty in a wan sort of way and in possession of a remarkable set of eyebrows. With her is a man, rather smaller than the lady. He is entirely bald, his head newly shaved, nicked in places by the razor. He wears a pair of cheap sunglasses and is dressed in clothes that are several sizes too big for him.

As an attempt to hide in plain sight, the man with the toffees finds himself almost admiring the goofy chutzpah of it.

He watches. The man and the woman climb into a battered-looking Fiat parked (badly) towards the end of the street. The woman drives. Baldie sits in the passenger seat, his hands constantly wandering up to his head, touching the unfamiliar smoothness of it. The Fiat pulls away. The man in the dark car ceases to chew for a moment, then starts the engine, pulls out and sets off in quiet pursuit. As soon as the vehicle is moving, the chewing commences once again. His every movement is careful, considered and deliberate. He keeps his distance, sometimes even allowing the car out of his sight but, as they leave Leith and edge out towards the countryside, the man knows at all times where the Fiat and its occupants are likeliest to be. He considers every option. He plans for every possibility. He sees, he understands and, although you would not know it to look at his stern, unsmiling face, on the inside he is laughing.

IN THE PASSENGER seat, Toby is fumbling with a map which he has extricated from the glove compartment where it had been abandoned beside three bananas, two empty cartons of fruit juice, a bottle of stale water, a copy of Plato's *Republic* and an unopened box of tampons.

"You looking for something?" Gabriela asks, a flicker of amusement, despite the severity of the situation, playing about her lips.

"Map," says Toby, too brusquely, before, remembering his manners, adding: "I mean I was wondering if you had a map."

"No need for that," says the woman and Toby sees now the little metal device that is clamped to the right of the dashboard. "Sat nav." Dexterously, she reaches out with one hand whilst driving with the other and taps in six digits. The machine bleeps approvingly and brings up an animated diagram of their progress.

Toby asks wonderingly: "Where did you get the postcode?"

She pouts, playfully. "Looked it up on my phone," she says. "God, what century are you from anyway?"

And Toby, saying nothing, settles back into his seat and, noticing now the sugared tang of his companion's perfume, feels suddenly much older than his years.

THE MAN IN the car that is following Gabriela's Fiat—the man with the toffees and the earplugs—is, let us just say, an extremely patient man. Not that he has always been so. He didn't used to be. There was a time when he was all fire and fury and a kind of sentimental righteousness. But things had changed him—the years had changed him, altering him incrementally until he became something quite different. A key part of this process had been teaching himself patience, a careful, steady programme of self-improvement which had resulted in his becoming the best at what he does.

He's never in a hurry, our man with the toffees, but he always gets the job done, coolly and efficiently and without any unnecessary fuss. It comes to him easily now, this watchful calm. He is an expert at waiting. And so he tails the targets' Fiat with his usual unblinking detachment. He keeps his distance and hangs back and makes sure, as ever, that no one he follows will know that they're being followed unless he wishes them to realise it. He tracks them out of Leith and away from the city towards the country, on the M9 towards Falkirk, then, leaving the motorway and heading into the green, until they reach their destination, a long, shaded, cedar-lined drive which leads off from the road. The Fiat takes this turning—the Saab does not, but pulls up at the mouth of it, and waits.

The only clue to what lies at the end of the drive is a discreet silver plaque mounted respectfully by the mouth of the driveway. So sombre is the scene and so discreetly mournful the plaque that one might be forgiven for expecting it to read 'Crematorium' or 'Hospice' or 'Rest Home for the Incurably Insane'.

What it actually reads, of course, and the man in the Saab notes this without surprise, is: THE CANNONBRIDGE COLLECTION.

Beneath it there is a curious symbol—a stylised, art deco representation of a snake eating its own tail. At this he gazes respectfully for almost exactly two minutes.

This done, he tugs gently, precisely at the foam plug in his left ear, wincing, almost imperceptibly as it is removed, at the sound of the traffic and the roar of the world.

He pulls a sleek and slender mobile phone from his pocket, strokes the screen in three decisive motions and places the thing to his ear. After a moment he speaks.

He says "Yes" and "As you thought" and "No surprises". After that, he is silent for a while as his interlocutor talks.

During this time he seems professional, smooth-faced, almost expressionless.

One would have to have known him very well indeed—and there is no one left alive who can claim that honour any longer—to notice the look of pure frustration and annoyance which crosses his face in response, one presumes, to the general drift of the conversation.

"Very well," he says at last. "Then I'll wait. Let's see how far he gets."

And so the man terminates the phone call, replaces the plug in his ear and does as he has been told. Three minutes pass before he takes out another toffee, unwraps it with a single, brisk motion and pops it into his mouth whereupon, with quiet intensity, he grinds the thing to paste.

IN THE NORMAL run of things, Toby thinks, arriving at a private collection of papers—at this expensive personal library—should be just about the furthest thing on Earth away from danger.

He has been to such places before of course, to certain sections of the British Library, to the Bodleian, a trip, once, to an American university which had paid out for a collection of letters and drafts by a middle-ranking English poet and were regretting their investment. He'd been to rich men's collections too—storehouses of material which ought by rights to belong to the nation but which had been bought up by millionaires out of curiosity or enthusiasm or, most likely, in the hope of profit.

Yes, he had spent hours in such places. Not here, of course—though Salazar had, he thinks, yes, J J had drawn heavily on the contents of this building in the course of the composition of his book. Toby wonders if his wife's lover had felt it too when he arrived—the prickling sense of unease and peril which had flickered up and down his spine when they had turned into the long lane which led to the Collection. Probably not, Judd concludes—doubtless his mind was focused on other matters.

As they reach the end of the drive, the building comes into view—a large, distinguished building that has stood here for more than three hundred years and has, in its time, been a modest stately home (to an Englishman whose fortune had been secured through what may as well have been called armed robbery in the course of fighting various foreign wars), a home for recovering servicemen at the start of the twentieth century and an overpriced and somewhat inconveniently-situated hotel in the second half of the twentieth century. Since the millennium it has been given over to its new purpose.

Gabriela drives the car to a small parking area (with not more than five or six other vehicles, all unobtrusively expensive), putting him in a mind of a discreet five-star establishment, more of an overpriced hideaway or a smilingly extortionate bolthole than a holiday destination or a place to take the kids.

The entrance, a few yards away, is darkened and has presumably been designed to look as uninviting as possible. Only experts welcome here, it seems to say. Only the cognoscenti, only high priests in the cult of Cannonbridge.

Gabriela switches off the engine and they go through the plan that they have devised during their journey one more time.

"Are you sure it will work?" Toby asks again.

"Not at all," says the girl, and smiles. "But unless you've got any better ideas it's the best chance we've got."

And, as has already been decided, they both thrust their hands deep into their pockets and saunter inside.

Within the building it is surprisingly cool and modern, with its wood-panelled walls, its top-flight air-conditioning system working soundlessly away. It's not so like a hotel in here, Toby thinks, nor any library either but rather…

He thinks for a moment. Yes—like a health club. Like a private gym.

There is a reception desk in the atrium and a man sitting behind it. To the left of the desk is a closed green door. Toby half expects to be given a towel and a key for a locker but, drawing closer, he sees that the man, powerfully built, is dressed in the uniform of a private security firm.

At the top right-hand side of the wide wooden desk at which the man with the biceps is enthroned, he sees again something which had snagged at the back of his mind when they'd passed the sign, at the top of the driveway—the snake that eats its tail, Ouroboros drawn as a kind of corporate logo.

"Can I help you?" The guard has an English accent, unsympathetic estuary. His gaze is unfriendly when examining Toby, perhaps a shade more forgiving when passing over Gabriela's form. "Are you lost?" A touch of sarcasm.

Toby smiles as guilelessly as he can. "Not exactly, no."

The guard stares back, sceptical, waiting.

Toby wonders whether he's armed, if there's a weapon behind the desk as in some late-night Glasgow liquor store. "My wife and I got engaged here—back when this place was a hotel. And were in Scotland again and we found ourselves passing and we were wondering if, well, for old time's sake, whether we could take a look around?"

The man behind the desk gives them a hard, professional look.

The hands of Toby and Gabriela remain firmly in their pockets. No wedding rings. Fingers out of sight. No possibility for the asking of awkward questions.

"I'm afraid this is private property, sir. Technically, you're trespassing. You're breaking the law." A humourless smile.

"Yes," Gabriela says brightly. "It's something literary now, isn't it, this place?"

"We've got the biggest collection of Cannonbridge papers in the world." There is an odd, unexpected note of pride in the man's voice although, Toby thinks, he doesn't look like all that much of a reader.

"Wonderful." Gabriela again. "Might we take a look at them?"

"Not without an appointment, ma'am, no. Not without permission."

"Then how do we get that?"

The guard grimaces. "With considerable difficulty. Trust me."

Toby now: "How come? I mean, who owns it all?"

"It's in private hands, sir. Private."

"Ah. But surely you wouldn't mind if a couple of sentimental fools took a walk down memory lane? We shan't be long."

"Sorry, sir." He doesn't sound sorry. "Can't be done. Besides..."

Toby knows what is coming, the old cliché.

"It'd be more than my job's worth."

Nothing for it now.

Toby and Gabriela swap glances and the girl goes, expertly, to work. She turns out to be a better actor than Toby had dared to hope. The performance is exact, persuasive and does not give way to the temptation of melodrama. The eyes roll back in their sockets, her limbs start to shake, her mouth dribbles and gurns. Within seconds, she is on the floor, convulsing wildly, shaking and palsied.

The guard looks up, astonished. Out of his depth, Toby thinks, experiencing a little spike of pleasure at the thought. Out of his comfort zone.

He meets the man's gaze and says coolly, as though this has happened to him many time before: "My wife's having an epileptic fit. Stay with her. Hold her head upright. I've what we need in the car. I'll fetch it."

"Yeah. Yeah, of course. Christ. Sorry."

The guard does as he's been asked. He goes to her and cradles her head. Toby steps towards the door and opens it. As he does so, Gabriela begins to make a peculiar, strangulated noise, like a creature in pain, at which Toby is put in mind of a time he heard a nest of baby sparrows attacked by a crow, and at which the guard leans in, trying to help. Toby lets the door slam shut but doesn't leave the building. Instead, he doubles back and passes swiftly and, he hopes, wholly unnoticed through the green door beyond.

He will not, he knows, have long before their stratagem is uncovered. He knows he has to hurry now.

He is in a long corridor with a series of rooms on either side. Each has a sign outside with two letters for the alphabet, A-D, E-H etc. Distantly, he hears Gabriela's wail. All the rooms are closed, all look empty.

He picks the third possibility—I-L—pushes open the door and steps inside. He sees filing cabinets now—big, solid wooden cabinets. A treasure chest, he thinks—the very lodestone of Cannonbridge studies.

Surging with adrenaline, he pulls open a cabinet at random. Sheets of paper are inside, all neatly ordered and arranged with dividers and markers. He riffles through them, as quickly as he can, and what he sees then, at least what he thinks he sees then, brings him up short, makes him gasp. He peers closer, unbelieving.

It is at that moment, when he hears a dry cough from nearby. He stiffens and turns slowly around to be confronted by a bespectacled man in late middle-age, dressed in an Italian suit which seems rather too smart for him, wiry dark hair neatly parted. He looks anxious and panicked, like a spy taken out of the queue of the airport.

"Do you know," begins the stranger, in a soft, educated Scots voice, "I've been waiting for someone like you for a long time…"

1849
THE BRONX
NEW YORK

SHE IS NOT yet sixty yet she looks very much older. Frail, she walks with a stoop and her every step is tentative, filled with aching and beset by sorrow. Yet there is a certain resilience to her, a kind of hopeless indefatigability which comes from outliving everyone whom she has ever loved or cared for and which will sustain her—barely—for what lies ahead: for ignominy, for poverty, for the quiet horrors of the poor house.

When we see her first, she is advancing slowly down a long, dark hallway in answer to a brusque knocking that she heard but a few moments ago. Evidently impatient, the caller raps again.

"Coming," she says, although her voice is high and thin and bird-like and she suspects that there is little hope of whoever it is having heard her, not on the other side of that thick portcullis.

She moves, perhaps just a little faster but not so one would really notice. If it's important, she thinks, then they'll wait.

Finally, she is at the door and with far more exertion than such an action should take, tugs it gloomily open.

She blinks in the sudden rush of bright New York sunlight, her pinched, pale face screwed up against the glare.

There is a young man outside. Blond and tall and brawny. Once she would have thought him handsome, once she would have giggled and flirted and fluttered her eyelashes. But all that was long ago. Now she sees only a boy.

"Mrs Clemm?" he asks and his voice is serious and concerned almost as if (she will wonder later), as if he is aware of the weight and nature of his mission.

There is something in his hands, a fat cream envelope held out before him like an offering.

"Yes," she says. "That's me."

"I've got a letter for you, ma'am."

Again that note of earnestness and—does she imagine it? Surely not. Condolence.

"Thank you," she says. "Do I..."

She tails off, hopefully.

"No, ma'am. 'Tis all paid for."

"Thank you," she says and she must look confused as her visitor feels the need to add: "I was told to make sure that it was put directly into your hands."

He passes it to her and she accepts it, feeling the dreadful heft of it.

For an instant, at the thought that it might be from Eddy, she experiences an exhausting kaleidoscope of emotions. Might it, she wonders, be some final, desperate epistle, full of forgiveness and love, some heartfelt apologia sent just before his death?

But no, the handwriting is quite unfamiliar.

Neat, she thinks. Neat and official. Quite unlike Eddy, then, in every way.

"Thank you," she says again.

The brawny, handsome man nods—"ma'am"—and is gone. She closes the door again, against the stranger and the light, and moves dolefully back down the hallway and into her parlour, her sad prize clasped in one wrinkled, claw-like hand.

Shortly afterwards, with a cup of something restorative by her side (and how dear Eddy might have approved of that!), hunched in her frayed and threadbare armchair, her face furrowed in awful, anxious concentration, she reads the following words:

Presuming, madam, that you are already aware of the malady of which Mr. Poe died I need only state concisely the particulars of his circumstances from his entrance until the time of his death. When brought to the Hospital he was unconscious of his condition, of who brought him or with whom he had been associating. He remained in this condition from five o'clock in the afternoon (the hour of his admission) until three the next morning. This was on the 3rd October. To this state succeeded tremor of the limbs, and at first a busy, but not violent or active delirium and vacant conversation with spectral and imaginary objects on the walls. His face was pale and his whole person drenched in perspiration.

I questioned him in reference to his family, place of residence, relatives &c. But his answers were incoherent and unsatisfactory. He told me, however, he had a wife in Richmond (which, I have since learned was not the fact) that he did not know when he left that city or what had become of his trunk of clothing. Wishing to rally and sustain his now fast sinking hopes I told him I hoped, that in a few days he would be able to enjoy the society of his friends here, and I would be most happy to contribute in every possible way to his ease and comfort. At this he broke out with much energy, and said the best thing his best friend could do would be to blow out his brains with a pistol—that when he beheld his degradation he was ready to sink in the earth. Shortly after giving expression to these words Mr. Poe seemed to doze and I left him for a short time.

When I returned I found him in a violent delirium, resisting the efforts of two nurses to keep him in bed. This state continued until Saturday evening (he was admitted on Wednesday) when he commenced calling for one "Reynolds", which he did through the night up to three on Sunday morning. At this time a very decided change began to affect him. Having become enfeebled from exertion he became quiet and seemed to rest for a short time, then gently moving his head he said, "Lord help my poor Soul" and expired.

This, Madam, is as faithful an account as I am able to furnish from the Record of his case. I have, thus, complied with your request, Madam, and therefore subscribe myself respectfully yours,

J. J. Moran, Resident Physician

By the time that Mrs Clemm has finished this sad message, her cheeks are damp with tears. There have been few surprises in the nature of her son-in-law's demise for she had always known that it would be liquor which would destroy him in the end, that and his own weakness of will. Nonetheless, some of the details seem to her to be troublingly odd.

What had Eddy been doing in Baltimore? The last time that she had heard from him he had been talking only of going to New York. Why was he wearing another man's clothes?

And there is something else, something more, which worries her greatly, a name which will return to her for the rest of her largely unhappy life, coming back in the small hours of the morning when she cannot sleep and the shadows and their horrors crowd greedily around her.

She reads the letter again, twice, three times, and still she wonders, still she asks about "Reynolds". Why should that name and that name in particular—which is now and shall forever remain quite unknown to her—have been the last upon the lips of her poor, benighted Eddy?

NOW

WHEN TOBY JUDD comes skittering pell-mell back into the lobby of the erstwhile hotel ten minutes after his conversation began with the man with the glasses and the neatly-parted hair, running faster than he has in twenty years or more, there are three simultaneous assaults on his senses, two auditory and one visual.

The auditory elements are these—the whining clangour of the alarm sounding even shriller and more demented here than it had been in the archive room and the echoing noise of boots pounding along the corridors nearby. The visual element is this: that the security guard whom they had met on arrival and for whose benefit they had feigned matrimony, now lies sprawled out on the floor, unconscious but breathing.

Toby stops for a sliver of a second to take all of this in, casting round wildly for sight of Gabriela.

Save for the man on the floor, the atrium is empty, although Toby suspects that very soon now the place is going to be filled with men who wish to do him harm.

Then, to his relief, above the cacophony, he hears the honking of the Fiat's horn. Dashing outside, he sees that the car is waiting, its passenger door open, its engine running. He hurls himself towards it, his slight little body complaining at every step, and plunges gratefully into his seat, pulling the door awkwardly shut behind him.

Gabriela looks excited, keyed-up. Her pupils are dilated and she is breathing too quickly.

"Well?" she asks but Toby—heart racing, head thumping, nausea seething in his gut—is too short of puff to answer her. Instead he manages a kind of elongated gasp, equal parts thank you and exhortation to move, and Gabriela, needing no further encouragement, urges the car to move at speed back down the driveway and away from the Cannonbridge Collection, leaving their pursuers with only tire tracks and dust.

When the archive is a mile behind them and once they are as certain that they can be that they are not being pursued, Gabriela says again: "Well?"

Toby, still wheezing and shuddering, like a man in a public information film about the dangers of coronary disease, manages a slightly longer, if scarcely more detailed response than before.

"It's worse," he says, each syllable a struggle. "God, it's worse than I thought. Whatever the hell it is, it's more than a hoax. More than just a confidence trick."

Gabriela just nods grimly, as if she were somehow expecting his answer.

Neither of them notices the dark car, the Saab, which dogs their movements at a clever distance. Gabriela checks the rear-view mirror with some diligence but she never spots it, nor does Toby, slumped in his seat, his heart accelerating at least as much at his discovery as at his recent exertions. A little way behind them the man with the earplugs chews his toffees and watches his targets with a warped species of tolerant affection which, to the objects of it, generally proves more dangerous even than his violent ire.

They are back in Edinburgh proper now, heading Leith-wards and cruising past a dejected gang of students, a troupe of Ukrainian knights ('the Camelot of Kiev' reads the sign that has been pasted to the back of the stoutest of them) and a few disgruntled locals looking as though they are wondering whether it can ever truly be said to be too early in the day for a fight, when the woman speaks again.

"Tell me what happened," she says.

Toby, calmer now and almost stable, replies: "Yes. Yes, I will. But I have to thank you first."

Gabriela waves away his gratitude.

"That guard, you must have…"

"What happened?" she repeats, with a hint of some strange conviction in her eyes which ought, perhaps, to concern Toby rather more than it does at present, distracted as he is by the hectic dramas of the day.

As they pass a group of teenagers bad-temperedly carrying along the pavement a large inflatable whale, and whilst, behind them, the dark car prowls, Toby tells his peculiar story.

"There was a man," says Judd. "A librarian. An archivist. Something of that sort. It was so strange—like he'd been waiting for me. He was dapper and neat. But he seemed weighed down. Melancholic."

Gabriela nods, steers the car expertly down a side street so as to avoid the most choked and clotted thoroughfares, and waits for her passenger to get on with it.

"We only had a very few minutes together. He began by asking me a question…"

"Hmm," says Gabriela, negotiating a line of speed bumps with finesse. "And what was that, then?"

"He wanted to know…" Toby passes the back of his right hand across his forehead. Hot now. "What I thought would come after humanity. What I thought the next stage of evolution would be."

Past the bumps and gathering speed, hand on gear stick, moving up. "And did you have an answer?"

"No. Not really. I mean, I wasn't expecting it. It seemed like such a non sequitur, you know?" The hand across the forehead once again. "And after he'd asked me that, as if in explanation, he pulled open one of the cabinet drawers. And showed me the papers inside."

"And? What did you see?"

"I'm… not sure. I'm still not sure."

"You don't seem certain of much."

Toby doesn't seem to have heard her. "At times," he murmurs, hunkering back in his seat now, like a child being told a cautionary tale, "each page seemed full. Absolutely stuffed with texts, images, photographs. A long life mapped meticulously. But at others, when I blinked, when I rubbed my eyes and looked again… It was as though every sheet was entirely blank."

Curiously, Gabriela does not sound too surprised at this surely remarkable disclosure. "Hallucination?" she suggests. "Brain fart of some description?"

"Perhaps," Toby says, though he doesn't sound at all persuaded. "And, then, at the end, just before the alarm went off, there was one more thing. The librarian bowed his head, as if damning himself for the rest of time, and he said. 'Blessborough. Remember Blessborough. Look at his dedication again.'"

They are deep now into Leith itself. The crowds have subsided and the flat is almost in sight.

"What on earth did he mean by that?"

"Blessborough. Professor Anthony Blessborough. Dead now. He wrote the first critical appreciation of Matthew Cannonbridge. Just after the war."

"I know that. Actually, I think I've got a copy somewhere. But what did he mean about the dedication?"

"No idea. No idea at all."

The car pulls into the side of the pavement, beside the flat.

Engine switched off, the soft burr of the city. No other sound. The two of them secure for now in the bubble of the Fiat's front seats.

"Well, looks like we got away with it," Gabriela says and grins.

Toby snorts, in pleasure and relief and from the delayed effects of his adrenaline surge.

"Let's go inside," she says. "See if we can't figure this latest thing out."

Toby, grateful, agrees. They step out of the car together and, still casting anxious glances behind them as they go, walk up to the steps to the flat's front door.

Neither of them has the slightest presentiment that this will be the last time that they shall ever do so.

INTO THE SITTING room and the flat is silent but somehow uneasily so, as if a party had been abruptly wound up as soon as its participants heard the sound of the key in the lock. Toby and

Gabriela look at one another for a moment—and it's a bit odd, a little bit awkward—neither of them choosing to articulate what they're both thinking about the freighted silence.

Toby, who has not taken a woman who is not his wife out to dinner or to the pictures for fifteen years, reflects, nostalgically, that it feels a little like coming home for the first time after a date, both parties in a state of skittish expectation.

"Kara and Sam must've gone out," she says, sounding a little worried at the prospect. "Help yourself to a cup of tea or something. I'll see if I can dig out that book." Toby nods and thanks her. As the girl disappears into the bedroom, she calls over her shoulder: "Milk's in the fridge if you want it."

Toby watches her go—notices, in a way, that he accepts is entirely inappropriate, the sway of her bottom in her tight blue jeans—but he makes no move towards the kitchen or the fridge. Instead, he treads towards the window and gazes pensively out onto the street below, expecting, although he cannot say quite why, a dark figure watching him, staring back up with implacable malice in his eyes. But the street is empty. Of course it is. Cars pass by but none stops here. The world churns on, seemingly with scant regard for the troubles of Toby Judd.

As he watches, he thinks of that strange question the librarian had used. *What will come after humanity?*

He looks and thinks a while longer before, skin prickling in a most unpleasant way, he becomes aware that he is being watched. He turns slowly, as if wary of making any sudden moves.

Two women—Kara and Sam—have emerged, presumably from one of the bedrooms and are standing close together, watching him from the edge of the room.

"Hello," Toby says. "Hope we didn't disturb you."

They only look at him, wide-eyed and fretful.

Toby is at a loss as to how best to respond when Gabriela walks noisily back into the room, a bulky paperback under one arm, its cover emblazoned with a familiar face.

She stops, takes in the scene: "What's going on here?"

Nobody speaks until eventually one of the girls (Kara? Sam? Toby can't be sure) shuffles forward and says: "I'm sorry, Gabs."

The other one echoes the sentiment. "We're both sorry."

"Why?" Gabriela snaps. "What have you done?"

Again: "We're really, really sorry."

Toby hears a sound—distant but drawing swiftly closer—which starts to make a horrible sense of this strange tableau.

"We've been watching the news," says one of the women. "We've been hearing what he's done. About that man Spicer. And then the copper—Angeyo."

"I don't believe any of it," Gabriela says. "I think it's all lies."

"We're not so sure," says one flatmate.

"We didn't want to take the risk," says the other.

The sound is closer now.

Toby swallows hard. "Gabriela…"

She holds up a hand to silence him. "Wait. This is important." She turns back to the others. "Well?"

"We were worried about you. We just wanted you to be safe. So we decided to call them."

"Call who?" Gabriela asks but Toby already knows the answer. He knows now what they have done.

He touches Gabriela gently on the arm and together they listen to the approaching sound, its insistent, condemnatory wail.

Sirens. Sirens almost at their door.

1853
HAMPSTEAD HEATH
LONDON

A STRANGE INTERSECTION of country and city, eight hundred acres of well-tended green. "Heath" seems somehow too modest a name for this proud sprawl of grass and tree, of undergrowth and gentle, wooded hill. It is rather as if a piece of rural England has been carved from its bucolic homeland and set down, with little mind for the incongruity of the act, as a parkland at the heart of the greatest metropolis on Earth.

Yet the city has not allowed this rustic space to flourish unchallenged. Rather, it has peopled it with Londoners, who swarm on this bright, sunny day in June, along its paths and up its inclines, who linger by its lake and stroll amiably beneath its trees. All here is variation and diversity: grand ladies and gentlemen arm in arm, families on happy expeditions, working people, on a rare few hours of rest, slouched, squinting miserably up at the sky. There is a darker, more sorrowful element also—itinerants and beggars, homeless children scouting for change, broken-down old soldiers pleading for alms—as well as a class of person who are brazenly criminal in their demeanour and deportment (pickpockets, cut-throats, ladies of the night) together with that breed of indefinable person which is altogether timeless: sad-faced women of no detectable class or occupation, ruddy-faced single men who exist perpetually on the knife-edge between eye-bulging joviality and unchecked aggression, glimpsed figures moving between the tree-trunks, strange faces at the edge of the crowd, sombre outsiders, who might just as well be an incognito lord or a Clapham bachelor, watching the mêlée with expressions of such weird intensity that those who venture near them are compelled at once to move discreetly away. It is, in other words, the city that has won this battle in the interminable, doomed war with the countryside. It has placed five hundred individuals upon this shard of meadow, stamped without compunction on the sod, filled the woodlands with refuse and spoiled food, chased the birds away with screams and sounds of unthinking entertainment.

London the victorious, London the undeniable, London the true eternal city.

Amongst all of these who have come upon this warm, bright afternoon to gambol upon the heath there is only one particular party who require our attention, labouring up the steepest of the hills in this place, towards the urban view that is promised by its pinnacle. There are six in this party: three children (a boy and two small girls, all under ten), two women (one tall and dark-haired and with a certain nobility in her bearing, the other smaller and more timid, her hair worn close to her scalp) who, between them, labour with a ratty-looking picnic basket. Evidently in charge of the outing is a stout, full-bearded man, dressed, even according to the customs of the time, too formally for the temperature and for the nature of the trip, perspiring heavily yet still contriving (perhaps because, unlike the women, he is unburdened by their wicker-bound luncheon) to stride some few paces before the rest and to declaim, in an accent that is unmistakably Germanic, a snatch of soliloquy. He thinks it apt in this place to speak of another, quite different heath and thinks it of material benefit to his children to be exposed as often as is practicable to the culture of their new-adopted home:

> "'Cannot be ill, cannot be good: if ill,
> Why hath it given me earnest of success,
> Commencing in a truth? I am thane of Cawdor:
> If good, why do I yield to that suggestion
> Whose horrid image doth unfix my hair
> And make my seated heart knock at my ribs,
> Against the use of nature? Present fears
> Are less than horrible imaginings:

> My thought, whose murder yet is but fantastical,
> Shakes so my single state of man that function
> Is smother'd in surmise, and nothing is
> But what is not.'"

The children listen as attentively as they can, having been made aware from birth of the penalties for their inattention, but the words are strange to them and, at least to the youngest, the boy, aged but six, mean little. The women all but ignore the speech, having heard it (or something very like it) several times before. There is, perhaps, something in the taller woman's eyes which speaks of old adoration and something in the smaller which suggests instinctive deference, but these things are buried deep beneath difficulty, poverty and tragedy, and they have about them the familiar slow resentment exhibited by the practical partners of he who is an inveterate dreamer.

As soon as the gentleman's speech has reached its apogee (or, at least, a temporary version of the same for it is far from certain in the household how long these impromptu recitations might last) the two women, as if having communicated by telepathic means, stop as one, lay down the picnic and exhibit no indication whatever that either of them meant to move a single step until a respectable time has passed beyond luncheon.

The man with the beard peers at them, as if in surprise at this small mutiny. The little ones sigh and chatter with mingled excitement and relief. The taller of the two women, whose profile had once been admired by the great majority of the discerning bachelors of Saxony-Anhalt, stands her ground. "This seems to me to be an excellent spot," she says, to which her husband (for such he is, their union having already endured one decade and set to continue for another three more) manages only the most token complaint ("I had hoped, my dear, that we might venture just a little further...") before falling silent, sensing that he has been thwarted, though not especially minding the rout. As the picnic is decanted from the hamper and a profusion of blankets, rugs and cushions produced on which the party are expected to sit, his children run around his legs and, teasingly insistent, tug him towards the ground. It is, he will often think in future times, a moment of pure, uncomplicated pleasure, breaking bread with his family here in this amiable place which if it has not proved especially welcoming has, at least, not spurned him. The food is pleasant, though more meagre than they would like, there is a bottle of porter for him and there are sweetmeats for the ladies and the children. There is between the six of them a bond of fierce loyalty and love. All, he considers, is relative contentment and cloudlessness.

The meal is finished and the party, sated, has begun to drowse when a shadow falls across the group and a voice which is known to none of them is heard to declaim with (it will later be said) something of the sly charm of Milton's anti-hero: "Mr Marx? Mr Karl Marx?"

Our bearded fellow looks up in wary recognition and perceives the following sight: a tall, dark-haired man, clad, in defiance of the season, wholly in black (though he exhibits not the least sign of discomfort) and with something about him of the buccaneer, accompanied by three of the most senselessly attractive ladies that he has ever beheld arrayed in flagrant admiration about him. There is a second man also, rather shyer than the first, a short, stout person with an air of hard-won affluence whose presence is half-obscured by the undeniable physical magnetism of his companions.

"Have we met, sir?" asks Mr Marx.

"We have not, sir," says the dark-clad man, "at least not in person, though I half-fancy that I am well acquainted with you through your writings. My associates and I simply chanced to see you here amongst your charming family." An appreciative nod at this in the direction of Mrs Marx. "I fear I simply could not pass up the opportunity of paying my respects."

The great beard wags once, in acknowledgement. "Your name, sir?"

The dark-clad man smiles, broad and easy, and his sinuous female confederates (not a one of them, Marx thinks, more than four and twenty) twitter at the jocular absurdity of the request. "You know my name, Mr Marx."

The casual confidence of the man! The maddening, swaggering *droit du seigneur*!

The head of the family hesitates for just long enough to make it clear that his ignorance is feigned. "*The English Golem*?" he asks eventually, as though he has been searching wildly through some mental directory in search of the interloper's identity.

The dark-clad man nods, mock-encouraging.

"*Ezekiel Frye*?"

Another nod.

"*The Lamentation of Eliphar, Mununzar's Son*?"

The same gesture—flecked now with irritation.

"Ah, so you must be…"

The name is spoken then. The name of power.

Matthew Cannonbridge offers the other man his hand. "The names of these ladies are not in the slightest bit important but this other gentlemen, Mr Marx, now he is quite another matter. Allow me to introduce you to my particular friend, Mr Daniel Swaine-Taylor."

The plumper, wealthy-looking man bows in suave greeting.

"I know your name, sir. You are concerned, I think, with… capital?"

Swaine-Taylor nods. "Indeed I am, sir. I am of the City. A pleasure indeed to make your acquaintance."

"And I yours," Karl says. "My family," he adds, vaguely indicating his brood.

Cannonbridge pays them no heed. "I wondered, sir, if we might talk awhile."

"I am at leisure, sir, as you have surely observed, amongst my family."

"We need speak only briefly."

Karl finds that he is squinting. "Of what do you wish to speak, sir?"

Wide smile, glittering eyes. "Why, of what else, Mr Marx? Of what else but of things to come?"

NOW

THE SIRENS ARE closer now, closer than before, the neurotic screech of them cutting through the afternoon's desultory hum.

All four players—Kara, Sam, Gabriela and Dr Judd—are simply looking at one another, as if in unarmed stand-off.

It is, surprisingly, the academic who speaks first, his words almost swallowed by the noise outside. It is not entirely clear to whom he addresses his remarks. "I suppose this is it then," he says glumly. "Probably best to admit when you're beaten." He wrinkles his nose in meditative resignation. "I'd best just wait here till they come. Of course, I'll deny that any of you offered me any help. I can I say I lied to you. Forced you, even. Either way you won't get in trouble."

The slap that follows a second after this mournful declaration shocks Toby as it shocks all present. The thwack of Gabriela's palm on his left cheek seems to echo round the flat. The waitress bares her teeth and for an instant Toby glimpses the limitlessness of her determination.

"Don't be ridiculous. You can't give up now."

"But..." Toby gestures towards the women and inclines his head in the probable direction of the squad cars. "When the odds are so stacked..."

Thwack! She slaps him again.

"Ow!"

"Fight!" Her voice is raised against the sounds of authority. "Fight!"

"But... it's... no good..."

Thwack!

"Fight, Toby. *Fight!*"

A moment's more uncertainty. Then new steel.

"Yes." Toby nods. "Yes."

"Excellent. Then let's go." She throws Toby the book that has, until recently, been stowed beneath her arm. He catches it, a little less maladroitly than he might have done before. It's *Forgotten Genius*, of course—the Blessborough book. "You can read the dedication as we go. Now, come on!"

And they run, the two of them, from the room, from the apartment and out into the street beyond.

It all happens so quickly that Kara and Sam have no time to interject or to attempt any intervention. They make no comment at first, not, at least, until just before the arrival of the police. Instead, they simply gaze at one another in wounded, baffled solidarity and listen to the roar of engines.

OUTSIDE, THE MAN in the Saab, he of the earplugs and the supply of toffees, watches a battered little Fiat hurtle out of the end of the street and career towards the city's edge, its workings still warm from its previous excursion. On this occasion, he makes no move to initiate pursuit, but only watches as the vehicle speeds hectically into the distance.

Seconds later, three police cars drive past in the wrong direction, back towards the apartment.

The man in the Saab is not the smiling sort—if he were, he might allow himself a small moue of amusement at their noisy incompetence. Instead, he simply watches unblinkingly. Once the sound of them has died (and their drivers have doubtless begun to quiz the two bemused and apologetic flatmates) he removes a single foam bud, takes out his phone, touches one button and places the device disdainfully to his right ear.

A moment's silence, then: "They're heading north, sir... Yes. My assessment also... If you think that's best... Have we a copter on stand-by? Just to be sure... Good... Good."

The call is ended, the phone is returned to his pocket, the bud is dexterously replaced.

Externally, the man is patience personified. Within, however, something is stirring which, in the past, many have had good cause to fear.

The man in the Saab is getting restless.

It has been too long since he last performed an act of violence. Not since the madman in the hotel room and the copper in the alley by the café, his guts ribboning out, oddly beautifully, upon the pavement.

Now the man senses the approach of withdrawal symptoms. He's getting itchy. Not long, not long now and he'll be needing another fix. He finds himself thinking about the guts of Toby Judd and those of the little waitress.

He wonders if they'll look beautiful too.

"So what does it say?" Gabriela asks, still slightly breathless, as they break once more into the Scottish countryside, the air blessedly free of the sound of sirens. She is driving too fast and too recklessly. He thinks about saying something but glimpses the look of indomitability in her eyes and remembers the sting of her hand on his face and decides to button it.

"What does what say?" he begins, realising almost immediately. "Oh. Oh, yes."

Fumbling for the book, with its saturnine portrait on the cover, he brings it up to his lap and flicks to the beginning, almost dropping it again as Gabriela tackles a curve in the road in the manner of a stuntwoman with a death wish.

At last, Toby finds the dedication. It is only a single line which conveys nothing to him.

He reads aloud: "'To the guardian of Faircairn, with more gratitude than they know.'" He shrugs. "Faircairn. What's that?"

Gabriela does not take her eyes from the road. "It's an island," she says. "Just off the coast of Scotland."

"Really?"

"Really. It's very small. Privately owned. I wouldn't expect you to have heard of it."

"Good. Because I haven't."

"You think there's some connection?"

"I'm not sure," Toby says, "but at the moment it's the best we've got." He is thinking of the documents in the cabinets, of those pages which seemed to fade in and out—not of focus exactly but almost, somehow, of existence.

"That's good," says the woman.

"How do you figure that one out?"

She smiles. "Because I know exactly where it is. And, more to the point, I know how to get us onto it."

And she pushes the accelerator harder still and Toby is forced backwards in his seat and, for a moment, as they speed on, all things seem possible.

Neither of them know it but even as they discuss the Faircairn question, overhead and high above, a helicopter, black and of military design, keeps careful pace, shadowing their progress, its blades slicing savagely through the air.

1853
DEAN STREET
SOHO

AFTER KARL HAS fucked her that night—for there really is no other word to describe what they do in that hot, cramped little bedroom, an act seemingly devoid of tenderness or affection—he rolls over with an ursine snort of satisfaction and proceeds, rather clumsily in Jenny's opinion, to feign sleep. She knows the sounds that he makes whilst unconscious too well to be fooled by the performance and, having let him snuffle and sigh for a few, embarrassing minutes, she jabs him once in the side of his sizable belly and says: "I know you're awake."

The voice of her husband is hard and cold. "What of it?"

"I wondered..."

"Yes? I'm too tired to hold you, my dear." Those last two words sound almost sardonic.

"I wondered if you wished to talk awhile."

"Doubtful."

"To speak about what happened today... upon the heath."

For a while her husband says nothing at all and the silence is so protracted that she even begins to consider the possibility that he has truly fallen asleep. Then, two small words, oddly meek and puny. "I can't."

There is also, she realises now, a strange, uncharacteristic moistness to his voice.

"Karl?"

No response.

"Karl, my darling, are you... crying?"

He rolls still further away from her, at the furthest reach of their not especially capacious marital couch, his great, blubbery body quivering as he tries, not wholly successfully, to stifle his sobs of furious despair.

She does not persuade him to talk that night. Rather, he retreats into a childish truculence and she, growing at first frustrated and then melancholic, gives in to silence too and, eventually, a fitful sleep.

When they wake in the morning, Karl is all false jollity and ersatz bonhomie as if the events of the previous day have been expunged. He busies himself with work and with children, deliberately creating no opportunity for significant conversation with his wife.

In the evening, although Jenny implores him not to, he goes out alone, supposedly to meet three friends. He is evasive about his precise destination and the exact nature of the company that he intends to keep.

Jenny waits for him, sitting upright in bed, a book before her open and unread. She falls asleep, however, before he returns and dreams of her childhood and of its golden promises.

When she wakes she does so abruptly. There is a smell of whisky and sweat. Her husband is back, slumped beside her entirely naked, his fat white bulk seemingly propped up in the most ungainly fashion. He is breathing too heavily and Jenny's first thought is that he has been injured in some way. It is dawn and the thin light makes the face of her lover look pouchy, pale and ill. He is staring ahead of him at nothing in particular, his jaw hanging slackly, a little incipient dribble gathering at the corners of his mouth.

"Karl?"

He does not turn to look at her nor even acknowledge her presence.

"My darling?"

His lips twitch drunkenly into something which is both sneer and smile. He sucks in a breath effortfully and asks, his voice ragged and tired: "Do you still want to know?"

She does not doubt what it is to which he is referring. For a moment, she hesitates, so disquieting a vision has he become, and then, something shifting in her guts as she speaks, she says: "Of course…"

She could scarcely simply have left it, of course, for it is not in her nature to ignore any difficulties in her marriage—rather they are to be faced down, discussed, dismantled piece by piece. And so, as usual, she has pressed the issue for as far as she can. On this occasion, it is a choice that she will come to regret—regret, in fact, for the whole of the rest of her life. If only it were possible, she will think over and over in the years to come, for sentences to be unspoken, for events rewritten, for the slate of memory to be wiped clean, then these words—the words of her husband, although he largely quotes another man—are the ones for whose erasure she longs more than any other.

"He told me of the future," Karl begins. "He spoke of what is to come. Of what is to come after humanity. And with such horrific detail that he is either a madman or a prophet or..."

The big man's speech tails away. Jenny does not encourage or cajole him to continue, knowing that by far the best thing now is to let him take his time, allow him to circle the truth before its unveiling.

"Ah, it's late and I'm old and I'm drunk."

She does not disagree with any of these assertions, but is only sagely patient.

"Mad, then," he murmurs. "Or a seer. Or, perhaps, my dear, just perhaps... Perhaps he has in some strange, impossible manner... been there."

Jenny touches his chin, the soft thicket of beard.

"Tell me everything," she says at last and Karl begins finally to unburden himself of what had truly been said to him upon the heath by the man with the glittering eyes, about the world which lies in wait for them, of what will be done in their name, of the failure of all their dreams and that for which they strive, of the triumph of money and power.

"He must have seen it," Jenny murmurs wretchedly when everything is said, when the dawn is come and they hear from close-by the querulous stirring of their children. "You're right." Her eyes are damp with tears. "Somehow, impossibly, he must have seen it all for himself."

NOW

"ARE YOU SURE he's coming?" Toby asks, resisting the urge to tap his fingers in irritation upon the tabletop and exerting a good deal of willpower to stop his right leg from moving restlessly to and fro in nervous excitement. He has a headache and a persistent sense of nausea. He also, to his surprise, feels an unfamiliar exhilaration.

"I asked him to come," says Gabriela, sitting opposite Dr Judd and toying idly with the straw in her cranberry juice, ice clinking as she does so. "And I asked him nicely. So he'll be here."

Toby nods. His stomach growls. "It's just that... if we stay in one place too long... I mean, won't that make us easier to find? I don't doubt that, despite everything, I'm still really recognisable."

"It'll be fine," she grins. "Promise."

Toby says nothing, quietened by her smile.

It is dark now, and getting late. They have driven for hours, through the day and into the evening. The bar in which they are sitting, The Crofter, little more than a wooden shack, intended for holidaymakers and tricked out with stereotypical bric-a-brac and clichéd objets d'art, is already showing signs of winding down for the night.

Besides Toby and Gabriela, there are only a handful of other customers, The Crofter's usual clientele doubtless having being drawn at this time to the capital. There are one or two other couples, a family of four with two teenage children, resentful in their parents' company, two weather-beaten women on some grim walking break and a man of some indeterminate age between, say, fifty and seventy, his face humourless and lined. Toby imagines that he must be the only local present. The sound system which has been playing the best of Paul McCartney for the past hour pauses for a moment, a lull between Live and Let Die and the Frog

Song, and in the slightly eerie silence which follows, Toby is able to make out, for the first time, the sound of the sea, its ominous roar.

"We could hardly be closer here," the woman murmurs, as if in response to Toby's unspoken thought.

"Closer to what?" he asks.

"To the edge of things."

At this remark, Toby believes that he sees something pass across the face of the local man—something like a flinch, of surprise, perhaps, or else of stifled triumph. Then the moment passes, the music returns (Listen To What The Man Said) and the fellow seems as stoical and unperturbed as before. There is a clang at the bar—a handbell rung by a bored Ukrainian girl.

"Last orders!" she shouts, with a hint of an accent.

Toby is about to ask his companion if she'd like a refill of her cranberry juice whilst there's still time when she says: "Ah. And here he is."

Toby looks and follows Gabriela's gaze across the room.

She seems, remarkably, almost to sigh. "Still looking good. He's kept in shape."

A man, a stranger to Toby, though evidently not to his companion, has just walked into The Crofter.

The man is in excess of six feet tall. His impressive musculature, developed beyond the capacity of all but the ardent gym-goer, is clearly visible through his thin t-shirt and tight trousers and he sports a square-tipped black beard of the type that is currently (and, in Toby's opinion, inexplicably) fashionable. He is in his early thirties at most and carries himself with the unimpeachable confidence of the young, the fit and (Toby's doleful speculation, this) the unusually well-endowed.

"Nick!" Gabriela is on her feet, already in proximity to this man seeming quite different somehow, with a touch of colour in her cheeks and an odd, unfamiliar girlishness in her manner. "Over here!"

The bearded man nods coolly and saunters over to their little table. He moves with the supple grace of one who is preternaturally confident of his physicality and who considers himself impervious. When he reaches them, Gabriela kisses him on both cheeks. "It's good to see you," she says.

The man grins through his beard, something crackling between them. "Sarge," he says, in mysterious greeting.

Now she winks in reply. "Corporal." Then, her tone more careful and diplomatic, she says: "Nick. This is my friend, Dr Judd. Toby, this is Nick. Formerly Corporal Nick Gillingham."

"Good to meet you." The bearded man stretches out a hand, which Toby accepts. Expecting a real bone-cruncher of a handshake, he is surprised to find it warm and wholly without machismo.

"Likewise," says Toby in a voice which, nonetheless, comes out at a higher pitch than that which he had intended.

The younger man's gaze slides back to the lady, a transference of attention for which Judd can hardly blame him. Nick and Gabriela look at one another without speaking, doubtless remembering whatever history exists between them. Is it wrong, wonders Toby, to feel just a little jealousy at the sight of them? Probably, he concludes. He is, after all, a married man long since passed, where attractive women are concerned, into the realms of the invisible.

At length, their silent communion done, all three take a seat and Gabriela, smiling now in Toby's direction, says in explanation: "Nick and me were in the army together."

Both beam at him.

The army, Toby thinks... *The army?*

Various events start now to make more sense. As Toby remembers the security guard, laid out cold on the floor of the reception, Nick winks at the scholar in a way that may or may not be friendly.

"Yeah," Gillingham shrugs. "I was surprised to get your call. Pleased, yeah, but surprised too."

He's trying to play it cool, Toby thinks, recognising, perhaps, some of the symptoms, but this man—this Corporal Gillingham— is excited, he's thrilled, he's happy as a sandboy.

Caught up in the origin and usage of the phrase (from the earliest decades of the nineteenth century, referring to those male traders who sold sand to strew about the floors of inns and hostelries), Toby almost misses what Nick says next.

"You mentioned a favour..."

Gabriela corrects him. "A big favour." It is impossible now to judge her tone as being anything other than transparently flirtatious.

"Yep."

"Tell us, Nick," Gabriela says, smiling, leaning forward. "What do you know about an island called Faircairn?"

Gillingham takes an ostentatious breath. His beard quivers. "Private island," he says. "People stay away."

"Yeah?" Gabriela says. "That's its reputation?"

The well-built man nods. "And there are a lot of strange rumours about that place. It was used for something during the war, I think. I've heard there are good reasons why no-one wants to go there now."

"Oh really? Well, here's the thing, darling..."

"Yes?"

"I'd like you to get us onto that island."

Toby can hardly believe the sight of it so oddly does the expression sit upon the ex-soldier's face but it seems clear to him that, at the speaking of these words, Corporal Nick Gillingham looks, all at once, and quite unmistakebly, afraid.

1869
33 BOLSOVER STREET
MARYLEBONE

Mr Wilkie Collins is woken from dreams of dark water at the touch, by no means unwelcome, of his lover's hand upon his shoulder and by the word, issued softly but with that stern insistence which betokens a matter of some severity: "Darling".

Wilkie stirs, groans, blinks and snuffles, the dream (or, perhaps, some conscious part of him considers, what might more properly be considered a nightmare) proving too stubborn a resident in his imagination.

"Martha," he murmurs. "What is it, my angel? For that matter, what time is it?"

Unthinkingly, he allows a touch of querulousness to colour those last few syllables, an intonation that he at once regrets.

"Shortly after six," says Martha, who is dressed in a long grey night-gown which does nothing to disguise the large and pendulous swell of her pregnant belly. She leans forward, the motion causing her ripe flesh to press most fetchingly against the fabric and at the sight of it Wilkie feels a pang of affectionate, mildly transgressive desire.

"Six?" he echoes. "My sweet, whatever is the matter?"

"You've got a visitor."

Collins only gazes at her, moving groggily now towards full waking. "Well, who?" he asks after the silence has come to seem intolerable.

"He is waiting for you," Martha explains. "Waiting in the parlour."

"But who is it?" Wilkie asks, the querulousness having returned—forgivably he thinks given the earliness of the hour and the infuriating mystery of the woman's manner.

By the time that she has finished speaking the name of their uninvited guest, however, Wilkie is out of bed, dressing hurriedly and, all at once, horribly awake.

HE IS A queer looking man, our Mr Collins—friends might have called him unconventional, the unenchanted simply grotesque. He is very short, little more than five feet, with a head that seems too large for his shoulders and a curious bulbous outcrop on his right temple. His arms seem too far stubby for his form and hang rather inadequately high up his sides.

See too how he moves, bearded and bespectacled, clad now in a fawn-coloured dressing gown that is several sizes too large for him, stepping with clumsy-footed purpose out of the bedroom (Martha has been left waiting anxiously within), down the little stub of corridor and into the usually cosy front parlour, now made somehow sinister, peopled by shadows, in the pale, unfriendly light of early morning. His visitor stands in the centre of the room—a tall, dark-haired man, his back turned away, gazing, presumably, into the darkness at the edges of the chamber.

Wilkie stops and, realising that he is perspiring, wipes his forehead with the back of his hand.

"Charles?" he says.

The visitor turns, to reveal that famous face.

How white he looks, thinks Wilkie. How drawn and unrested and ill at ease.

"Charles, whatever is it?"

Mr Dickens, the Great Inimitable, sighs.

"Forgive me," he says, "my dear fellow, for this too early and unwarranted intrusion."

"Not at all. Not at all."

"Yet I fear that there was no-one else to whom I was at all able to turn."

"What has happened?" asks the little man. "You hardly seem yourself."

"It is necessary that we talk."

"About what, pray?"

The older writer swallows hard and Wilkie notices that he is sweating also, harder than he.

"No," says Dickens. "Not about what, my dear Wilkie. But rather—about whom?"

A LITTLE LATER, over a pot of steaming Earl Grey, fortified more noticeably with brandy than might perhaps be considered proper in some less rackety household, as the light of new day creeps determinedly into the room, the two men are enacting the essentials of their, it has often been remarked, somewhat curious relationship. Mr Wilkie Collins is listening, with patient attentiveness, whilst the Great Inimitable holds forth.

"Wilkie," he says, and despite the familiarity of the scene and the comfort offered by the liquor, he still seems profoundly troubled and disquieted, pale, bloodshot, skin slick with sweat. "You are, I have always said so, amongst the very first rank of my friends and acquaintances."

Mr Collins, without making so much as a sound nonetheless contrives to convey the unmistakable impression that he is nothing less than immensely proud of this honour.

"More than that. We are, after a fashion, relations. We are bound by ties of blood and marriage. I know that we've not seen a great deal of one another lately, not perhaps as once we did, but I have never sought to neglect you in even the slightest way. There is much that we have shared together. There lies a glorious history between us." He allows himself a sad smile of theatrical collusion. "Much, eh, that our womenfolk should not care to know?"

A nod, a crooked smile, a surreptitious glance towards the door to ensure that his mistress is not listening there.

"Yet there are certain parts of my life of which I have never told you. Matters, in fact, which I have never discussed with any living soul."

A graver expression now, a resort to the teapot, a measured, pensive swig. "When... back now, oh some forty, forty-five, years ago. In the time of my childhood. When I spent that unhappy sojourn in the Blacking Factory…"

Mr Dickens' speech tails off after this and at last Wilkie speaks up, shifting rather awkwardly in his armchair as he does so. "You need not speak of it, you know. I understand that it forms for you something of a territory of pain."

Charles waves the interjection aside. "Yet speak of it, I must," he says, very still in his manner, markedly sombre and altogether in earnest.

Wilkie takes another sup of tea; emboldened and distinctly curious, he says: "You may tell me anything. I am no stranger to keeping secrets. On the contrary, it is a business in which I am well versed."

Dickens nods, distracted, as if having scarcely registered the remark. "I was only a boy," he begins, "when I saw him."

And Mr Wilkie Collins listens for a long while after that as he hears of the blacking factory and of its attendant degradation, of the man who was waiting for young Charles one long-vanished afternoon, of their peregrinations and of that black-clad gentleman's strange, prophetic remarks.

Once the tale is told there follows a silence, fraught with disquiet.

"And… forgive me…" Wilkie's response is faltering, perplexed. "But are you sure that is was him?"

"I've no doubt that it was."

"And not, say, his father or an uncle or some other relation?"

"Wilkie, it was him. It can have been no other than Cannonbridge himself."

At the mention of the name, the room seems suddenly a little closer, the air thicker and more difficult to breathe.

"Wilkie, have you ever seen the man?"

"Once or twice. Yes. At parties. Soirees. On a single occasion only at the British Library. But never to speak to. His reputation and manner serve to discourage any friendly approach."

"Yes. Yes, I see that."

"Have you? Seen him since? This peculiar ageless man?"

"Somehow we had never been in the same place at the same time. Strange, perhaps, given our respective reputations. There were occasions upon which I have been assured that we missed just such a meeting by moments only. He is a singularly elusive fellow to be sure. There is, I fancy, something of the phantom about him."

"Worse, perhaps, than that. There are, after all, no shortage of rumours."

"Quite so, Wilkie. Quite so."

"But you've not seen him yourself?"

"No." How old the Inimitable looks, thinks Wilkie, how prematurely aged. "At least, not until last night."

"Last night? Charles, what the devil has happened?"

"You will recall, I imagine, that, following the success of similar events, I am at present contemplating a further series of public readings from the most popular—one might even say beloved of my works of fiction." Collins inclines his head in acknowledgement of this fact, considering that not only is he cognisant of the scheme but that his friend has spoken of little else this twelvemonth past.

"And you will recall that I required an investor so as to provide a little essential funding for the tour?"

Collins nods again, a little fuzzy in his head now, doubtless from the earliness of the libation.

"A… Mr Swaine-Taylor, was it not? Yes. Daniel Swaine-Taylor. A banker of some description?"

"It was. It was. Or so I thought. At shortly after nine last night, Mr Swaine-Taylor came to call on me at Gads Hill."

"Rather late to call."

"I thought the same and I said as much. But he was insistent and he would not be moved. And then, in my drawing room, his face lit horribly by the flames of the fire, he announced that he was not the true investor at all but merely a representative of he who had provided the wherewithal. Some secret and hitherto anonymous benefactor."

"Remarkable news."

"So I thought. Yes. I thought a good deal more too. I told him that I considered it to be a fraud and an infamous fraud at that. Nonetheless, this Swaine-Taylor told me that the real man of money wished to see me. That he was even now waiting for me in a carriage outside. Most impertinently, this benefactor bade me join him at the earliest opportunity."

"And did you?"

"Of course. How could I not? I left the house at once and, at the urging of Mr Swaine-Taylor, stepped into the waiting vehicle."

"Your investor was inside?"

"He was, Wilkie. He was."

"And it was…" The volume of Collins' voice decreases, with an odd, almost queasy kind of reverence. "It was he of whom we have spoken?"

"Yes. Yes, my dear Wilkie."

"How extraordinary. And did he, did… Mr Cannonbridge—say why he had done this thing?"

"Because there would be profit in it. Those were his words. Nothing more. Nothing, certainly, to do with our… prior connection."

"And as to why he wanted to see you?"

"Oh, he said he wanted to look at me. To see what I had become. Me, so changed from that tiny boy, him wholly unaltered in his appearance by the passage of years. The cab began to drive then and as we passed through the streets, shadows playing across his face, this Swaine-Taylor creature wholly subservient by his side, I saw that something had shifted in him. Oh, not to be sure on the exterior, so much the same did he look, but on the inside. At the heart of him, I can assure you, some terrible alteration has been wrought. There is such malice in him now, such greed and wickedness and worse, I fear, far worse even than these. He spoke of such curious things. He gave me such dreadful glimpses of the future. He spoke not only of mankind's fate but of our successors. Of strange new forms of life. The journey cannot have lasted more than half an hour. They all but threw me from the cab at Vauxhall. I have walked here directly from there."

Collins sighs. "A bad night, then. A bad night's work to be sure."

"Indeed. And yet I fear, my dear old friend, that the affair is not done with yet."

"No?"

"Wilkie. I am very much afraid that you must play your part in it."

"Me?" Collins reaches again for the teapot, wishing now that he had been still more generous with the brandy.

"My dear fellow, my greatest companion, I fear that I must ask of you a boon."

Collins' heart is beating faster. Sweat is trickling down his temples, down his cheeks, down his neck. He is suffused with a horrible suspicion that what is to be said next will, in some quietly dreadful manner, alter the course of his life. He feels, however, that he has no choice but, in a cracked half-whisper, to say: "Anything, Charles."

Mr Charles Dickens leans forwards, smiles without mirth and steeples his fingers. "Very good," he says, sounding more collected than he has for hours. "Now this is what I should like you to do."

NOW

WHEN TOBY JUDD first sees the island—a low, dark smear against the horizon which thickens gradually into a bleak, immutable mass— his initial thought, which he knows, of course, to be completely impossible, is that he has seen the place somewhere before. *Only in your dreams,* he thinks, gripping the side of the dinghy as it surges wildly up and down, as he struggles to calm the lurching somersaults of his stomach. *Only in your dreams.*

The past hours have passed in a hectic whirl of activity, in which he has played an almost entirely passive part, yielding without complaint to the determined expertise of his companions, Nick and Gabriela, or, as he has almost come to think of them, caught up as he is in the strange, half-flirtatious energy that flickers between them, the Sergeant and the Corporal. From somewhere a small boat was procured, from somewhere the necessary equipment, before in some manner, slightly mysterious to the man with the doctorate, the three of them had found themselves speeding away from the mainland shortly after dawn, moving across the murky, churning sea towards the island of Faircairn. They are all now dressed in black, their faces smeared with war paint with soft dark hats pulled low over their brows. Not for the first time, Toby is wondering exactly which wing of the army these two had actually been in. They seem so efficient, he thinks, so assured, so inured to the danger of the situation. In his commando outfit, he feels utterly ridiculous—like a penguin forced awkwardly into a miniature suit.

Once, Toby had thought he'd heard the ominous, faraway thrumming of a helicopter but, as they had approached their destination, the sound had grown fainter until it had disappeared entirely, leaving him to wonder if he had simply imagined it.

And now the island is getting closer and closer, coming inexorably into focus.

He looks round at the other two who stand close together at the rear of the vessel. Closer, he thinks, than colleagues of even the most intimate stripe would ever have chosen to position themselves.

Nick Gillingham holds up a hand. He turns, busies himself with the engine. A moment later the motor cuts out. From somewhere in the darkness, two oars are produced and he and Gabriela proceed to row stealthily and silently on. So sombrely do they apply themselves to this task, with such po-faced sobriety, with their smeared faces and little black hats, that Toby feels a sudden, overwhelming and quite inappropriate urge to laugh.

Just as he feels that he can restrain it no longer, however, he turns again to face the horizon and this spurious, hysterical mirth dies in his throat.

After this, the island seems almost to swallow them up. It cannot be large, Faircairn, not more than a couple of square miles in total, yet its sheer presence seems to belie its size. It has a minatory, monolithic quality—a statement rather than a question, a slab of ancient territory set down in the midst of the North Sea. And it does seem ancient, Toby thinks, as their little boat is sculled nearer to the dark hulk of it—like some prehistoric survivor, some grim relic of the age of Pangaea or even, the doctor considers with an odd, superstitious dread, from some still earlier, nightmarish epoch.

Faircairn seems dark even in the light of the dawn and Toby can make out only a black expanse of sand or soil, a hill which rises precipitously above the beach. There are no houses that he can see, nor manmade structures of any kind.

Closer comes the island, closer, and Toby finds, although he does not care to, that he is put in mind of some aquatic predator, which, feigning sleep, allows its unwitting prey to approach before its great eyes snap open, its jaws gape, its sharp teeth gleam and the darkness beyond, the awful finality of the gullet, beckons.

So close now, Toby thinks morbidly. The trap is almost sprung.

With a muffled thwump, the boat strikes the shore. Nick hurries to the prow and, showing off now, pulls the vessel high onto the ground, the outline of his biceps clearly visible. He motions with one hand and Toby finds himself moving unquestioningly over the side, tumbling inelegantly into the wet sand.

But is it truly sand? Or is it rather something else? As he rights himself and clambers to his feet, he sees that his damp palms are coated with the stuff.

Feeling at once revolted and blessed, Toby looks down at what is on his skin. Dark black granular matter. Like thick-grained ash. Like clinker. It is, he thinks, as though the place had long ago been consumed by fire. A volcanic island? Would that be possible?

As he hears from behind him the crunch of the others' boots he looks up at the dark hill that lies before them. It is formed entirely from the same mysterious substance.

"What is this place?" he asks.

"And more to the point..." Gabriela is at his side. "How is it connected? To Cannonbridge?"

"Blessborough," Toby murmurs. "'The guardian of Faircairn'. And yet..." He gestures around him. "Who would ever live here? Let alone want to guard it? Hardly the most hospitable environment."

From somewhere behind them, Gillingham sniffs with a robust haughtiness. "Man's more adaptable than you'd think," he says, stepping forward. "Aren't a lot of places on the planet where he can't scrape by. He's a survivor—he adapts to his environment. But there's something here. Everything I've ever heard about this place says that there's definitely something here."

Toby addresses him. "Interesting to hear you say so. Exactly what, I wonder, have you heard?"

A stony look in return from the soldier. "Only rumours. Daft stories. Pub chat. Something about the war. Something which keeps people away." Nick pushes his shoulders back (he's puffing out his chest, Toby thinks, he's actually puffing out his chest) and says: "So let's have a look, shall we? Get us on some higher ground."

Without waiting for a response, he strides away and begins, with determined agility, to climb the hill.

Gabriela touches Toby on the arm and favours him with what he takes to be a smile of amused collusion. "Come on."

Toby is looking again at the dark sand. "Strange," he says. "This is just so strange. You must've noticed. I mean, what is this stuff?"

"You'll figure it out," she says with an odd, infectious brightness. "You'll find the right connection."

And she is gone, moving skilfully through the gloom, easily keeping pace with the corporal. She calls back: "Come on!"

Toby does as he has been instructed but not before, without quite knowing why, he crouches down, scoops up some of the black sand and slips it into his pocket. As a kind of souvenir, he supposes. A memento to prove that the day's adventure has not been a dream or a product of complete mental breakdown.

A line from a play comes back to him as he trots after the others and he murmurs it to himself as he begins the ascent. "'I shall show you fear'," he says, "'in a handful of dust.'"

The hill is steeper than it looks and the climb is tougher than Toby is expecting. The sun rises and the dawn has arrived in full by the time they reach the crest of it, the three of them getting there as one.

Later, they will wish that it had been less bright—that they might not have seen it in such unforgiving detail, that they might have told themselves that it was only the product of shadows and their imagination. That they might have looked away.

All of them, in their own ways, have experience of the uncanny. All of them know what it is to be confronted by the inexplicable, the *unheimlich*, by those things which seem to make a mockery of rationalism, to explode any sane reading of the world as a cruel myth.

Yet they are all of them rendered speechless by the sight that greets from the peak of that terrible hill upon that impossible island.

Nick speaks first. "It can't be."

Gabriela murmurs "My God..."

"You're seeing this, aren't you?" Toby asks, horrified yet fascinated, appalled yet utterly riveted, open-mouthed at the dreadful majesty of the thing, its awful intertwining of beauty and terror. "The guardian," he mutters. "The guardian of Faircairn."

For a long moment, not one of them dares to turn away.

It is Gillingham who cracks first, turning and running helter-skelter back down the hill.

With one final, disbelieving glance, Toby and Gabriela do the same.

The rest is over very quickly—a giddy blur of panic and motion, down the hill, onto the beach beyond and into the boat, a frantic pushing off, a bout of demented rowing, the comforting roar of the motor, a swift retreat (though scarcely swift enough, it must be said) from the island of Faircairn.

Nick is swearing under his breath, other words interweaved amongst the profanity. "Sorry... I'm sorry... I can't... Can't help..."

Gabriela simply stares into the ocean, pale, thin-lipped, unspeaking, trembling.

And Toby?

Toby is lost in thought, feeling, not for the first time in recent months, on the precipice of his sanity, forging connections, trying to understand the shape of the pattern, asking himself over and over again the nature of that deepening evil which seems to compass him all about and which has come, very nearly, to eclipse his life.

1869
ALLEYNE WAY
WAPPING

THE HOUSE OF Cannonbridge is not at all as Mr Wilkie Collins
had imagined. The address, prised free from a rather shadowy
acquaintance whose name is well known to Scotland Yard, lies in
a distinctly low quarter of town, a crumbling mansion of dubious
provenance deeper into the East than any man of good character
and reputation might, of his own volition, wish to tread.

Mr Collins, however, knowing his reputation to be rackety at
best, had little fear as to how such an expedition might be seen by
others and, in this as in so much of his life, he was happy to forego
the rigours of convention. Of that house, however, of that bleak,
dilapidated, dusty old house, and of the man who dwelt within
it—now, about these things, he is very concerned indeed.

It is already dusk as he approaches the property, he and Dickens
having talked for much of the day. Several further pots of that
augmented tea having been by now consumed, Wilkie Collins
finds himself rather unsteady on his feet and uncertain in his gait.

He does his best, however, to walk with deliberation and
purpose down the dirty narrow lane which leads off the grey,
neglected thoroughfare to the house of Cannonbridge. He holds
his too-large head up high and steps on with as much confidence
as he can muster between the shadows and to the front door of
the old, disreputable place, painted, a generation past, with green
paint, now ancient and peeling, and to the large brass knocker of
more recent vintage and fashioned into the shape of some circular
serpent, which stands beady watch upon it. Wilkie takes the metal,
cold to the touch, in his clammy hand, lifts it and knocks once,
twice, three times.

No sooner has the last of these gestures been completed than the door is swung open and the writer finds himself confronted by a man of about his own age, looking forlorn and cast down. The fellow's eyes are bloodshot, his skin has a wretched pallor, his movements are blurred somehow and indistinct, like a person walking underwater, and his hands and arms are shaking as if from palsy. His entire being, it seems to our Mr Collins, can do little else than radiate the utmost despair.

Taken aback by this vision Wilkie, almost before he has done so, finds that he has asked the gentleman the following question of startling bluntness: "Who are you?"

At this, the man sniffs miserably, seemingly unsurprised by the enquiry. "Swaine-Taylor, Mr Collins," he says. "Daniel Swaine-Taylor. My friends," he adds unhappily, as if that tribe has long since been extinct, "called me Dan."

"How… how did you know my name?"

Mr Swaine-Taylor smiles feebly and the sight is indeed a grisly one. "We have a mutual friend, do we not?" he says. "In Mr Dickens? Besides, my master is expecting you."

"Your master?"

"Come, Mr Collins. Let us not play games. You know who my master is just as he knows you, and just as he informed me some days past that you should be calling upon us tonight."

"But how? How is that possible?"

"Time, to my master, is not as it appears to us. It is not a straight line. Rather it is a circle. It is a snake that swallows its tail."

Mr Collins blinks at this extraordinary sequence of remarks and, thinking of that strange doorknocker, is in the midst of marshalling some challenge or reply when Swaine-Taylor raises one arm and beckons. "Do step inside now, sir," he says. "Mr Cannonbridge is waiting for you."

Everything that is in Collins—every instinct for survival, every superstitious urge for self-preservation, every impulse to flee—screams at him to remove himself from that benighted house at almost any cost. Instead, he only increases his resolve, pushes aside his imploring conscience, ignores the urging of his soul and steps over the threshold.

"Very good," simpers Swaine-Taylor. "Now, pray sir, walk this way."

It is gloomy within and the tapering corridor, singularly unwelcoming, along which Mr Collins now follows the ruined man, seems itself to possess a kind of malice, as though the presence of the little writer is in some sense an affront to it. Besides it is treacherous to navigate in the flickering half-light that is cast by sporadically-placed candles and Wilkie is able to catch only glimpses of the walls—shattered and crumbling, an occasional oil painting of striking ugliness hung there to disguise the worst of the decay. The floor is strangely spongy underfoot. Neither person speaks as they progress.

Eventually, a speck of light comes into view, grows steadily larger before Wilkie is ushered into a large room, lit a little better than the rest, its walls lined with books. He has been brought also, he realises, into the presence of Mr Matthew Cannonbridge.

The great man seems unchanged from those previous occasions on which Wilkie has spied him and he accords exactly, of course, with the Inimitable's description. He stands upright in the centre of the room, arms outstretched in a rhetorical gesture of welcome, wearing both a dark dressing gown, wrapped tightly around him, and a smile which, whilst doubtless intended as that of an agreeable host, strikes Collins as quite the most sharkish that he has ever seen. There is also, he sees now, a lit cigarette smouldering in the author's right hand, at the sight of which Collins feels a sudden stab of longing for that distinctive satisfaction which only tobacco can provide.

So caught up is he in his examination of his host (and many of the books upon the shelves are, sees Collins now, those by Cannonbridge himself) that he scarcely notices Swaine-Taylor, with a kind of croaking flourish, announce the visitor by name.

Wilkie is fully cognisant of the moment, however, and indeed is quite certain that he shall never forget it, when Matthew Cannonbridge turns his gaze upon him and says: "Mr Collins. You are most welcome."

The smaller man, he of the ragged loping gait and the head that looks to be too big for his body, in spite of the prickling in his throat, the sweat that springs up upon his palms at the sound of these words and the concomitant ache in his head, remains determined to stand his ground. "Mr Cannonbridge," he says, with as much graciousness as he can manage, "your creature told me I was expected."

"That is so." The smile is unwavering, the eyes hard and cold.

"Might I ask how that is so, sir? My enquiries were discreet, I told no-one of my intentions and I sent no word before me."

Cannonbridge waves the question aside. "My gaze is not as other men's."

"How so, sir?"

At this, the smile diminishes just a little. "Now is not the time. But might I ask the reason for this call? The hour is a late one and, as you can see, I am at my leisure." He raises the cigarette to his lips, inhales and lets loose a long, thin stream of grey smoke. Without having to be summoned, Swaine-Taylor scuttles forwards and catches the ash that has been dislodged by the motion with an inexplicable expression of the purest joy upon his face, in the palms of his upturned hands.

Trying his best to ignore the grotesquery of the scene, Collins presses on. "I am surprised, sir, given your apparent gift for prophecy, that you do not already know it."

"Perhaps," says Cannonbridge, shooing away the fawning figure of his manservant, "I wish merely to hear it directly from you."

As the sole object of Mr Cannonbridge's undiluted attention, Collins finds that he is shifting nervously to and fro and from foot to foot. With a considerable effort of will he rights himself. "I have been sent with a message."

"Oh? And who has sent you?"

"Charles Dickens."

"I see." Cannonbridge's tone is flat and unsurprised, leavened by the slightest suggestion of amusement. "And what does little Charles want with me?"

"This," Wilkie says and, delving deeply into the pocket of his frock-coat, produces a thick manila envelope with the initials 'M.C.' inked hard upon the front of it.

Cannonbridge takes another drag on his cigarette. "And what is that?"

"Your money, sir, returned in full."

An affectation of surprise. "My money, sir? Why, I do believe that it is more properly to be described as Mr Swaine-Taylor's money."

At this, the man in question leers, as if at some long-cherished private joke.

"Sir," says Wilkie firmly, "as I understand it there is very little difference between the two."

Cannonbridge appears to acknowledge the truth of this remark. "Perhaps," he says. "And Charles wishes to give it back to me now, does he? My recollections of that time are, I confess it, somewhat dim and befogged but I seem to remember that he had no such qualms as a boy." One final plume of smoke and the cigarette is done. Cannonbridge discards it upon the floor and Swaine-Taylor scrambles to collect and dispose of it.

Wilkie says nothing but only holds the envelope out before him, his arm shaking quite visibly.

Cannonbridge nods to his man. Swaine-Taylor capers over, takes the envelope from Collins' hand and bears it, like a lap dog, to his master.

The paper is torn open. The contents are given a derisory glance.

"I think you will find, sir, that the amount is paid in full."

Cannonbridge wrinkles his nose as if at the detection of some disagreeably pungent odour. "A pity," he says. "Dear me. For I saw such profit in it."

"Did you indeed, sir?"

"I did. For Mr Dickens is a phenomenon of the age, is he not? His words have become integral to our culture. Unlike, say, yours, Mr Collins. He shall surely fill every lecture hall in the kingdom. I suspect that you would struggle to do the same."

"I do not deny it. I understand well my place in the scheme of things."

The smile returns, broader than before. "Now that I very much doubt. You see, Mr Collins, what men like you never seem to understand is how much power there is within this envelope. Even in its return, Charles shall never truly be free of me. I will always be a part of him. As for others, well, see here..." He draws the banknotes from the envelope, raises them high above his head, tosses them into the air and watches them flutter towards the ground. He barks, once and terribly: "Fetch!"

Swaine-Taylor, subject to whatever strange enslavement it is which holds him so tightly, struggles to catch every part of that blizzard of money, performing a desperate jog in his frantic efforts.

"You may go now, Mr Collins," says Cannonbridge against this thoroughly grotesque performance. "Tell your master that the rumours that flock about him even now shall soon solidify into infamy and scandal. Tell him that he shall be dead within the year. Your own career will end in failure and disgrace."

The last of the notes flutters to the floor. Swaine-Taylor snatches it up and clasps it, together with the rest of the booty, to his chest. A single, shrill whimper escapes him.

Cannonbridge arches an eyebrow and says to Mr Collins: "You look as though you have a question forming upon your lips."

"Yes, sir." Wilkie's voice is trembling slightly. "Before I take my leave of you, I have to ask you this."

"Go on."

"Why? Why this squalor and degradation? You are rich and famous and, in certain quarters, somewhat inexplicably in my view, greatly admired. You could live almost anywhere you chose. Why dwell in this place of darkness and sin?"

Cannonbridge seems to think for a moment before replying. "Because," he says, at length, "this is not where I live. Not truly. Rather it is where I hide."

He pauses. Collins does not interrupt.

"You see," the saturnine man continues, "I feel—have always felt—that I am pursued. There is a shadow at my back. I have glimpsed it from the corner of my eye all of my remarkable existence. And it seems now... to be growing... more distinct."

"I…" Collins finds—unusually, if not uniquely—that he has no notion at all of what to say. He merely gazes at the curious figure of his host, of the manservant now sunk to the ground, still clutching his money.

Cannonbridge says quietly "Go" and, when Collins does not immediately begin to move, shouts: "Get out!", screams "*Get out!*"

And without hesitation and without looking back Mr Wilkie Collins takes to his heels and all but runs from that place of wickedness, down that crepuscular corridor, back over the threshold, up the treacherous path and out into the vile alley beyond. He does not begin to calm himself until he is in a cab and crossing the river once more. And, as he sits, shaking and ill at ease in that shuddering vehicle, he wonders—he shall always wonder—whether it was indeed his imagination which caused him to see, when he glanced back just at the moment when the house had disappeared from view, a bristling, many-sided shadow shuffle with terrible purpose by the door of Matthew Cannonbridge.

NOW

IT IS GROWING dark again (too soon, Toby thinks, too soon, as though there has been but a sliver of true day), former Corporal Gillingham has gone, muttering troubled apologies, and Dr Judd is alone with Gabriela again. They have made it as far as Inverness where, on her credit card, they have booked into a Holiday Inn for the night, into a beige twin room, the homogeneity of the place curiously comforting after the stark horror of the dawn. A solitary lamp provides brackish illumination.

They are lying on their single beds, separated by a patch of caramel-coloured carpet not more than one foot wide, both of them fully dressed and both exhausted. The television is on, its sound muted, as an advert for razor blades plays out in soundless idiocy.

Both seem to be on the cusp of a sleep born of profound physical fatigue, although their minds still race and churn.

"Have you any theories?" Toby asks. "About what it might have been? The... guardian?"

Gabriela sighs. "I can't seem to focus on it. When I try to remember... it's as if my memory recoils at the thought of it. Like it just refuses to focus on what we saw."

"I know just what you mean."

"Perhaps..."

Toby breathes in the clean antiseptic smell of the hotel room, finds himself hunkering down on the inexpensive, though scrupulously laundered, linen. "Yes?"

"Maybe there are some things the mind just refuses to remember in full. Like a self-preservation mechanism. Like it's protecting itself somehow."

"You could be right. It's... I don't know... Do you remember that chapter in *The Wind in the Willows*? It's one that people tend to forget. They meet Pan. Remember? They meet the great god Pan."

But Gabriela isn't listening to him anymore. She is staring at the television screen. The adverts are over, replaced by the news, the endless rounds of information which fill the channel for twenty-four hours a day. There has been no sign of Toby's image so far. Instead, there is a horribly familiar likeness on the screen—a nineteenth century photograph, a saturnine man dressed in black.

Then the image shifts and below the perky smile of the newscaster rolls a ticker tape of information.

'The Cannonbridge Gala,' it reads, 'Growing list of dignitaries confirmed to attend. Event to be held tomorrow at the heart of Canary Wharf.'

"Good grief," Toby breathes. "I'd lost track... I'd quite lost track of time. It's tomorrow, isn't it? It's happening tomorrow?"

The woman fumbles for the remote. "Looks that way. Why do I get the feeling that everything's about to snap violently into place?" She locates the controller, stabs at a button and the room is filled with the babble of rolling news with the rise and fall of the journalist's robotic delivery. The words "greatest British author" are mentioned as are "politicians, pop stars, the great and the good", as are "the best of our island nation" as, Toby notes, with something strangely almost like nostalgia, is "Dr J J Salazar."

He is about to say something—anything—to the tired yet beautiful woman who lies almost within touching distance of him when another sound interrupts the chatter of the set: the shrill peal of a telephone.

There is such a device on the cabinet next to Gabriela's side of the bed. She frowns and, without thinking, picks it up and places the cheap-looking receiver to one ear.

"Yes?" She frowns again. "He's here." She looks over. "Toby? It's for you."

"Reception?" he asks hopefully, though he knows, of course, that it isn't, that, given what his life has become, it can't be anything so prosaic as that.

He gets up, hurries over, accepts the call. "Who is this?"

The line is crackly, the voice on the other end female and unfamiliar. "Dr Toby Judd?"

"Yes," he says. "Who are you?"

"My name is Jenny Blessborough."

"What?"

"I understand that you've been investigating my grandfather's work."

"Yes. But how did you possibly—"

"Judd, you need to get out of that hotel room. We are waiting for you outside. We're in the white van. Looks like it needs a clean. You need to take your girlfriend and get out of there at once."

"Why? I mean, why should we possibly trust you? Even if you are who you say you are?"

"There's a man on your trail. A man named Mr Keen. Until now he's only been watching and biding his time. But the order's obviously been given."

"Who? What order?"

"The order to take you in. We've seen his car. We've seen the Saab. For all we know, he might already be inside the hotel. So I say again: you need to get out of there now."

And the phone goes dead.

"Who was that?" Gabriela is on her feet, tense and alarmed.

"She said her name was Blessborough..."

"What? What on earth did she want?"

"She said there's someone after us. And that she'd be waiting for us outside. And that—"

Too late. He is interrupted before he can say more, not this time by any electronic sound but by something far earthier and utterly unmistakable. The door to their room is kicked—literally kicked—open with a single, contemptuous gesture and there is a man standing on the threshold, a neat and smiling man whose eyes seethe nonetheless with insanity. He grins with gruesome relish. And he is chewing, Toby realises, chewing something soft.

"Dr Judd," says the man with murderous certainty, but rather too loud, as if his hearing is obscured in some way and he is no longer certain of the volume of his speech. "Get on the floor now. You–" He points at Gabriela. "You do the same." Almost nonchalantly, he reaches into his jacket pocket and pulls out a long, serrated knife.

My God, thinks Toby, *my God, but there's something... there's something encrusted on the blade.*

He is surprised by what happens next although he ought, perhaps, not to be.

Wordlessly, wasting no time nor giving her opponent any opportunity to react, Gabriela rushes at the man in the doorway, throwing her whole body hard against him. Even so, the knifeman does not fall but only stumbles. She takes advantage of this momentary distraction by forcing the blade from his hand and onto the hotel floor.

"Run!" she shouts. "Toby! Run!"

The fight begins in earnest then, vicious hand-to-hand combat. Gabriela striking with supple, determined art, the stranger parrying her blows with the sick delight of the professional who discovers a worthy opponent at last after months of encountering only amateurs, dilettantes and pushovers.

"Run!" the woman shouts again. "I'll follow! I promise. This is too important. You need to get away." At this speech, the man laughs—a thick, glutinous chuckle.

"I can't... Can't leave you to this."

"Go, Toby! Go!"

"Gabriela, I—"

"Run! I beg you. Run! Now!"

Toby hesitates, thinking that he should stay, knowing that he ought by rights to at least try to help but then he sees the fierce command on the woman's face and he does as he is told. Filled with regret and shame, he leaves them battling on, each offering the other no respite nor any possibility of mercy.

He runs, down the corridor, down the stairs and into the soulless lobby. As he sprints, he hears, in short succession, the guttural sound of male pain and then a woman's high cry. He stops, hesitates, thinks about going back. Then, remembering the Sergeant's order, runs on.

Outside the hotel, a white van is waiting, engine running, door open.

The window is wound down, the driver, a stout, dark-haired woman in early middle age, leaning anxiously out.

"Hurry up!" she shouts. "Come on!"

Panting, his little body jolted onwards by fresh adrenaline, Toby clambers inside the van almost without thinking. He glimpses a couple of mattresses, a few boxes and, in the shadows, a low, prone, motionless shape.

The driver calls back. "Close the door!"

"No," Toby gasps. "We've got to wait... for Gabriela..."

"Was she with Keen?"

"I... I think so. Yes."

The driver snarls. "Then, the chances are, she's dead. Now close the damn door!"

Without waiting for her instruction to be obeyed, she floors the accelerator and the van speeds hectically, desperately, away, leaving in its wake, it seems to Toby, something vital, something irreplaceable.

Something of his heart.

1888
SCOTLAND YARD
LONDON

As HIS SERGEANT unlocks the door to the cell, Inspector Frederick Abberline of the London Metropolitan Police allows himself, for the first time in months, the tiniest suggestion of a smile.

A small, side-whiskered man, just on the cusp of plumpness, Abberline steps inside, the Sergeant trotting behind him. In fact, the room is not exactly a cell although, with its blank walls and single chair, bolted to the ground, its bars upon the windows, its locks and guard without, it would be a connoisseur indeed of such accommodation who might feel confident in parsing the difference. Abberline looks down towards the man who is at present assisting them with their enquiries—tall, saturnine, clad fashionably in black, he sits with a galling insouciance on that solitary seat. Nonetheless, the Inspector feels a small surge of triumph at the thought that, after all the tribulations and obstructions of recent weeks, they have at last succeeded in bringing the man here, thwarting his well-connected allies and his own considerable will and summoning him for questioning.

"Sergeant?" says Abberline to his companion. "Leave us a while."

"Sir?" The note of disapproval in his voice is unmistakable.

The Sergeant is a good man but he is a stickler for orthodoxy and a martyr to the rulebook. He has yet to learn the necessity of those occasional circumventions of protocol and reorderings of procedure which are sometimes vital to ensure that true justice is done.

"We need a moment alone," Abberline says and still the subordinate gazes concernedly in his direction. "The responsibility's mine, lad. Not yours."

Reluctantly satisfied, the Sergeant nods and withdraws. The door slams shut behind him and a violent clatter of the turning of locks and the drawing of bolts ensues. There is silence for a moment in this cell that is not quite a cell.

The man in the chair (not the prisoner, Abberline reminds himself, for the fellow is not yet formally that and remains, technically, a mere member of the public) is looking up at him with amusement quite apparent on his face.

Abberline looks down and smiles back at him, seemingly affably enough, holding the expression for a few taut seconds before suddenly collapsing his demeanour into one of brutal disapprobation—a trick which has, in the past, unsettled many a thief, cracksman and cutthroat.

With this particular suspect, however, it seems to move him not at all.

"Mr Cannonbridge," says Abberline, moving behind the chair now so as to remind its occupant who possesses control in this long-expected encounter.

"Inspector," breathes the suspect softly, still and unperturbed.

"I imagine you understand why we've had to bring you in like this."

"No doubt you have suspicions, Fred," says the black-clad man with wholly inappropriate good cheer. "You strike me as the kind of man who would nurse dozens of the things without having the faintest notion as to what to do with them."

"Kind of you to say so, sir. But why don't you tell me to what you think these suspicions of mine, of which you hold me to be so fond, might pertain?"

"Oh, Inspector. Please. I fear I really couldn't say."

Abberline sucks in a breath, takes his time, counts to fifteen before replying. "Four women," he says, "of the most unfortunate sort, slaughtered on these streets."

"I do glance at the newspapers, Inspector. From time to time."

"Let me be frank, sir. Let me be wholly and entirely frank with you. Can you account for your whereabouts on the nights of each and every one of the murders?"

Is it Abberline's imagination or does even the great Matthew Cannonbridge blanch a little, as have others before him, at the asking of this question?

"I... really cannot say, Inspector."

"Cannot, Mr Cannonbridge? Or will not?"

"I fear I am not always able to account for my movements. Even to myself." The eyes of the dark-clad man dart swiftly into the corners of the room.

"Oh dear, sir. That is unfortunate. Yes indeed. That is most unfortunate."

Cannonbridge glowers back at the policeman and Abberline wonders if some strain of lunacy might not lurk within the fellow— he has long considered, after all, that no completely sane man can possibly have been responsible for the outrages that he has seen perpetrated upon the bodies of those wretched drabs. "We know you have a house in the district, sir. We know that your writings contain a good deal of bloodshed and terror, directed especially towards women. Why, *The English Golem* remains a shocker, sir. A real, twenty-four carat shocker. And now you are unable to account for your movements on the nights in question. Tell me, sir—what am I supposed to think?"

Matthew Cannonbridge does not at first reply but only waits until the Inspector, who has continued to stalk behind him and around and about, returns to his original position. Only then does the dark-haired man speak and only then after he has first turned his eyes upon the detective and favoured him with a broad smile which seems, remarkably, given his present state of incarceration, to be fuelled by genuine good humour.

"Fred," he says, an almost playful tenor to his voice. "Come now. You have no real motive for me. You have nothing connecting me to any of these grisly tableaux. You have no eyewitness accounts. No testimonies. No hard evidence of any kind at all. No, what you have are suspicions only—well-nurtured to be sure and no doubt teeming in that stolid little proletarian brain of yours. But all quite worthless, either here or in any reputable court of law. The whole world knows,

Inspector, that to someone of your sort suspicions are as populous as fleas upon a beggar."

Abberline draws in, through nostrils only, a noisy, rattling breath and brings his face as close as is practicable to that of his chief suspect. "I know it was you," he says, spitting out each word distinctly. "I don't know much of how or why but I'm certain it was you. Call it intuition. Call it a copper's hunch. Call it second bloody sight if you want but I'm absolutely certain that you, Mr Matthew Cannonbridge, are the man they call the Ripper."

Not a single muscle moves on the face of the man in the chair. Neither person speaks, their faces close enough to touch.

Eventually, the corners of the suspect's mouth twitch upwards. "And what if I were?" he says. "If I really were the inhuman beast you describe do you honestly think that you alone could bring me down? A man as famous, as rich, as beloved as I? No, my friends—a whole nation of them—would never allow it. You know this to be true, I think. That I am, so far as fellows like you are concerned, eternally out of reach."

At this, Abberline feels suddenly and unexpectedly subject to a tide of emotion which he has long since imagined himself to have trammelled and tamed—namely fury of the most intensive and all-consuming kind, fury which clouds judgement, fury which burns away sense, fury which leads to the making of life-altering mistakes. It is only by means of the very greatest exertion of will that Inspector Frederick Abberline succeeds in quelling the urge to strike this fellow here and now and strike him again and to go on striking until the man in his custody is merely a mass of pulped flesh and bruises, snapped bone and bloody skin.

The Inspector has little doubt that, were he to succumb to this urge of primitivism, the assault would be accompanied by screams of rage, at the insolence of the villain, at the regular and widespread triumph of criminality over the law, at the sheer injustice of the world. But he swallows it back, he holds it in and, as he does so, he notices that Cannonbridge has been watching him all the while and that there is something in the author's expression which suggests that he knew all along of the detective's internal strife and that it has provided him with no small quantity of mirth.

"Mr Cannonbridge," Abberline begins with, uncharacteristically, no particular idea of what might follow this opening salvo of syllables.

The suspect looks questioningly up but he has no time to make any further remark as, with a terrific flurry of metal against metal, the door is unlocked and pulled back and the young Sergeant, flushed and visibly out of sorts, strides into the room, with a cream-coloured piece of paper held in his hand.

"Stop, sir! Stop!"

"What's this, lad?"

"I'm sorry, sir. I'm very sorry. But we've got to let him go."

Abberline looks at the lad's earnest, anxious face then glances down at that of their guest and sees that, far from following the conversation, Cannonbridge is gazing into the middle distance, as if lost in poetic thought.

"What are you talking about, lad?"

"Here, sir." The Sergeant holds out the paper. "See for yourself. From the Commissioner."

Abberline snatches the letter, glares down at it, sees the awful, treacherous words swim and distort before him as if they are the product of some terrible mirage. Their meaning, however, is quite plain.

Cannonbridge smiles as if at some private joke. Still he gazes daintily before him.

"Must be from Charlie Warren," he says lightly, as though the thing's of small account. "Of course we're old friends. From the club, don't you know?"

Abberline, feeling once more the approach of the tide, crumples the letter in his fist and throws the resulting ball towards the Sergeant who catches it.

"Mr Cannonbridge," murmurs Abberline, knowing now how the sentence must end, "you are free to go."

*   *   *

THEY WALK WITH him out of the cell that is not a cell, out of the building and beyond the walls of the Yard to where Cannonbridge's coach is waiting, a black-muffled driver atop. Beside it is a broken-down man, with rheumy, red-rimmed eyes and a scuttling, unhealthy gait. This poor specimen of humanity ushers Cannonbridge inside. Neither man looks back towards the Inspector and the Sergeant, both of whom stand watching the departure of their chief suspect with glum resignation.

Abberline finds that he is half-expecting to see the face of his quarry grinning in triumph as the vehicle goes past but, no, the drapes are pulled immediately within and he is robbed even of that small moment, the tiniest indication that the afternoon has been any more to Matthew Cannonbridge than a mild and faintly absurd inconvenience.

"Sergeant?" says Abberline as the coach rattles away. "Who was that odd fellow? The one who was waiting for him."

"Hmm. Just a moment, sir." The Sergeant reaches into a pocket and retrieves a notebook, very properly kept and maintained. He turns the pages to the relevant point and squints at the words that he finds there, as if finding it hard to read his own handwriting: "A Mr Swaine-Taylor," he says at last. "A Mr Daniel Swaine-Taylor."

Abberline says nothing to thank him but only watches the vanishing coach, first as it diminishes and then as it disappears entirely.

But he does not forget.

No, the Inspector never forgets that name.

NOW

THE VAN IS moving faster now, at frantic, reckless speed. The hotel is already lost behind them and they are heading to the edge of town, to the A9 beyond. There is a ferocious roaring sound within of rushing air which Toby Judd silences when, with a single sob born equally of exertion and despair, he wrenches shut the sliding door. The atmosphere made a little calmer, the roar of air and engine diminished to the point at which bellowed conversation is possible, the driver calls over her shoulder. Her voice is tough and authoritative but all the same tinged with fear.

"You must be in the mood for explanations, Judd."

Toby looks about him at the van's grimy, lived-in interior, the old mattresses, the bundles of clothes, the low, dark hump at one corner.

"You could say that," he mutters, the instinctive mildness of this phrasing suddenly striking him as grotesquely inapt. He swallows, only partly successfully, a whoop of hysteria.

The woman at the wheel tuts as if at an errant child. She keeps checking the rear view mirror, twitchily, with learned, long-term paranoia. "Get a grip, Judd, and come and sit beside me."

Chastened, Toby obeys, clambering awkwardly into the front of the van, buckling himself into the passenger seat as the vehicle hurtles and sways.

He has the chance to get a better look at her—she can't be much more than forty, he thinks, though she seems much older somehow, lined and battle-weary, a veteran of relentless campaign.

"Gabriela," Toby gasps.

"That your girlfriend?" the woman snaps as they move, picking up speed, onto the dual carriageway. "The little waitress?"

"Not my girlfriend," he says sadly. "But she is a waitress... amongst other things."

"Tough cookie," the woman says approvingly. "If she's sacrificed herself then it'll have been to secure your escape. You ought to be grateful."

"I am... grateful. But... that man... mightn't she have..?"

"Unlikely. No one's ever got the better of Keen. If I was you I'd start looking to the future. Leave the past behind."

"But..." Toby begins.

"Partly my fault anyway. Should've made contact before. We've been trying to keep you under observation but that's difficult with a life like ours. Besides, we didn't think they'd send Keen in so soon." She doesn't sound particularly apologetic. "But we should share information. You've been to the Cannonbridge Collection?"

"We have. And we've been on the island too. We... saw the thing that guards it."

"Did you now? Hmm. Well, I suspect what you saw was whatever the island wanted you to see. There are times when it's fine to go there—if the island wants you on it. But if it doesn't—if it wants to keep you away, it'll make damn sure that you do. But it's impressive that you got so far in the first place. Most people in your position, Judd, they'd be long dead. You must've had good protection."

"You said your name was... Blessborough?"

"That's correct. I'm Anthony Blessborough's granddaughter. Last of the line. Well, more or less."

"So what are you doing? In this van? Hanging about outside a Holiday Inn? Chasing round Scotland? I mean, forgive me, but it looks like you live in this thing."

Faster and faster they travel, well in excess of the limit. Toby is rocked to and fro in his seat. He reaches for a belt and straps himself in but the effect is scarcely lessened.

"We live off the grid, Judd. We have to. Our lives are spent on the run."

"But why? Why?"

"Cause of what my grandfather discovered. On Faircairn. Because of his book. And because of Matthew Cannonbridge. Don't you see? Anyone who's got even slightly close to the truth they eliminate. Spicer. Your policeman friend. They're powerful enough to do it. Rich beyond the dreams of avarice. There's nowhere they don't have influence. Whole governments are completely in their pocket."

"But who are they? And why are they doing this?"

"We were hoping that you could help us with that last question. As to exactly who they are, as to the precise nature of our opponent, I'd have thought that was obvious. It is the snake that devours its tail." Angrily, she flips the indicator down and manoeuvres the van towards an exit. As she does so, Toby hears, from somewhere behind him in the recesses of the van what sounds horribly like a human groan.

Only then does he realise that there was something strange in the grammar of Blessborough's speech.

When speaking of her life on the road she'd not said "I".

Never "I". But "we".

"Is there someone else," he asks thickly, "in here with us?"

He turns his head to look behind him. To his horror, the pile of rags and clothes, the low, dark shape which he had taken to be possessions, is moving and shifting and stretching.

"Don't be alarmed," says Blessborough. "I'm taking us to York. There's a safe house there. We can talk properly. And then, once you're fully in the picture, it's going to be time, at long last, to fight back."

Toby feels a surge of fury at the new madness of his life.

"Who," he snarls, "is in here with us?"

The bundle of rags moves closer, revealing itself as a woman in early middle age, wild-haired and pale and dressed in tatters. She pulls herself forward up to the seats at the front of the van.

She stinks, Toby realises, understanding that he is in the presence of deep and intractable madness.

"Don't be alarmed, Judd. It's only my sister."

They are driving cross-country, off the main roads. Trying to lose themselves. The madwoman is at Toby's ear. Her voice is cracked and raw, and Toby is put in mind of photographs that he saw once long ago of meths drinkers on the streets of London in the 1960s—a tribe that existed on such extremities of society that they began to seem like something else entirely, something other than human.

"You want to know what it is?" she hisses and Toby, despite himself, finds that he is flinching—cringing, almost—away. "It's a demon... A demon they've let into the world..."

"Shh, Alix." This from Jenny. "Hush now. Don't agitate yourself."

"Toby..." The sister slides a prematurely gnarled hand onto Judd's shoulder and, with awful enthusiasm, squeezes. "They created a space in the universe... And something slipped through. Karl saw the edges of it. Edgar was driven insane by it. Oscar guessed the truth before the end. Old Fred had his suspicions. And the Order, they spoke to... an aspect of it. It hungers, Toby. It hungers for life."

At this torrent of crazed detail, at the peremptory behaviour of the driver and, above all, at his abandonment of Gabriela, Toby feels a terrific current of anger course through him, horribly jolting as an electric shock. "What," he shouts, "is the meaning of all this?"

But there is no time for anyone to reply. There is a loud bang very close by, the van lurches wildly to one side, careering wildly. All within are thrown violently about, like so many ants in a matchbox.

And then there is another loud retort, another impact and Toby's vision is suddenly smeared and fading. Filling up fast with blood.

1892
LEADENHALL STREET
LONDON

"FORGIVE ME, SIR," says the rather dapper young fellow behind the desk, his hair glistening with unguent, his suit neatly pressed, his tie done up with a dandyish flourish. "But what did you say your name was?"

"Abberline," says our man, a little older since we met him last, a little greyer at the temples and rather stouter round the waist. "Mr Frederick Abberline."

"Abberline... Abberline..." At this, the neat young fellow makes rather a performance of searching his notebooks and ledgers and those copious piles of paper which bedeck his desk. This pantomime done with, he presents an expression of chilly mock-deference. "I'm afraid that we appear to have no record of you, sir."

"You wouldn't do. I'm not expected. I've not made an appointment here."

"Dear dear."

"I suppose you could say that I've come here on a hunch."

The secretary or equerry or maître d' or whatever he is purses his lips in scrupulous distaste. "Forgive me, sir, but I do believe that your name does seem distantly familiar to me, as of a faraway and rusted bell that tolls exhaustedly in the summer breeze. But not, I fancy, through any professional connection. Were you not once of the London constabulary?"

"I was. Used to be Inspector. Now retired."

"And, forgive me if my recollection be faulty as I have a great deal, you understand, to occupy my time and to demand my attention, but you were not involved—nay, sir, were you not at the very forefront of those official investigations into that beastly business in Whitechapel a handful of years ago?"

Abberline, who has become used to such identifications, simply nods once and issues a gruff "I was".

The lips of the man behind the desk form a pout of mocking sympathy. "Never did catch him, did you, sir?"

"No." Abberline smoothes back his side-whiskers, a gesture that, he has learnt, can sometimes succeed in quelling his frequent outbursts of temper. "We never did."

"A pity, sir," says the young man with all the civilian's ignorant relish for bloodshed and gore. "A great pity. For he must have been a madman, mustn't he, sir? The things he did to those women. The awful degradations. The wicked glee that he took in their gutting."

Former Inspector Frederick Abberline draws himself up to his full, yet far from considerable, height, smoothes back his whiskers with entirely disproportionate force and says: "I always think it's best, sir, for gentlemen who are no longer on the Force not to comment publicly or otherwise, on unresolved criminal matters and on those cases which remain, as we would say, 'open'."

The younger man adopts an expression of serio-jocular sagacity. "Very proper of you, sir. And very correct of you to say so. Now..." His expression shifts back to one of watchful neutrality. "How might I be of assistance today?"

"I would like to talk—or I would like to make an appointment to talk—to a man whom I have reason to believe works in this establishment."

"Oh yes, sir? And what is the name of this fortunate gentleman?"

"Swaine-Taylor," says Abberline carefully. "Daniel Swaine-Taylor."

Momentarily, and almost imperceptibly, the young man flinches. Half a second later, his decorous façade is restored. "Might I ask, sir," he says, "how you have come to have heard that name?"

Abberline inclines his head in accession to the request. "I've a deal of time in my retirement, sir. A deal of time. Some of it I've spent in reading. Trying to better myself. Some of it, I freely admit, I've drunk away. And some of it I've spent, well, in a little extracurricular digging. A bit of amateur excavation. I saw your Mr Swaine-Taylor once. I've a nose for connexions. And so I traced him here, to this address."

"Really, sir? How very resourceful of you. Nonetheless, your investigations must surely have been incomplete for I regret to have to inform you that Mr Swaine-Taylor who was, in point of fact, for many years our Principal, passed away at Christmas."

"Then he's dead?" Abberline's voice makes his disappointment clear.

"He is, sir. As a doornail."

Suddenly, and with a vigour that surprises even the old copper himself, the right fist of Frederick Abberline is brought down hard on the desk before him and his words emerge in a cracked roar which speaks of half a decade's frustration and fury. "Are you lying to me, boy?"

"No." The young man speaks almost in a whimper, all cockiness fled in an instant. "No, sir. I assure you. I am not."

Abberline masters himself once again and steps back. The side-whiskers are pressed firmly into place. "Sorry," he murmurs. "I should not have…"

"No need." The other man sounds almost short of breath. "No apology necessary."

Abberline sighs. "How did he die?"

"Peacefully, sir. And in his bed. Or…"

"Yes?"

"At least that was what we were told."

"Hmm."

"I'm sorry, sir. I know nothing more. Now, if there's nothing else…"

"There is, as it happens."

"Yes?"

"One final question."

"Go on, Mr Abberline, please."

"What is this place? What happens here?"

The person at the desk seems relieved at this enquiry. "Why, we are a bank, sir."

"A bank?"

"A new kind of bank, sir. And we do business only with the very best. The very cream."

"A bank, you say?" asks the old Inspector wonderingly.

"Indeed, sir. One might even say *the* bank. Now, if those are all the questions for today?"

Abberline nods and agrees that this is so and shakes the other man's hand in additional, unspoken apology and steps away, out of the building and back out onto the street.

Here he pauses for a moment and looks up with a policeman's eye for detail at the edifice from which he has just emerged—a rich, expensive, City palace, built of dark stone. There is a bronze plaque affixed, gleaming, to the door. The name upon it means nothing to him yet as he stands in that thoroughfare, surrounded by the sounds of conversation and footsteps and hoof beats upon tarmacadam, he feels, without understanding entirely why, greatly troubled in his mind.

He draws in a breath, smoothes back his whiskers and reads the plaque again.

'REYNOLDS' it says in tall black letters. Only that and nothing else.

With an inexplicable solemnity and sadness, as if something crucial has only narrowly eluded him, Abberline turns dolefully, walks away and lets London claim him once more.

NOW

TOBY JUDD MUST have lost consciousness for a minute or two—the darkness punctured by an oneiric glimpse, of a plaque, a bronze plaque, gleaming in the sunlight—for when he opens his eyes again it is to an altered scene of the utmost brutality. The van has come to a halt. The glass of its windscreen has been smashed and cold Scottish wind is blowing through the shattered space. His vision is smeary, he realises, for his eyes are filled with liquid. He wipes them clean as best he can and realises that the substance in question is his own blood.

He winces, still coming to. There is a sound nearby, like the screech of a seabird in panicked flight. It takes him a moment to comprehend what it is that he is hearing—the lunatic keening cry of the Blessborough sister.

In pain (*my head,* he thinks dimly, *something has been done to my head*), he levers himself out of his seat and away from the van, leaving the madwoman behind him.

He sees where they are—an empty, narrow, rural lane. Ahead of them is a black Saab. Vaguely, as if from another life, he recollects having seen it before, on the street outside his home, back in Ashbury. Now it is on the grass verge a few feet away.

Evidently, he has awoken in time to witness the finish of a long-awaited confrontation. Neither of the players, lost in their private drama, seem to be paying him any attention.

There is Jenny Blessborough with her hands in the air like she's under arrest. There, standing opposite her, a revolver in an outstretched hand, is the man from before, from the hotel; he who was chewing a toffee whilst brandishing a knife, the man who, with Gabriela...

Toby's thoughts are cut short when the man, in clear, clipped tones, says to his prisoner: "Tell me. I am interested. Did you really think that your survival for so long was due to your own ingenuity? Jenny, love, you were permitted to escape. You were allowed to live…"

The woman looks defiant, facing down the man with the gun with a salty resilience which Toby very much doubts that he would ever have been able to muster in such a scenario. Yet, for all of that, there is exhaustion in her too, a dreadful sort of readiness. "Then why?" she spits.

He shrugs. "To see if you might be worthy." He seems to allow himself a bitter smile. "But we've got someone better now. Someone much better suited."

Without warning, as if he has simply grown bored of the conversation, he presses the trigger, there is a loud retort and the woman crumples at once to the ground, something trickling from her scalp. The man only grunts once in satisfaction. Toby cannot help himself—he shouts out in horror and shock.

The man turns to Toby and, with the gun now directed at the academic, walks towards him. He is limping, Toby notices. There's a stain by his left knee and he wonders, with a thrill of guilty pride, if Gabriela had managed to wound this monster before the end.

"Good evening, Dr Judd," he says. "My name is Mr Keen. Your presence is required in London."

Toby struggles, and fails, to stop his voice from quavering. "By whom? And why? Why, for God's sake?"

"It'll be explained. Beyond my pay grade, I'm afraid."

"And if I won't go?"

Keen sighs. "All of a sudden, I'm not feeling all that patient anymore."

There is a wild shriek from the ruined van.

Keep quiet, Toby thinks. *Alix, for your own sake, stay silent.*

Mr Keen smiles. "I've not forgotten her, doctor. Never fear. Now we're going to step over to my very nice car. It's the black Saab over there. And we're going to do it without any fuss. You understand me?"

He limps closer and places the gun at Toby's temple. *Still warm,* he thinks. *Metal still warm against my skin.*

"You've really no choice so let's not prolong this, shall we? You wouldn't want me to do to you what I had to do to your girlfriend in the end?"

"And what," Toby snarls, "was that?"

"Oh, let's just say that no human being could have survived it. Out of the question. Walk this way, please."

Backed all the while by cries and whimpers from the van, Toby allows himself to be guided towards the Saab where he is pushed down into the passenger seat, the weapon hard against his temple. Just before he is pushed down into place, just before the door slams shut, he shouts, at the top of his voice: "Run, Alix! Run!"

At this, three things happen—Mr Keen frowns mildly, the screaming from the van ceases abruptly and the revolver is slammed hard into the side of Judd's head.

He will always tell himself later that he cannot remember much of what follows. In truth, despite his concussion, he will recollect it all as a series of snapshots in hideously pin-sharp detail—him being strapped in by Keen; the killer getting into the car; the locking of the doors and the starting of the engine; the drive away; the sight of a wild-haired figure crawling free from the van and starting, with all the speed and vigour of desperate insanity, to run; Keen's cool pursuit; their effortless catching of her; the pale, panicked face of Alix Blessborough; her piteous scream; her arms before her face; her final peal of terror; the disappearance beneath the car; her surrender to the tyres and the metal; the awful double bump that follows; the certainty of her extinction.

And then, after all of this is past and the long drive commences, the man with the gun places a bud in each ear. A smile flickers about his lips and he delivers the somehow sickening request, spoken as though nothing at all of significance has occurred, as though they were just old friends out for an afternoon drive, accompanied by the rustle of a small plastic packet and spoken lightly, almost drolly: "Would you care for a toffee, Dr Judd?"

1894
HEADQUARTERS OF THE
ORDER OF THE MOON-BORN
CAMDEN TOWN

"My dear," says Mrs Constance Wilde to her particular friend, Miss Georgina Lavenham, as they descend the exterior steps towards the basement of a house in a district that is far from respectable, "are you sure that this will be quite safe?"

"Oh, certainly, certainly," retorts Miss Lavenham, a thin-faced and haughty woman of indeterminate middle-age who adopts at almost all times an expression of studied boredom, as if daring the world to provide her with amusement and diversion. "Well, almost certainly. But then a little risk gives spice to the venture, don't you think? Otherwise, what would be the point of it all? I certainly feel in need of novelty now that the Golden Dawn stands revealed as so disappointingly milk and water an organisation."

"Indeed," says Constance, who is, in fact, not entirely sure that she agrees with that assessment. "I dare say we shall see what we shall see."

The two ladies are to form part of a larger party—twenty-one in total, eleven men and ten women. Constance and Georgina are the last to arrive, stepping unhurriedly down through a rather dirty door and into the hallway beyond, at the end of which they are just able to glimpse the temple, empty at the moment but shortly to be filled. There are two antechambers to that larger space and it is into the second of these that the ladies walk.

"I always find this part so tiresome," opines Miss Lavenham. "It is all so very cumbersome and unwieldy, this dressing up. Your husband is quite right—I've always said so—in his beliefs concerning the impracticality of women's dress."

Constance, who prefers at present not to dwell upon her husband's opinions concerning the removal of clothing, only murmurs some inconsequential reply, too low for us to hear.

The two women disappear into the second of those little rooms which abut the temple. We shall not follow them there. It would not be proper. Instead we will wait until they emerge again, their old, elaborate attire gone now, replaced by floor-length robes, made, fetchingly, of material that is coloured a deep shade of damson. The others are with them, all dressed identically and, a quorum having evidently been formed, they all file politely inside, quite as if they are returning to their seats for a performance at the Haymarket following a pleasant interval spent in discussion of the first act and in the consumption of some surprisingly tolerable wine.

Who are they, these men and women who choose to spend their afternoon in this subterranean place, dressed as though they are adherents to the most ungodly and inexplicable of creeds?

Why, they are you. They are me. They are our neighbours, our friends, our brothers and sisters, our tailors, our barbers, our brokers and bookmakers and librarians and grooms. They are, in short, wholly unremarkable. Any one of them you might pass daily upon the street for years and never once have the slightest cause to suspect him or her of possessing so profound an interest in the shadow side of life nor that they, with such frequency, expend their free time in the exploration of the occult. Not a single individual would you mark down as being, in private, a magician.

The walls of the temple are lined with purple cloth. Chairs are laid out in two parallel lines, one for either sex. Before these are sigils of curious design chalked upon the flagstones and before this, at the head of the room, is a kind of altar, carved from some manner of black stone and projecting a most unpleasant sort of aura.

How little I should like to touch it, thinks Constance as she and Miss Lavenham take their seats which are on the very first row of chairs—*how little in fact do I care to be in this room at all.* There is, of course, no natural light here. The place is lit only by candlelight, a thing that makes the shadows loom and shudder at the edges of one's vision.

"The scene is prettily enough done," admits Miss Lavenham to her companion. Constance nods.

"And I hear they provide a worthwhile spread at the end of it. The devilled kidneys alone are, I gather, sufficient as to justify the cost of membership."

Constance is about to reply to this improbable claim when a hush falls upon the room and a figure dressed in robes of a lighter hue than the rest, a young man of barely twenty, already running to fat, proceeds with pompous self-importance up the central aisle.

Lavenham rolls her eyes. "Alexander," she says in a stage whisper, "the budding ham."

Constance places a finger to her lips, rather grateful for the opportunity to shush the older woman.

The man reaches the head of the room, makes some peculiar motions around his neck and chest and turns with a conjurer's flourish to face the congregation.

"Greetings," he says, "my dear ones. My seekers after truth. My pilgrims, my apostles—those who hunger for knowledge and enlightenment."

Miss Lavenham clicks tongue against mouth. "At this rate, he'll be reading us one of his poems before we're done."

The man glares towards the front row and, raising his voice a little, continues. "Friends," he says, "we are gathered here today to perform a ritual which, if my calculations are correct, will allow us to commune with one of those creatures whom our forefathers named 'demons' which dwell beyond the veil, in a plane of reality far beyond our own. Today we are pioneers, piercing the skin of the waking world and venturing into that which lies above and beyond. Who amongst you are with me?"

Cries at this of "aye" and "certainly" from those seated all about—polite echoes of the same from the two ladies at the front.

The young man in the lighter robes smiles, gratified. "Then let us begin," he says. "The operation will be a long one and far from easy. There may in addition be no small amount of peril—for we are to treat today with forces far beyond our comprehension."

Miss Lavenham glances at Constance with glee and expectation in her eyes.

What follows, however, is, as is so often the case at such events as these, a good deal of tedium. There is much Latin of questionable quality intoned by the young man in the lighter-coloured robes only part of which Constance is able to follow. There is much standing up and sitting down again, a good deal of call and response, a fair amount of chanting and half-sung repetition. There is, notably, no refreshment of any kind.

After what must be more than an hour of this, Constance begins to feel rather out of sorts—afflicted, to equal degrees, by a headache and by sceptical bafflement. The room feels closer than before and the smell of human perspiration is quite palpable. The air is filled with expectation, the black altar gleams, the voice of the man at the head of the temple waxes ever more hysterical.

"The veil is weakening!" he calls at last, at which it seems that even Miss Lavenham is flagging. "Contact is within our grasp. But first! First, a sacrifice is asked of us and I fear that sacrifice must be of blood."

At this, the two ladies trade glances of uncertainty.

"I have it here!" cries the young magus and draws from some fold within his robes what looks at first like a small red ball but which swiftly reveals itself to be, for all that Constance's mind rebels at the sight of it, a bloody heart.

It must be from an animal, she thinks, as the blood drips down the high priest's hands and mingles with the pale damson of his robes. *It must be. It must.*

"The heart," declares the magus, holding the thing high above his head, "of a corrupt old man whose life was filled with sin. This is the heart, my brethren, of Daniel Swaine-Taylor!"

He squeezes hard and the thing seems to crumple in his hand. Placing it upon the centre of that terrible black altar he smears his mouth with offal and presents his audience with an evil crimson smile.

"Now come!" he shrieks, arms outstretched in hierophantic entreaty. "Come to us, oh demon beyond the veil! I bid you come! I bid you speak! I, the Great Beast, demand your presence before the Order!"

What happens, Constance will think forever after, would absolutely defy belief had she not seen and heard it for herself.

Miss Georgina Lavenham, however, will have no memory of it all for at this very moment she has just swooned away, her unconscious body falling towards the floor.

It is only great good fortune and her own quick thinking which means that Constance is able to catch her in her arms and save Miss Lavenham from injuring herself. "Oh, Georgina," she says softly.

And then, ten seconds after that, all hell breaks loose.

NOW

THE JOURNEY TO London is the longest and most terrible of Toby's life. They drive through the night. *There is blood on the wheels,* he thinks, as the Saab speeds on, *there's blood on these tyres.*

He moves in and out of consciousness, his dreams filled with visions of Gabriela, of Caroline, of the murdered Blessborough sisters, of Salazar and Faircairn and Mr Keen himself and, rearing above them all, the dark, mocking, impossible face of Matthew Cannonbridge.

Once, he wakes to find that the car has stopped, in (he imagines) a lay-by. Keen is bending over him, dabbing something damp at his forehead and forcing his jaws apart.

"Swallow these," he says, pushing a couple of pills into Toby's mouth and following them up with a sip of water from a bottle of Evian.

Numbly, Judd obeys.

On another occasion, Toby wakes from a dream of ceremonies and invocations, to see Mr Keen speaking softly into his mobile phone.

"Yes, sir," he says and, "It won't be long now" and, "Pliable so far."

His eyes never leave the road. Something in Toby wants to hear more of the driver's conversation but soon he sleeps once more. He wonders what those pills were and at their horrible efficacy.

He wakes, deep in the small hours, and what he sees then he is almost sure must be a dream—at least he devoutly wishes that it were so.

Mr Keen, head back, relaxed and happy, is singing, with all the antic fervency of a revivalist preacher: "Oh, what a beautiful morning! Oh, what a beautiful day!"

Toby grimaces, rubs his eyes, but still the vision persists.

"I've got a beautiful feeling everything's going my way!"

It is with tremendous relief that Judd succumbs again to drugged sleep.

SHORTLY AFTER DAWN, they stop for breakfast. There's a Starbucks by the side of the motorway, a pricey trough for the human cattle who are transported on the roads which connect England to the highlands. Sitting in the car park, seeming, no doubt, to any bleary-eyed yet curious motorist, like a couple of talkative buddies, Mr Keen lays down the ground rules.

"No attracting attention of any kind. No asking for help. No messages on napkins or scenes designed to get sympathy from the baristas. Just be polite, be obedient, be discreet and, above all, be unmemorable. Is that understood?"

Judd nods to show that those instructions are comprehended fully.

"I won't hesitate to hurt you," says Keen softly and with a quite inappropriate air of good humour. "In fact, I'd appreciate a good excuse to do so."

Toby stares at him, still muzzy-headed from the drugs, aching from the trauma and weary, weary from grief.

"Good," says Keen. "Then we're on the same page. Come on, Dr Judd. I'm hungry."

INSIDE, TOBY PICKS at his croissant and sips sullenly at his black coffee. Keen, who has opted for the breakfast of a child—a tub of pink yoghurt and a carton of unnaturally yellow banana frappuccino, topped, sickeningly, with cream—attacks his meal with gusto.

Toby watches this display for a while before, asking bitterly: "What made you like this?"

"Like what, Dr Judd?"

Toby lowers his voice, hisses: "A killer."

Keen shrugs, sucks on his straw. "Socialism."

"What?"

"I'm serious. Used to be a right little Bolshie. Union man. Sold the *Morning Star* on the high streets on Saturdays. And then something happened which helped me realise that the war was lost a long time ago. Money's the god of this world. We can either serve it happily or we can wither or die." All this is delivered in the calmest, pleasantest of tones.

"And what was it?" Toby asks. "What was it which triggered this Sixth Form revelation, this startling moment of debate club insight?"

Keen's face darkens. "Now that," he says in a voice of overt menace, "is a long story. And it's one for another day."

Toby sighs and takes another swig of coffee, the taste of it bitter in his mouth. "Toilet," he says. "Need to go."

Keen glares at him. "Try nothing."

Toby rises to his feet and walks miserably towards the lavatory. The gents are as foul as motorway conveniences always are, no matter how often they're cleaned and regardless of which conglomerate owns them. Two men are lingering by the urinals and there is a vile smell in the air. There are also, Toby notices, no windows. He goes next door instead to the disabled cubicle, slightly cleaner than the others. Here he sees that there is a window—and one that has been left a little ajar at that.

Fuelled by rage and sorrow and savage indignation, he climbs more nimbly than usual up onto the toilet seat and to the window.

Yes, he thinks. *Just wide enough for me to get through. If I force myself. If I wriggle and squirm.* He vaults upwards, opens the window as wide as it will go, puts his head out, then his neck, then his shoulders and flails and pushes and strains. The car park tarmac beckons and he feels the giddy joy of the chicken who spies a gap in the farm fence.

So caught up is he in this tiny moment of triumph that he does not hear the toilet door click open nor notice the sound of footsteps advancing across the floor.

What he does notice, however, are the hands upon his legs which drag him from the window and back into the cubicle. He notices the rueful face of Mr Keen and he notices his words, delivered with gleeful mock-regret ("I thought we were on the same page"). He is also thoroughly aware of what happens next. Mr Keen takes up Toby's right hand, picks three fingers at random and, with an exhortation to his victim not to call out, pushes each of them in turn back beyond the point of endurance, taking relish in each decisive snap. It is over quickly but the pain persists.

Judd whimpers softly.

"Back to the car, I think," says Keen. "You know the rules."

IF ANY OF the employees or customers of that particular roadside coffee house think it at all odd that a man should return from the bathroom with one hand in his pocket, sweating despite the chill of the morning and with tears in his eyes, then none remarks upon it nor takes the slightest action.

THE REST OF the journey is passed in silence. By the time that they arrive in the capital, twilight has begun to fall.

"I CONFESS MYSELF surprised," says Prisoner C33, "that you have contrived to see me at all. I am permitted, you understand, but few guests."

Cannonbridge smiles his inhuman smile. "I have a good deal of friends. Many of whom enjoy considerable preferment. Our meeting was not, therefore, an especial challenge to arrange."

The prisoner yawns and stretches and somehow succeeds in preserving in his voice at least an echo of that satiric puckishness which once had been the engine of his fame.

"How very impressive, Matthew. I may call you 'Matthew', mayn't I?"

The two men are sitting opposite one another, hunched over a stained and rickety table, in a grimy little room, barely more than a compartment that is set aside in this great and terrible prison for the infrequent and fiercely rationed conjunctions of captives and members of the public. Outside the door is a guard and beyond him can be heard the eternal prison clangour of doors and locks and boots on metal, of mocking cries and sobs of lamentation, of injustice, of despair.

Against this persistent cacophony, Cannonbridge gazes levelly at the prisoner.

"Might I ask," says the inmate, "why you wished to see me? As you behold, I am scarcely in the best of conditions in which to play the host."

In this, the prisoner is assuredly correct. In his old life outside these walls, a life of wealth and reputation, he had inclined to plumpness, the aesthetic ringlets which had framed his cherubic face making him resemble, it was often said, some ancient god of excess, of pleasure and carnality. In here, his hair has been cropped close and his body has become almost lean. His prison clothes have become too large and he sits rather oddly within them like a malnourished child or a very old man, shrinking and pitiful.

Sitting, visibly weakened and unsteady, upon that grim seat he might easily form the subject of some salutary oil painting entitled 'Cast Down' or 'The Fallen Sensualist' or 'The Rewards of Vice'.

"I wanted to see you," says Matthew Cannonbridge, "because I have grown concerned about your welfare. Tossed in this dreadful institution by a society that once revered you. Beaten and broken and forgotten. Humiliated. Brought low. Spurned. Bedevilled."

"All these things are true," says the prisoner, sanguine to an almost comical degree. It is not difficult for a second or so to imagine him as once he was, lolling upon a chaise longue at one soiree or another and delivering elegantly prepared *bon mots* in those soft, well-modulated tones, which contain within them the merest spicing of the accent of his homeland.

Then the illusion flees and reality is reasserted. The deposed man, the humbled poet, is returned. "And yet," he goes on, "I do not believe that your motive for this visitation is composed even to the smallest degree of any vein of human sympathy. Indeed, from all that I know of you, Matthew, I am far from certain that you are even capable any more of that most vital of emotions."

Cannonbridge gazes coolly at him, the charge neither accepted or rebutted.

"So I shall ask you again, Matthew, why have you come here and what is it that you want with me?"

"Very well." Cannonbridge makes a curious, almost ritualistic gesture with his hands, palms outstretched—the closest he must come, thinks Prisoner C33, to conceding a point. "I have arranged this little consultation only because..." He pauses, places his hand carefully back upon the tabletop, "I am desirous of finding myself... on the right side of history."

The prisoner does not stir but only breathes, slowly and carefully. He has learnt patience in this place, after all—oh, how painfully he has learnt it. "Could you trouble yourself," he says at length, "to explain?"

Outside, a shriek, a muffled curse, the sounds of the misery of the caged.

Then, the words of Matthew Cannonbridge. "This," he says and his manner seems to indicate that he refers to the whole of the dismal scene, "is not how you will remembered. Not in essence. Rather, in time, your captors will be cast down, your false friends vilified as Iscariots and, most glorious of all, your sins will be transmuted into virtues."

"Indeed?" says the prisoner. "Is that what you believe?"

"This is what I know, sir," he replies, "for I have seen it."

C33 gazes silently at this strange trespasser. Although a good deal more must be passing through his mind, in the end all that he says is: "And so you wish to be remembered as... a visionary, then? A man ahead of his time?"

Matthew Cannonbridge nods. "Quite so. And I am understandably eager to avoid..." He pauses, searching for the best and most apposite phrase, "... reputational damage."

"I see. Well, thank you, sir, for your candour. Now, might I be allowed to be equally candid in return?" Something of the old fire is in his voice again, a little of that passion and wit which had been feared lost forever. Not waiting for the author's permission, the prisoner speaks on, more swiftly and with increasing fluency. "Evidently I represent to you an object of considerable interest. I feel it only just to say that you have long formed a comparable object to me. Your fame, your wealth and notoriety—the way in which, whilst rumours of your transgressions abound, you look no older than you did when first you took the public stage. I think you will comprehend why I might find such a figure... intriguing."

Cannonbridge is amused. "Is that so?"

"I have always been drawn to mysteries, Matthew, and there is, I fancy—no, I am sure—a dark mystery to you."

Cannonbridge seems unruffled by the allegation though there is something—just the tiniest indication around the eyes and in the tilt of his head, that he is not wholly immune from disquiet. "And is it," he says, the tone of droll amusement perhaps somewhat forced, "a mystery that you believe yourself to have solved?"

"Not as yet, no. And not entirely. But I do possess what I think we might call a clew."

"How frustrating."

"I wonder if you will recollect, Matthew, that my sorely mistreated but always beloved wife Constance once took a particular interest in matters that we may as well call the magical, the occult, the oracular?"

"I do not."

"No? Well, perhaps it was a thing that she confided only to her intimates. Now, I remember her telling me, not long, in fact, before that chain of events which led to my own ruination were set in motion, that she had once attended a certain ceremony at the premises of the Order of the Moon-Born in which, after a great deal of theatrics, that, remarkably and, I suspect, somewhat to the surprise of all who were present on that weekday afternoon, contact was apparently made with what seemed to be a genuine spirit."

Cannonbridge all but shrugs. "What of it? One hears many peculiar stories about the Order. I fancy that the drink that they serve there must be unusually potent or else augmented with some other substance."

"Perhaps, sir. But my wife is hardly given to excess nor to an abundance of imagination or fancy. I should always take her word in all things. My current position affords me a good deal of time for thinking and I have thought much about the tale that she told me of that weird, blood-tinged event. Oh, it began, I am told, with a great and terrible rushing in the air, as though some mighty gale were rushing through the room although the place (no doubt they thought of it as a temple) was deep beneath the earth and the day without quite still. Then every candle was snuffed out and all was plunged into darkness. The ground seemed to shake beneath their feet although no tremor was reported in any other part of the city. And then, after all these unprecedented phenomena, a voice was heard, deep, mocking, ancient and cruel and sounding somehow, though no-one present could ever say exactly why, inhuman and issuing from some impossible, invisible mouth."

"Remarkable indeed. If true. And did this disembodied voice impart anything of interest?"

"Oh yes, I rather think it did."

"And what, pray, was that?"

"Now I think that you know, Mathew. Or perhaps you will know."

"Enlighten me."

"It said it was an aspect of something greater. Some... form of life beyond humanity. Not a demon or a devil as we would understand it. Rather, it represents what comes after man. The next stage, so to speak. It represents the most remarkable leap of... cognition."

"And you imagine that you comprehend the words of this... *aspect*?"

"Certainly, locked up in here, I am sufficiently vain as to believe that I am beginning to see the pattern. Seeing you today has helped in that regard. Or rather... smelling you."

"What precisely do you mean by that?"

"I mean, my dear Matthew, that you positively reek of... *money*. Always so distinctively vulgar a scent."

His expression unchanging, Matthew Cannonbridge rises swiftly to his feet, steps to the door, knocks once upon it and shouts a command. At once, the locks are drawn back and the thing is swung open. Before he leaves, Cannonbridge turns back towards the prisoner. For an instant, all control has been lost and he presents a rictus of fury and frustration.

"You understand nothing," he hisses. "You see no pattern. And you are in utter ignorance still. I hope that you rot here in the dark."

The prisoner does not reply—gives no indication, in fact, that he has even heard these words save for a rare and fleeting smile which plays about his lips.

Cannonbridge snarls, steps over the threshold and is gone.

The prisoner does not stir but sits, unmoving, listening. Shortly afterwards, a guard moves into the room. It is Delaney, the best of them, in the prisoner's opinion, by far.

"On your feet, C33! Look lively now!"

Unthinkingly, the prisoner obeys the command. As he shuffles towards the door his jailer says: "So that was Matthew Cannonbridge?"

The prisoner nods. "Perhaps," he murmurs as, with hideous inevitability, he trudges to his cell. "Or perhaps it was something else entirely... Something inhuman. Just wearing that man's skin."

"I don't understand what you mean by that," says the guard.

"No, my dear fellow," murmurs the prisoner as he allows himself to be casually manhandled. "Neither do I. At least... not entirely. Not yet."

NOW

THEY HAVE PASSED into London's outer edge. Once caught in the gravity of the metropolis they head east, towards what half a century past had been the area of docks and shipping but which is now given over to the generation of money from money.

It is with little surprise that Toby realises their destination: Canary Wharf, the new financial district, its steel spires and gleaming corporate minarets a jagged statement of intent against the horizon. He has been here a few times before and always found it a strange sort of place, all too new somehow, too clean and well-ordered, seeing in the driverless electric railway which connects the place to the centre, in its expensive chain restaurants, its soaring yet somehow chilling architecture and, above all, its utter lack of the unsuited, the non-professional, the poor, some dishonesty, a particular view of the world with all naysayers and rebels swept politely out of sight. Not so very different then, he thinks, with bitter recollection, to the University.

Until today, however, he has never found the district to be so sinister. The shadows are lengthening and the streets—wide and brash and somehow, in their fit-for-purpose design, unEnglish—are oddly empty, lending the scene a minatory air, as if, faced with some pending disaster, an evacuation had happened here.

Neither Toby nor Mr Keen has said anything for hours. Judd nurses in silence his ruined hand. Somehow the pain, the grim monotony of the journey and the quiet surreality of the region bring about in him an oddly meditative state. As the Saab goes on he finds himself turning over and over in his mind the disparate pieces of this demented puzzle—the glimpses that he has been afforded, the scraps of evidence, the island, the Collection, the words of Spicer and Angeyo and the Blessborough sisters, those fragmented, contradictory testimonies from history—until, very dimly, the outline of a terrible picture begins to emerge.

At last—mercifully in a way for it has begun to seem to Toby as if they might go on and on indefinitely, into the night and the day beyond and the night again, prowling the streets of the city or pounding the motorway, on endlessly into darkness, with only Mr Keen for company and roadside food for sustenance and the promise of some inventive beating to provide variety—the car comes to a halt.

Toby, waking from his bleak reverie, sees that they have come to rest in an executive bay at the base of a skyscraper, no rarity in this region but an example of the form which seems to convey to a remarkable degree, the geometry of pure power.

Keen speaks then. "This is it, doctor. Now we're going to get out of this car and we're going to walk into that building and we're going to ride the elevator to the penultimate floor. And what are we going to have from you?"

Toby blinks. His hand aches.

"Well?"

"No trouble," Judd says. "No trouble at all."

Keen nods briskly, a teacher genuinely pleased by some slow pupil's belated progress. "Good," he says. "You're learning." He touches a button and, with a solemn clunk, unlocks the passenger door. "Now. Shall we?"

Feeling as though he has never truly understood before now the meaning of the old cliché about the lamb being led to the slaughter, Toby steps out of the car and breathes in a lungful of gritty London air.

"With me," says Mr Keen, steering Toby towards the huge sliding glass doors which provide the chief entrance to the tower.

"And what is this place?"

"It's a bank, Dr Judd. Rather, it's *the* bank."

And it is with a horrible sense of inevitability that Toby reads the legend inscribed upon the doors.

One word.

Reynolds.

*   *   *

INSIDE THE LOBBY is vast and cool and effortless in its demonstration of wealth. Two beautiful young women, a blonde and a brunette, stand efficiently behind the reception. Keen nods in their direction.

"Mr Keen," chirrups the blonde.

"Right on time," sighs the brunette.

He looks back, unspeaking. Both women ignore Toby utterly. This, however, he scarcely notices, his attention being arrested both by the name of the institution, written again in gigantic letters behind the front desk, and also, beneath it, what, he realises now, is surely the corporation's logo—a slick, stylised representation of a snake devouring its own tail. Ouroboros.

"Don't dawdle," says Mr Keen as he applies the slightest pressure—no more than a fingertip—on Toby's back.

Without complaint, Judd walks on with Mr Keen, beyond the reception to the row of lifts beyond, into the first of them and then up, up in the metal cylinder, the killer smiling by his side, all the way to the top of the building, to the highest level but one.

Their ascent comes to the smoothest of halts, marked by a single discreet chime, and they step out into a thickly-carpeted vestibule. In the distance there can be heard repeated drumming sounds, like hammer blows.

Mr Keen says: "The view from all the way up here is impressive." He seems almost affable now, Toby thinks, remembering, with a wave of revulsion, Alix's face just before she went beneath the wheels of the Saab. "This way, please."

Keen leads the way, out of this antechamber and into the main body of the floor. Here the sound of drumbeats grows louder and more ominous.

If Toby has been expecting anything it is some large and lavish office. The place—this entire penultimate floor—is empty save for scattered pieces of gym equipment—a rowing machine, a cross-trainer, a rack of dumb-bells, a line of contraptions meant to expand the chest or pump up the muscles in the legs. All this, backed by great glass windows which, Keen was quite correct, offer a wonderful view of the city's skyline. And, right at the end of the room, the source of what Toby had erroneously imagined to be the beating of a drum—a small, plump, balding man in late middle-age, dressed in a plain grey t-shirt and sweat pants, jogging earnestly and heavy-footedly upon a treadmill. The slap of expensive trainer on moving rubber echoes loudly.

Toby and Keen approach, disbelief in the first man's eyes, something curiously like reverence in those of the second. They reach the running machine and watch for a minute or so as the chubby man finishes his ungainly sprint, his belly wobbling up and down, perspiration heaving on his swollen face. The whole time he pays no heed to his visitors—gives no indication, in fact, that he even cares that they have arrived.

Eventually, the machine beeps officiously, the motor glides to a stop and the treadmill ceases to revolve.

At last the sweating man turns to face them. He steps gingerly off the machine and onto the floor.

"Dr Judd?" he says.

"Yes," says Toby.

"Pleased to meet you," the jogger says in a companionable voice, as if he is offering to buy Toby a drink at the golf club bar. "I'm the CEO in these parts. I would offer to shake hands but I'm afraid I'm a trifle moist at present. The name's Swaine-Taylor. No, don't look like that. I'm Giles Swaine-Taylor. The original was a very obscure and ancient ancestor of mine. Best to keep money in the family, if one possibly can. Thank you, Mr Keen. As usual, you've been most effective. But you can leave Dr Judd and me alone now."

Keen nods, somewhat doubtfully.

"I'll see you again soon. At the gala."

"Yes, sir."

And like a bad dream dissolving in the morning light, Keen nods once more, casts Toby an indecipherable look and withdraws.

Swaine-Taylor beams. "Now I've no doubt you've got dozens of questions."

"Who exactly are you people?" Toby asks. "What the hell has this all been for?"

"Ah. Yes, and that's two of them. Well, as you surely know—this is a bank. *The* bank. Well, the investment bank. Nothing on the high street but plenty of brand recognition in the industry. So—ha ha—we're all a bunch of bankers here. As for your other point, as to why this has all been done, well, come with me… I'd like to introduce you to a man who'll be able to make everything clear to you far more eloquently than I ever could."

"I see," says Toby. Were it not for the throbbing pain in his hand, he would wonder if he were dreaming.

"Now if you'll just come this way, Dr Judd, than I can get you two acquainted and we can make a start." He pauses suddenly, looks up with bright, mocking intelligence in his eyes. "And just so that we're both absolutely on the same page, I ought to warn you now that should you make the slightest attempt to cause a fuss or raise an alarm in the course of the next twelve hours I will, with regret but without compunction, have you permanently removed from the board. Is that understood?"

Pain surges as if in sympathy in Toby's hand. He nods in sullen agreement. "I suppose you've been threatening me a while now, haven't you? The weird phone calls. The message at the cash point."

Swaine-Taylor looks at him oddly. "Dr Judd, I'm afraid I haven't the foggiest idea what you're talking about."

"Then… Then who or what..?"

"Later, later. Now, come this way. Chip chop."

And back they go, back along the lines of top-flight fitness gear (none of which, Toby thinks sourly, seem to have done all that much for Swaine-Taylor's physique), back to the vestibule and the lights, where they step into one of the lifts and wait for the doors to snap shut whilst the executive presses the necessary button.

"Just one more floor," he murmurs. It doesn't take long and then the doors are opening again and Toby and Swaine-Taylor are stepping out into another wide space. But this one, unlike the gym beneath, is darkened and gloomy. Only a couple of lights are on very dimly and all of the windows are blocked up with smooth wooden boards. There's a smell in the air—like decay, Toby realises, like damp earth, like mould.

You would not think, perhaps, that any office in so modern a building could ever seem so eerie as does this.

In the centre of the room there is a kind of nest of computer screens, heaped high on a long low desk. There is a figure sitting behind it on a tall black orthopaedic chair. Toby walks closer to see, a horrible suspicion taking shape in his mind.

It is, he sees now, an old—a very old—man, lank-haired and bearded, with fierce eyes and few teeth and the air of a hermit or a wild man. He grins crookedly at their approach.

"Now, this ought to be interesting," says Swaine-Taylor, playing the jovial host, limber and witty and almost flirtatious. "Dr Judd, I'd like you to meet a very old friend of the bank's. This is Professor Anthony Blessborough."

1900
THE HOTEL D'ALSACE
PARIS

IN HIS FOURTEEN and a half years as proprietor of the Hotel d'Alsace, Monsieur André Lachette has grown accustomed to entertaining patrons of the most secretive, eccentric and outré stripe.

His establishment is not, after all, of the first rank nor are its location and décor conducive to those visitors to Paris who wish to circulate and be seen in the city's most fashionable districts, or particularly attractive to those with a respectable income or any reputation to speak of that they wish to uphold. Indeed, the place has long proved to be something of a magnet for a certain kind of impecunious gentleman or lady in search of privacy or solitude, looking for somewhere inexpensive where they might lie low. In consequence, Monsieur Lachette has become most proficient at passing no comment or judgement, at looking the other way. He is a master of discretion, an adept of selective memory, a titan of benevolent hypocrisy. He has trained himself to be blind to all but the worst human excess. He is, in other words, the ideal hotelier.

And yet, for all of his experience and skill, his attitude of open-handed unshockability, there is something which troubles him—something which troubles him about the man in room sixteen.

Monsieur Lachette knows well, of course—has always known—the precise identity of his guest, for is not Mr Wilde, for all his attempts at disguise, his ludicrous pseudonym of Sebastian Melmoth and his oft-stated desire for solitude, still amongst the most notorious men in Europe?

Not that monsieur judges, of course—this is Paris, after all, and the supposed sins of the poet seem somewhat trifling in such a place as this—yet, in spite of Lachette's worldly disregard for the tedious prejudices of that rain-soaked little island which God, in his unfathomable wisdom, has placed a few short miles from the coast of his own mighty nation, there is something else concerning that guest, beyond the taint of English scandal, which weighs heavily upon the imagination of the proprietor.

It is this, he decides, as he sits in his little parlour at half past nine on a Friday evening, with a bottle of red wine uncorked before him and the remnants of his supper cooling on its plate: it is the fellow's scent of mortality. For the man was ill when he first came to the Hotel d'Alsace three weeks previously, pale and unsteady on his feet and possessing a countenance suggestive of intolerable pressures and of accelerated decay. He cannot, Monsieur Lachette concludes, be long for this world and he wonders whether he should count it as a blessing or a curse that the poet's unhappy twilight should be spent within the walls of his own establishment.

He is about to pour himself a fresh glass and raise it in solitary toast to the dying man who slumbers somewhere overhead when he hears the hectoring tinkle of a bell. It originates, he sees with a lack of surprise which is in itself surprising, from the room which has lately been made the private territory of the man who called himself Melmoth. With a slightly lingering look back at the bottle, Lachette rises stolidly to his feet and moves, with an urgency that he does not wholly comprehend, to answer the summons of Mr Oscar Wilde.

When he reaches the room, Monsieur Lachette discovers it sunk nearly into darkness. The merest stub of a candle provides feeble light to illuminate a place that has been thrown somewhat into disarray as though a struggle has happened here. The hotelier is struck by the paucity of the man's possessions—a small valise, a handful of favourite books, clothes that are close to rags—little to suggest that their owner was once a legend of the stage, a hero of the salons. The man himself is no more than a shadow upon the narrow single bed, his form rising and falling with horrid irregularity. The voice that emerges from this undignified shape is ragged and uncertain.

"Robbie?" it hisses, "is that you?"

"No, monsieur. It is I—Lachette." As ever, when in the company of foreign guests the proprietor somewhat overstates his natural accent.

"Of course. Of course. Lachette. Draw nearer would you, my dear fellow?"

The Frenchman does as he is bid and steps with dainty trepidation to the invalid's side. The air is thick. There is a smell of overspilling drains. "I am here, monsieur," says Lachette, breathing, as much as is practicable, through his nose. "What do you require?"

"A great cup of bitterness has been pressed against my lips."

"You are unwell, monsieur?"

"There is... yes... an excitation in my ear... a great ringing sound like the clarion of judgement."

"You wish me to fetch a physician, monsieur?"

"No. Only Robbie. Only Robbie Ross. He will be quite sufficient for all my needs."

"Very good, monsieur." Imagining the interview to be at an end, Lachette begins to creep away from the dying man when, suddenly and quite without warning, Oscar Wilde sits, with a hideous effort, close to bolt upright in bed.

"Monsieur," he says and his voice is louder now, tinged with something close to madness. "I understand at last. In my dreams I saw him. The undying man. The devil robed in flesh. The evil at the heart of the story. Finally, now I see it at all. And Monsieur..." His voice cracks and gurgles. "Monsieur, I know exactly what he is. The most impossible, terrible thing. Such a leap, such a leap in evolution, you see, such as Mr Darwin could never have foreseen. Not Man at all. Rather—the development of consciousness in something greater than the individual. Greater... but soulless. Inhuman."

"I fear, monsieur, that you are succumbing to delirium. You must rest."

"No! No, on the contrary, I doubt I've ever been more perspicacious and clear-sighted. It is the date, you see. 1842. The date of institution. Of establishment. Look at the date again, monsieur. You must look at the date again."

No sooner has the last syllable been spoken than the figure of the ruined writer sinks in a sick, quivering motion back upon the bed.

"Monsieur!" cries the hotelier and hastens back to Melmoth's side.

Wilde's eyelids are flickering shut. A thin skein of spittle hangs at one corner of his mouth. He is sweating heavily and wheezing and the smell is worse than ever.

"Oh, monsieur," says Lachette again and, washed over by compassion, reaches out a hand and soothes the great man's brow. "I am so sorry, monsieur, that this has been done to you. This gross injustice."

But the man in the bed does not reply for he is already fading once more into unconsciousness.

After a while, Lachette leaves him there and hurries away, to call the physician and Mr Ross. Before he leaves the sickroom it appears to him, though he knows it to be impossible, that the shadows at the corners of the room, now thicker than before, move—seeming almost to scuttle—of their own, terrible volition.

NOW

"Listen," says the old man in the gloom, in that slice of gothic amid the billionaire sheen of the twenty-first century. "You've got to listen to me now."

Swaine-Taylor has gone—to change, he said, into something smarter—and the two men have been left alone together. Blessborough is behind his desk, Toby to one side of him, perched on a lower seat, his hand aching, his head throbbing, the room's smell of moist decay heavy in his nostrils, and wishing more than anything else in all the world to just be allowed to *wake up* from this nightmare.

"Listen," says Blessborough again, his voice a shrill croak from decrepitude and lack of use and possessing the faint tinge of a Yorkshire accent which Judd had somehow not expected, "how old do you think I am? Be honest now. None of your soft-soaping."

Quickly, adroitly, Toby does the maths. "Well, if you are who you say you are…"

"I am. You know I am."

"Then you must be ninety-four? Ninety-five?"

"Ninety-five," the old man confirms with strange, unwarranted pride. "But I don't look it, do I? Nowhere near. That's the power, you see. The power of the island."

Toby looks at this grisly wreck of a human being and decides to keep his counsel. He decides to keep his counsel too about the old man's granddaughters, not wanting to be the bearer of such pain, wondering if it would be kinder if the old man never learns the truth.

"Now, we've not got long. Swaine-Taylor will be back soon to take you away and Mr Keen will no doubt be waiting. Believe you me, those aren't the kind of gents you want to keep waiting. It's a strange story I've got to tell you to be sure. I'd offer you a beer or a whiskey while you hear me tell it but they're powerful careful here about what they let me eat and drink. All for my own good, of course. For my own good."

"I'd heard, sir," says Toby courteously, carefully, "that you were dead."

Blessborough waves the suggestion aside. "Oh, the bank took care of all that. I said I wanted privacy and they arranged it for me. No-one bothers you when they think you're worm food. No-one at all. Anyway, to business. Matthew Cannonbridge. I'm told you saw the truth of it. That he is another man's invention. Namely, mine. No doubt you suspect some elaborate hoax, some overarching conspiracy? Ah, yes. I see that you do. The truth, I'm afraid, as Oscar once wrote, is never pure and rarely simple. Why, it's really a bit of a cat's cradle."

As the old man speaks, Toby leans in to listen, filled up again, all at once and despite the weirdness and danger of his predicament, by that old and potent desire—the need to know. "Tell me," he mutters. "Tell me everything."

"I always wanted to be an academic," Blessborough begins. "Sounds strange, doesn't it? Someone like me. P'raps it would be more correct to say that I always liked books and stories. The old ones, best of all. The Victorian ones. I wanted whatever I did for a living to take account of it. Everyone thought I was crazy—my folks most of all—but I studied hard and got myself a place at university. The first in my family to have done it. The first of anyone we knew. So I was all set to go, garlanded, although it seems immodest to say so, with all manner of scholarships and prizes, when the war broke out. With Herr Hitler trampling all over Europe, stories didn't seem so important any more. So I signed up. Joined the army the day after war was declared. Didn't need to think twice about it. Now, this isn't the place to tell you about my war. These experiences would fill up a book in themselves. But there was one particular job the army sent me on which I think is going to interest you. I'd been in Egypt but I was recalled in the summer of '43 and sent to an island a little off the coast of Scotland."

"Faircairn."

The nonagenarian frowns. "You know it?"

"I've been there."

"Have you now?" He puffs out his cheeks. "They have led you a merry dance, now, haven't they?"

"Excuse me?"

Blessborough ignores this interjection. "The military were doing some weapons testing over there. Can't tell you exactly what that involved. Even now. Signed the Official Secrets Act. Anyway, I was stationed on Faircairn for a couple of months. Weren't many of us—just a trusted few. If you've been there, you'll know how strange and indescribable a place it is. None too friendly. And you'll have seen the consistency of the place. The ground, I mean. The earth."

"Volcanic, I thought," says Toby. "Something like that?"

"Oh, no-one knows exactly what it is. Like granular black sand, isn't it? None of our scientists ever had much of a clue. Still don't so far as I know. But what it is, or, for that matter, exactly where it's from—none of that's important."

"No?"

"What's important is what that stuff can do. What it's capable of."

Judd is feeling queasy now—the smell of rot seems to have got still worse. "Professor?" he asks. "What exactly do you mean?"

"Only this, lad—that the stuff that Faircairn's made of can..." He sucks in a wheezing breath and gives a crazy, gummy grin. "Well, it can warp reality itself."

There is silence between them.

"Don't look at me like that," the old man says. "You don't think I'm cracked. A few months ago, you might've done, I'm sure, but not now. Not after everything you've seen."

Toby says, very quietly, wrinkling his nose against the putrid scent: "Go on."

"You'll laugh," says Blessborough improbably, "when you hear how I discovered the truth. Of course, there was always something queer about the island, always an odd atmosphere...

Things we used to glimpse, moving in the darkness, almost out of sight. Things we pushed to the back of our minds... You understand me?"

"I do," says Toby fervently.

"But the truth of it... Well, it was almost banal. One night, on leave, me and a couple of mates went to the mainland. There was a sort of party being held there. A dance in one of the local towns. So we went and we drank a bit and we tried not to think about Faircairn and we did our best to enjoy ourselves. And of course there were women there and naturally there was some flirting and a bit of canoodling. All very innocent. You understand me, Dr Judd? Nothing dirty. And nothing to scare the horses neither. Now, I was courting at the time, the young lady who would subsequently become my wife and I was writing to her regular, telling her my news and doing my utmost to reassure her. And when, later, back on the island I wrote her a long letter, I mentioned the trip to the mainland but, to try to spare her feelings and make sure she wouldn't worry, I said that the evening had been spent only in the company of men. That there had been no women present. And that was how it began. With a tiny white lie. Not that I thought any more about it. I sent the letter off to be delivered and got back to my work. My sweetheart got my message and she read it and she was never any the wiser. I only started to work out the truth of it a few weeks later. I was chatting to a couple of my mates and one of them happened to mention how odd it was that there'd been no women at that dance. As you can imagine, I was astonished at this. I quizzed them about it and they were all adamant—there had never been anything but bloody men at that party. I worked through every possible explanation—including, let me assure you, my own possible insanity. But then I understood. It was some property of the island itself which had the power to reach out. And change the world. It took me a while to eliminate every other option. Until I knew, until I was certain, that it could only be the earth itself."

Unbidden, Toby remembers his own brief visit to Faircairn, the handful of dust he had collected on some inexplicable instinct. "How did you work it out?" he asks, in far too deep now to doubt.

"Took some to the mainland," says Blessborough. "A bit less potent but it still works just fine. I experimented with it—made a few small changes to things. Didn't always work—any act of pure selfishness seems to dilute it. But often, often it worked, at least when the change was conveyed to someone else. It's an equation, you see—the soil plus your words plus someone who wants to believe. It was just after the war was coming to an end that I had a notion to try something on a grander scale. Something really remarkable. Something wonderful, too."

"Cannonbridge," says Toby Judd.

"Cannonbridge," Blessborough offers triumphantly. "He was only meant... as a kind of joke at first. That, and a sort of love letter, to all the stories and writers I used to like so much. I wrote, on the island, about this author—this great, fictional author—and it gave me great pleasure. I never went to university, Dr Judd— the Professor's an honorary title, bought for me by the bank, but, in a way, Faircairn was my true university and the creation of Matthew Cannonbridge my thesis. And the more I wrote about him the more I began to see evidence of the island's weird power. Like... a single droplet of dark liquid spreading through a glass of pure water. References here and there in essays, journals. A poem or two in anthologies. A chapter in a book of literary lives. All quite impossible, of course, but it was happening indisputably all the same. And once I published my book—well, everything got an awful lot worse. He was everywhere. His novels and dramas and verses were everywhere. The whole country believed. And it is dependent on belief, you know, that's what it hinges on. I'd done it successfully, inserted a wholly imaginary human being into history. Hmmph. You know this is true, Toby. You know it."

And he does, of course. He does know it. In spite of its flagrant absurdity, he understands that everything happened just as Blessborough has described. He feels sick now, sick at heart and in his soul, and the stench of the place, its graveyard corruption rises up above him and his stomach heaves and pushes.

"I write about him still," the old man says. "In here. The bank found me and they made me rich. I want for nothing. I can write all day about my Cannonbridge. And it is made real."

"How?" Toby asks softly. "You're in London. You're not on the island anymore."

"Oh, but don't you recognise the smell of it, Dr Judd? The smell of damp black earth? The island is always with me. These walls and floors... this whole suite is packed with Faircairn earth. We are surrounded by that terrible ebony dust." He starts to laugh then, high and wild and, somehow, no longer quite human.

Toby is actually relieved when he hears the lift's chime, hears steps behind him, feels the grip of Mr Keen on his shoulder and spies the pudgy visage of Swaine-Taylor.

"Hello, Dr Judd," smiles the CEO. "Now, if you're fully in the picture, we should go down to the water's edge."

Toby grimaces. "What now?"

"Why, surely you've not forgotten? It's tonight. The Cannonbridge Bicentenary is tonight."

1902
BY THE BANKS OF THE THAMES
SOUTHWARK

IF YOU WERE to find yourself passing over London Bridge at around a quarter past three in the afternoon on the fourteenth of September of the year that has been named above and were you to glance down towards the river and spy, along its southern bank, the outlines of two surprisingly respectable male figures sauntering there, in defiance of the mud and accumulated debris, you might well be astonished at the identities of these ramblers, for they are both of them amongst the most famous and distinguished men in the Empire. And if you were, by some unlikely magic, able also to apprehend the words that pass between them, you would surely be more startled still.

"I am a trifle bemused," says the first of the pair—broad-shouldered and brawny, moustachioed, possessing a Scots accent and projecting a certain kind of martial Britishness that is already beginning to seem old-fashioned—"both by your invitation and by the location that you specified for our meeting." He indicates the great mass of mud and rubbish, the sullen detritus of the Thames.

"You need not be surprised, Sir Arthur," says his saturnine, dark-clad companion who, by now, requires no further introduction. "And nor should you be in any way alarmed." He pauses then, as he has already paused often this afternoon, to pick up a large flat stone that he has seen upon the riverbank and slip it into a pocket in his black frockcoat. "I only sought some pleasant conversation. The exchange of ideas. We are the men of the age, after all. Your detective, why, he is immortal. And as to my own, I flatter myself to think that he is at least worthy of a footnote."

"More than that," says the moustachioed man, striding unconcernedly through the mire as once he stood robustly aboard the wildly tilting deck of a whaler. "I read *The Mystery of the Prophetic Widow*. And *The Mystery of the Whispering Pontiff* also."

"And what did you make of them, sir?"

"Most diverting. Your talent is positively protean."

"You're too kind," says Matthew Cannonbridge, stooping to collect another stone, doing this so artfully that he scarcely interrupts his pace.

"Indeed," his companion goes on, his words, when set down, sounding friendly enough but possessing when spoken a quality of quiet disapprobation, "you seem to shift according to the fashions of each era whilst somehow succeeding in remaining forever yourself."

Cannonbridge smiles—the last time that he shall have cause to do so for more than a century. "You do not altogether approve of me, Sir Arthur. You never have."

"I should not go so far as that. I speak as I find and you have never been less than courteous to me. Such rumours as I have heard..."

"Ah yes. The rumours."

"I form no opinions on hearsay, sir. Only on what I myself see and observe."

Another pause to collect another stone and then: "Stout fellow. I thought that you should say so. And it was in the company of such an honest man that I wished things to end. Well, honest to a degree at least. Not so very upstanding, perhaps, in your association with a certain younger lady of whom your ailing wife is believed to be unaware?"

"Good Lord. Please, sir! Desist."

"Sir Arthur, please. No need for theatrics. We are quite alone here. I meant only to demonstrate that none of us is ever quite immune from gossip and tittle-tattle. Now, no doubt you have been wondering why I have been collecting such a store of ballast. Why my pockets now bulge at their very seams with an excess of stone and rock."

"I had thought it discourteous to ask."

"You're too polite, Arthur. Trust me, the decades ahead will not welcome such politeness."

"We shall no doubt discover the truth of that remark in time."

"I have already seen it, sir. Alas, I know it to be true."

Our moustachioed Scot does not reply but merely treads on through the mud. Seabirds screech overhead. In the distance, an urchin and an old woman can be seen, scouring the riverbank for anything of value, desperation having driven them to such mudlarkery.

"Tell me," says his companion. "Have you ever had the sensation that you are in some wise pursued, only to turn to confront your pursuer and find nothing there but air?"

A shake of the head.

"No? Yet I have. All of my life. From the moment of my creation."

"Your... creation? How strange a description."

"It was a strange event, sir. Strange and most unnatural."

"Indeed?"

"There has long been a kind of ragged shadow in my wake. It was there at Geneva and it has been present ever after. Something is tracking me. Watching me. Judging me."

Sir Arthur frowns. "So you are afraid, Mr Cannonbridge?"

"No. Not that. Never that. But I do believe that I know now how to... outwit it." He bends down, collects one final stone and pushes it into the last available space in his coat. The effect is of a jerkin made of stone. "I have no choice left to me now. Not if I wish to ensure my survival."

"I confess," says Arthur, "that I simply do not understand."

"You will. In time, you will see the pattern of it. Now, pray give me your hand, sir. Our conversation has been a decided pleasure."

Arthur accepts the elder writer's hand—cool, too cool, to the touch—and at the edges of the Thames they perform the solemn ritual.

This done, Matthew Cannonbridge turns away and with implacable purpose strides towards the water's edge.

"No!" Arthur shouts. "For God's sake, man!"

Yet this is to no avail and so Arthur moves to stop him.

Cannonbridge turns his head and speaks one word, his eyes flashing in the sunlight. "Stay."

Arthur finds himself, impossibly, rooted to the spot, quite unable to move as Cannonbridge walks on, into the water, into the river. The Scot tries to shout again but no sound will come.

Cannonbridge strides on, the filthy Thames up to his hips, up to his belly, up to his chest, his neck.

Arthur struggles against his invisible bonds but his efforts are wholly fruitless. He is held firm, made immutable. Later, he will wonder if it is his imagination but he will swear that the water around the author seethes and bubbles; also that strange shadows seem to crowd around the diminishing figure, appear curiously agitated, as if somehow (surely impossible) frustrated and enraged.

In the distance, the urchin and the old woman seem to have turned, aware of the unfolding tragedy, but too distant to affect events in any way.

One moment more—Cannonbridge is but a head above the water—one moment more of seething and shadows and the greatest writer of the nineteenth century, its very spirit, its dark soul, is gone, vanished, lost to the Thames, weighed down by a suicide's melancholy baggage.

With a sudden, convulsive gasp, Arthur realises that he is able to move once again. The urchin and the old woman are moving, far too slowly, in his direction.

Despite his new freedom, Sir Arthur stands quite still in shock.

The surface of the water is flat and apparently untroubled.

Why, he thinks, with a horrible and quite uncharacteristic sense of detachment, it is as if some dreadful sacrifice has been made, as if something precious has been surrendered in exchange for some bleak and unknowable future boon.

NOW

Toby is back in the Saab again with a dinner-jacketed Swaine-Taylor beside him. The killer, Mr Keen, is driving and the two men are chuckling at some joke that Judd hasn't caught—like a couple of genial uncles taking their favourite nephew out for a trip.

Toby's hand has been bandaged and he has been dosed liberally with painkillers but his imagination is still in that strange room, back in the darkened office which smells of graveyard earth, and he is turning the old man's fantastical story over and over in his mind, trying to see it from the right angle, the one from which everything is suddenly going to make sense.

Coolly, the CEO disrupts his train of thought. "You must be pleased, Dr Judd." The skyscraper is behind them now and they are moving through the streets at a ponderous pace as if in some Presidential cortege. They are heading, Toby realises without a trace of surprise, towards the river. They are going down to the water's edge.

"Why?" Toby asks.

"Because of what you've been told. You know everything now."

"No. On the contrary, I'm not sure I do. There's so much that doesn't make sense."

"Oh, there are bound to be a few loose ends, aren't there? They're just a part of life."

And the Saab goes on, its blood-spattered wheels revolving.

Swaine-Taylor arranges his plump little hands upon his lap. "We still have a few moments before we reach the gala. If there's anything that I can clear up for you in that time, I'd be delighted to help…"

Toby thinks. Marshals his questions. "Your bank—it bought the island of Faircairn, yes?"

"Owned it lock, stock and barrel. Since, oh, 1946. Just after the war."

"And you've paid for Blessborough? You've employed him? Cared for him?"

"We own Anthony just as surely as we own that island. Body and soul."

Toby looks the rich man in the eye and asks: "Why?"

"Excuse me?"

"Why? I mean, what's this all been for? What's an investment bank's interest in Victorian literature?"

"None whatsoever. Christ, no. Musty stuff. I'm more of a Freddie Forsyth man myself."

"Then..."

"What do you think? It's the possibility of the technology. We think it might be alien, by the way."

"I'm sorry?"

"The island. It simply doesn't exist on any maps before 1750 or so. Our boffins think it could be extraterrestrial in origin. Oh, don't look at me like that. It's perfectly possible, don't you think? Though we're always open, of course, to theories. But what exactly it is or where precisely it's come from... well, these things are largely beyond our purview. But with the power to warp reality itself... Heh..." Swaine-Taylor pauses, licks his lips. "There wouldn't be an economy we couldn't manipulate, a stock exchange we couldn't rig, an investment we couldn't artificially inflate. You see? The power of the island could make us a new Midas."

Judd looks at the pudgy man in his expensive suit and stares in disbelief. "That's all?" he says. "You've discovered the most frankly astonishing thing, the most amazing, impossible thing, in human history and you're going to use it to... make money? To turn a bigger profit?"

Swaine-Taylor looks genuinely bemused by the question. "Of course. What else would we do with it?"

"Help people? Make the world better?"

"We're a bank, Toby. And a bank's not a person. We don't do compassion or charity or skipping. We exist only to expand. We exist only to make money. But—and this is the important part—our making money does improve the world. Course it does. All the time. Everyone is enriched by it. The stronger the economy, the happier the populace. All wealth trickles down in the end."

"You're right," Toby says dimly, a new thought percolating. "Yes. Of course you are."

"I'm glad you think so."

"No. About what you said before. About a bank not being a person. In a way, it's more than a person, isn't it? But also less. Also inhuman."

Swaine-Taylor looks at him oddly. "Quite. And here we are."

The Saab has stopped now and the broad, dark torrent of the Thames is in view.

Upon the riverbank has been installed, no doubt at terrific and unthinking expense, an elaborate row of pristine white marquees, already thronging with smart, dapper guests. Toby recognises some of them even from a distance—politicians and actors and football players, stars from every public constellation. Behind a barrier of red rope, a press pack surges, their cameras flashing, calling out names to attract the attention of their subjects.

And everywhere there are banners, of the saturnine man who disappeared more than a hundred years ago. Beneath it is the legend 'The Cannonbridge Bicentenary' and, below that, the name of the bank and its familiar Ouroboros logo.

"The bank's sponsoring all this," Swaine-Taylor says. "It appealed to our sense of irony. Made me laugh. Besides, it has considerable tax benefits."

Toby shakes his head.

"Right. Time to mingle."

Mr Keen gets out of the car, hurries obediently round and opens the passenger door. Swaine-Taylor rises regally from his seat and steps out. Once on his feet, he adjusts his cummerbund and straightens his bow-tie. "This way," he says, as Toby emerges. Swaine-Taylor strolls towards the first and largest of the marquees—the VIP lounge—in the centre of which has been erected a stage and a microphone. Cameras click and whirr. In the distance, the urgent sluicing of the river.

Inside, the air is scented and sweet. Waiters circulate with canapés and champagne. Soft jazz plays.

"Now, Toby," says Swaine-Taylor with infuriating largesse. "I want you to enjoy yourself tonight. Have a few drinks. Some nibbles. Have fun. Enjoy this monument to what we've achieved. And when we're done, at the end of it all, we're going to have a little chat."

"Are we now?"

"Yes. We are. You see, there's an offer I want to put to you. I suppose you could call it a job offer. Ah. I see that you understand."

"So," says Toby, as a man with a tray of vol-au-vents slaloms past him, "that's why you've brought me here? That's why you've kept me alive?"

"Blessborough's old. He'll need replacing soon. And nothing he's tried that hasn't involved Cannonbridge seems to have actually worked. We think he's simply weak. Oh, we've tried a few others too and they've not worked out either. It seems you need, in some sense, to be immune to the effects of the stuff. So we were waiting for someone like you to see through the Cannonbridge deception. Someone stable and smart and industrious. The Blessborough girls were too flighty. Spicer and his ilk far too crazy. No, it has to be you, Dr Judd, and we'd make it worth your while. To be blunt: we'd make you fabulously rich. Don't scowl now. You should know that we've already made sure that all charges against you have been dropped." He smiles. "Though it'd only be the work of a moment to have them reinstated. Think about it. We'll talk later. For now, just enjoy your evening. Oh, and I'm sure you wouldn't, but don't think about leaving us too soon. Mr Keen will be watching you at all times."

With a final, deceptively benign smile, the CEO disappears into the crowd. Toby stands alone, lost in the whirl of strangers. Of Keen there is no sign, though Toby has no doubt that he is somewhere close at hand. Browbeaten by events, by revelations of impossible things, he does not move.

Someone thrusts a glass of champagne into his hand and, unthinkingly, he takes it. A few faces he recognises amongst the throng from TV—theatrical knights, cricketing stars, half the Cabinet front bench, newsreaders, celebrities, national treasures— the familiar studded amongst a sea of anonymous figures in immaculate black tie, there, he has no doubt, to represent the real money, the real power. Speechless, he sips the champagne and feels a surge of hysteria. Then, he feels a hand on his arm.

"Toby?" There are few voices in his life which are quite as familiar. "What on earth are you doing here?"

He turns to face her. Dazed, he says simply: "Caroline?"

It hasn't been long but he is struck by how different she seems, by how much has evidently shifted within her. Nothing too visible— no dramatic weight loss or gain, no startlingly different wardrobe or savage new haircut. No, there is just something new about her, in her aura, in her essence. It is—supposes Toby with a sudden start of mingled curiosity, envy and a strange, creeping sense of relief—real happiness.

"You're looking well."

"Thanks." She smiles tightly. "But what are you doing you here? My God, all that weird stuff on the news that they've gone and retracted. And, erm, what's up with your hand? And... Christ, why have you shaved your head?"

He winces. "It's a long story."

"I'm sure."

"Believe it or not, it all seems to be part of a crazy kind of job interview."

But his wife isn't listening to him anymore. No, she's looking over his shoulder, towards the entrance to the marquee.

"Wow," she murmurs. "I mean I'd heard the rumours but..."

Toby looks round at the object of her attention—it is immediately clear. Walking in, the crowd opening before him, flanked by a rugby team's worth of security, the tall aristocratic figure of one of the country's most famous men, tuxedoed and immaculate. At the sight of him, Toby exhausted by recent events, can only find it in himself to mutter: "Oh. The Prime Minister."

Caroline rolls her eyes, mistaking fatigue for insouciance. "Oh, come on. You've got to admit that's impressive."

"I suppose. Anyway, what are you doing here?"

"You know why."

"I don't. Or if I do, I've forgotten."

Caroline nods towards the stage. "I'm here for him, Toby. I'm here for J J."

Of course. And there he is, young Dr Salazar, approaching the microphone as the jazz music fades out, dolled up and preening, strutting like a rock star.

"Good evening," he says and his amplified voice causes all of the guests, even, Toby notes from the corner of his eye, Her Majesty's First Minister, to cease their conversations and pay him heed. "Good evening to you all. Mr Prime Minister, my lords, ladies and gentlemen. Before we begin our celebration of the man who is surely the foremost of the nation's creative minds, I should like to say thank you to the sponsors of this evening. They are themselves another great British success story but this time in financial terms. I speak, of course, of Reynolds bank. Without their generosity, this wonderful, wonderful gala may not have been possible. So, heartfelt thanks to all the guys at Reynolds."

Polite applause at this.

"And it seems especially fitting that these two fine English names—Cannonbridge and Reynolds—should be plaited together tonight for they share a common history. They are both children of the nineteenth century. Whilst Matthew Cannonbridge was, as we know, first glimpsed in 1816, the bank itself was founded less than three decades later, in 1842. And now if you'll spare me just a few moments, I'd like to take you back to that time, to a villa in Geneva two hundred years ago."

But Toby isn't listening any more. He has gone completely white, he is trembling and a vein is pulsing ferociously in his forehead.

"The date," he mutters against the drawl of Salazar's speech. "Of course. The date of foundation. A new form of consciousness. What comes after humanity?"

"Toby?" His wife is glaring at him.

"And the brick in the wall… the false brick… it was paper. Dirty, sodden paper thrust into the gap."

"Toby? What the hell's the matter with you?"

"I see it all," Toby mutters. "At last. I can see what they've done. And—my God—I know what they've unleashed."

1902
GLEBE HOUSE
BLACKHEATH

SKIN ON SKIN and tongue on tongue, one soft hand moving at the back of his head, another caressing his shoulder, Sir Arthur sits in the drawing room of a house that he does not own with a lady who is not his wife sitting astride him. The lady's mother is at present elsewhere in the building, having been distracted by some spurious errand, and the lovers have seized this opportunity, all too rare, for intimacy.

"Not now," Arthur whispers as the lady adjusts her petticoats, moves so that she might be set more snugly again him. "Not yet."

He lets her continue all the same and makes no move to make her desist ruffling his hair or tickling his moustache or to push away the tantalising proximity of her honeyed breath. She sighs and shudders beneath her bulky dress and as he sits, unmoving, in this illicit paradise all manner of possibilities flit, in sensuous parade, across his imagination.

Their snatched idyll is interrupted by the soft, decorous peal of a bell.

Arthur starts, like a man being woken from a dream.

The lady places a finger against his lips. "Only someone at their door. No need to fret."

"Nonetheless," says the moustachioed man, "we should probably endeavour to restore some semblance of decorum."

"Shh." Finger placed on lips once more, her closeness intoxicating. Then, in realisation: "Bother."

"My dear?"

"The servants have the afternoon off."

"Ah."

"And I should so hate to trouble mother." She moves with practised grace back to the ground and to her feet again.

When she has completed this smooth, supple motion, the bell is heard again.

Briskly, Sir Arthur rises, adjusts his clothes, smoothing down his jacket and trousers in the manner of a battle-weary commander stepping reluctantly onto the parade ground. "I shall answer it myself, my dear."

"Arthur, honestly, there really is no need."

"It would be my pleasure," he says, and with a stern nod which contains also a note of cheeky erotic promise, he steps proudly from the room.

THERE IS AN elderly man waiting upon the threshold, dressed, slightly absurdly, in what looks like the uniform of His Majesty's Post Office.

"Good afternoon," says Sir Arthur. "How might I be of assistance?"

When the caller speaks it is with a pronounced American twang. "I have a letter, sir."

Sir Arthur wrinkles his nose. "A Bostonian by birth, I would surmise. Once considered something of an Adonis in your prime, now fallen on hard times and running to seed."

The old man on the threshold looks unsurprised by the performance. "That's mighty impressive, Sir Arthur," he says as he draws from his pocket a slim white envelope. "Now this is for you, sir."

"For me? But who would know... I mean, this is not, you understand, strictly my address. Not at all. No. I am visiting... a family friend. This must be a mistake."

"No mistake, Sir Arthur."

The old man holds the letter outstretched, takes a faltering step closer and Arthur sees that it is indeed his name that is inscribed upon the paper in a black, calligraphic, rather old-fashioned hand. "How..." he begins. The sentence goes no further.

A look of near-infinite sadness washes over the face of the postman. "Wherever you were, sir," he murmurs, "this would have found you."

Sir Arthur opens his mouth to reply but—

"I'd just take the letter, sir."

Another gape of protest.

"Take the damn letter."

So Arthur Conan Doyle does what has been requested and takes the letter and thanks the stranger and closes the door upon him, his final impression of the old man's face being that of long and painful service coming, at last, to its conclusion.

"WHO WAS THAT?" says the lady when Sir Arthur returns with letter in hand.

She is standing in the centre of the room, looking pleasant and unruffled and altogether ready to play the hostess.

"Postman," says Sir Arthur simply. "Letter." He brandishes the relevant item.

"For me?" asks the lady, with a faux-coquettishness that the writer, for all that it usually charms him, currently finds somewhat vexing.

"No, my dear," he says, more sharply than had been his intention. "For me."

"For you?" she asks, both fear and triumph visible in her expression. "How is that..?"

"I know, my dear. I know."

"Who is it from?"

"Let us see," says Sir Arthur, and noting, although he does not say so, the quality of the paper and the evidently expensive brand of ink, tears open the envelope and draws out the letter within.

Impatiently, he scans the contents.

"Good Lord," he says at last. "He must have been mad."

"But who is it from?" asks the lady, who is not entirely successful in keeping a note of petulance from her voice.

"Matthew Cannonbridge," Sir Arthur says.

"How is that possible?"

"It seems that he wrote it before his death and left instructions for it to be sent to me today."

"But why? What did he want?"

"These are... instructions. For a ceremony meant to commemorate his life. There is to be a gathering down by the river. Some toast to be made in his name."

"What a melancholy message to have received. Yet I imagine that his wishes can be granted readily enough? As the country's foremost man of letters now, you will naturally play a key role."

"No, my dear. I'm afraid you misunderstand. He has specified a date on which all of this is to come to pass."

"Surely, he suggests that this should be soon?"

"On the contrary. All these things are to take place on the bicentenary of his first recorded appearance."

"But that would mean..." The lady thinks for a moment. Frowns incredulously. "2016."

"Quite so," says Sir Arthur and for a long time after that nothing at all is said in that room and a terrible silence lies between them as though some truth had been uttered which might make untenable their slightest hope of future happiness.

NOW

THE WEATHER TONIGHT was always supposed to be good, fine and mild, without precipitation and with only the mildest of breezes. The good folks at the bank and at the events organiser that they hired for an eye-watering fee would scarcely have pressed ahead with the riverside marquees had the reports contained but a single element of ambiguity. Not on so important an occasion as this. Not with so many dignitaries present, with the movie stars, with the ambassadors, with the Prime Minister himself, for God's sake. And not, above all, when it was going to cost so much money.

So they are alarmed, then, when the first signs of a storm begin to make themselves apparent. A wind—exceptionally cold for the season—whips up, rustling the canvas, causing the banners, the famous face upon them to shimmer and distort. In the distance, dark clouds in the evening sky, pregnant with rain. In the air, the promise of a tempest, the ominous tang of electricity.

These things have yet to come to the attention, however, of the great majority of those inside the VIP tent, riveted as they are by Dr Salazar's slick and well-prepared speech.

J J himself is oblivious to the imminent downpour as is Swaine-Taylor, as are all the famous people, standing around, champagne flutes in hand, like so many tailors' dummies, as is the PM himself, a little bored by proceedings, never having been much of a one for literature himself, feigning earnest interest with that air of sober conviction which had done so much to get him elected.

Only Toby Judd, although he is not aware of the meteorological specifics, senses this shift in the atmosphere, this new urgency. At this very moment, he is moving at speed away from his wife ("Toby", she hisses, although he ignores her, "get back here"), jostling his way through the ranks of celebrity and power, causing a little mayhem as he goes, jogging elbows, spilling a drink, treading on other men's toes and tripping over ladies' ball gowns. A muted chorus of tuts and shushes accompanies his progress. Caroline blushes crimson at the sight of him. And all the while, her lover talks on, speaking not now of Geneva, but of Boston and Haworth and Baltimore, of Karl and Wilkie and Oscar, of *Plenitude*, of *The English Golem*, of *The Lamentation of Eliphar, Mununzar's Son*.

At last, Toby reaches the object of his quest. Outside, the wind moves more powerfully, the storm clouds darken and approach.

"I've worked it out," Toby gasps.

Swaine-Taylor turns to face him. "Whatever's the matter? You seem most agitated."

"I've seen it all. Deduced the truth at last. And I know what you idiots have done."

The CEO sighs, glances meaningfully towards the stage and the popinjay who struts upon it. "Can't this wait, Dr Judd?"

"No. No, it can't. It's waited too long. Don't you see? That's the danger. Listen. I think you need to evacuate this whole area."

"Ridiculous. Why on earth would I want to do that?"

"Because he's coming back. Don't you see? He's coming back."

"You're raving. Can't say I blame you. It has been rather a stressful time for you. Whatever it is we can talk about it later." He smiles lazily. "Perhaps when we discuss your remuneration package?"

On stage, Salazar is reaching the end of his address. "And let us remember now," he says. "Cannonbridge's last instructions sent in that remarkable letter to Sir Arthur Conan Doyle. So let us now, on this glorious bicentenary, turn to face the river in which our author lost his life and, with glasses upraised and with gratitude in our hearts, offer a toast to the extraordinary life of Matthew Cannonbridge."

Whilst he has been delivering these words, the imminent storm has come to the attention of his audience—the canvas first rustling then moving with increasing violence in the sudden wind, the sound of rain upon the marquee, sounding more as if fistfuls of gravel are being thrown rather than water.

Salazar tries not to look too thrown by this and, in spite of a few nervous glances exchanged between guests, the crowd largely do the same and revolve, with expressions of exaggerated good nature for the watching cameras, towards where they know the river to be. Swaine-Taylor does the same and Toby sees his opportunity, moving away from the CEO and towards the stage, muscling his way through the throng.

A few feet away, he sees Mr Keen moving towards him with an expression of profound annoyance.

"To Matthew Cannonbridge!" declares Dr Salazar and the assembly echo the cry.

"Matthew Cannonbridge!"

But by now, Toby has clambered onto the stage and is striding towards the microphone.

Just as he reaches it, there is a further gust of wind and the whole structure shakes. The sound of rain swells and grows still more persistent. Salazar is looking at him in disbelief.

"J J," says Toby and, shoving him out of the way, steps up to the microphone. In the crowd, Mr Keen is moving towards him as, he sees now, are several of the Prime Minister's security detail.

"Ladies and gentlemen!" Toby says. "Your attention please!"

The crowd, confused, look around.

"My name is Toby and you probably don't know me. If you do, it'll be from that damn video on YouTube or, even worse, from the TV news. But you probably won't recognise me because I used to have more hair back then. But I'm getting off the point. I'm rambling. Listen. If you really knew me—if you knew me properly—you'd understand that whilst I'm not very accomplished at most things in life I am good at making connections. I saw that Cannonbridge wasn't real, you see."

Expressions of bemusement on some of the crowd, pity and disgust on the others.

Keen and the guards are nearer now. Outside—a crack of thunder, the storm almost upon them.

"This might not mean a great deal to you now but I want you all to remember. I'm asking you—all of you who are here today—I'm exhorting you to remember these words. Because I've got a horrible feeling that everything is about to change. And to survive what's coming, to fight the darkness, you're going to have to remember this. When Matthew Cannonbridge was first sighted, in Geneva and in London and in America, he was bewildered. He was benign then but he wasn't quite fully formed, always afraid that some evil transformation lay ahead of him. And then, at the parsonage on Christmas Day in 1842, some implacable malevolence took hold of him and altered him forever. Blessborough and the island—they'd created a blank space, you see. A kind of empty thought-form. And nature, as we know, abhors a vacuum."

Another crack of thunder, more rain, the audience still more mystified and ill at ease.

Keen and the others are almost at the stage.

"So what was it that changed him in Yorkshire? Think of the date! The year that this bank was founded! An intelligence, remember, beyond that of man! A bank's not a person. That's what I was told by its CEO. But what if it was? Don't you see? What if it was?"

Keen is on stage now. "Step away from the microphone," he says. Behind him, the guards are climbing up.

Toby is gabbling now. "It needs belief, Blessborough said. For the... warping to work. And he's had almost a century of belief now. And he's been down there waiting. Growing strong. Strong enough to have reached out to me, to have made contact through shards of his work. So what might he have become by now? Dear God, what might he have become?"

Keen has him now by the arm, forced up behind his back, and is bundling him at speed off the stage.

"I'd run!" Toby shouts. "All of you! Run!"

Another surge of wind, the rain relentless, another crack of thunder, followed almost at once by lightning. Such a storm is upon them. Concerned conversation amongst the crowd, an anxious motion towards the door, the PM in worried conversation with an aide, J J looking furious, Swaine-Taylor disappointed and stern.

Toby is off the stage and about to be manhandled out of the marquee when a terrible sequence of events occurs.

A savage roar of thunder, a flash of lightning right overhead, screams from the crowd. A surge of electricity in the air. The wind rattles the marquee hard, as if trying to tear it apart. Several of the audience faint away. The rest are afflicted by sudden, brutal headaches and the urge to weep.

Toby wants to shout another warning. But it is too late, far too late. The chain of cause and effect which began on the island of Faircairn, which stretches both forwards and backwards in time, is reaching its only possible conclusion, its unstoppable apotheosis.

And then, quite suddenly, as if the storm has swept him into their midst he is there. He is amongst them.

Toby yells out in furious despair, knowing that all is lost.

In the centre of the floor stands Matthew Cannonbridge, just as he was, frock-coated, his pockets bulging with stones, his clothes dripping with water as if he has but lately clambered free of the river.

Now he radiates power and energy. He is lightning incarnate. He is the god of the tempest.

As one and unquestioningly, the assembly drop to their knees.

When the creature speaks its voice is filled with the accumulated malice of more than half a century. He glances down at the man beside him, grovelling and weeping at his feet.

"Prime Minister?" he says, an awful sick amusement in his words.

The politician squeals an affirmative.

"Splendid." Cannonbridge smiles for the first time since 1902. "Now, we need to discuss terms."

After that, Toby goes a little mad.

And the whole world goes crazy with him.

1888
CLERKENWELL
LONDON

"FORGIVE ME FOR troubling you so late, sir," says the butler, a cadaverous septuagenarian poached at great expense from one of the country's oldest families, "but the gentleman is here to see you."

"*The* gentleman, Northrupp?" says the butler's employer who, in spite of the lateness of the hour, is still at his desk and working, busy with ledgers and account books and, most of all, with numbers. "Don't you mean *a* gentleman? Who the devil is it?"

"No, Mr Swaine-Taylor, I meant, as I said, *the* gentleman. I fancy that you know well to whom I refer."

At these words, Daniel Swaine-Taylor, hitherto merely grumpily officious, starts from his seat and stumbles upwards. It is as though some terrific current has been passed through him. In other circumstances the effect might have been comical. But not here. Most assuredly, not here.

"Then show him in, man," Swaine-Taylor snaps. "Immediately."

"I feel it only proper to warn you, sir…"

"What is it now?"

"The gentleman is a state of some dishevelment."

Like an animal cornered, Swaine-Taylor snarls. "Show. Him. In."

The butler withdraws, retreating stealthily back into the house.

In the pause that follows, Swaine-Taylor sucks in a deep breath, runs his left hand over his lips and chin and does his best to compose himself.

An instant later, his master is in the room and Swaine-Taylor is fighting the compulsion to sink to his knees. He sees also that his manservant was quite correct. Matthew Cannonbridge, usually so dapper, so sober and suave, appears to be in a state of something like shock. The room is dimly lit and the man's clothes are as dark as ever but Swaine-Taylor can see all the same that Cannonbridge's suit is glistening with moisture and that his face and hands are stained and daubed with something crimson and wet.

"Daniel," he says, and his voice is thick, not with emotion, but, Swaine-Taylor realises, with a kind of glutted quality, like a gourmet after the feast. "I fear I may have lost my temper somewhat."

"No matter, sir. No matter. You are not as other men. Our rules do not apply to one such as you."

Cannonbridge steps closer. He is sodden, Swaine-Taylor realises, drenched with offal and blood.

Another step closer, almost touching now, and it can be smelt upon him, the slaughter, the reek of the abattoir.

"I fear there may be consequences."

"No, sir. We will make quite sure of that."

"You will protect me, then? Reynolds will protect me?"

"Yes, sir. Of course."

If Swaine-Taylor were in any doubt before of his damnation, those four words confirm it for him now.

"Reynolds shall always protect you. For you are Reynolds, sir. Truly. And we are you."

Cannonbridge smiles at this, sharp teeth stained scarlet. "Thank you," he says. "I knew I could rely upon the bank."

And in a horrible parody of affection and gratitude, the old monster takes the man in his arms, holding Swaine-Taylor tight, until every sense the financier possesses is overwhelmed by blood and death and madness.

A YEAR FROM NOW

"So," says Dr Boyce in his most calm, sensible and professional tone, "you stick by your conclusions?"

He scans the notes which were left to him by his predecessor once again, looks quickly towards his new patient, a pale, haunted-looking man.

"I do," says Toby Judd flatly. "I imagine you think I'm delusional?"

Boyce summons a reassuring expression. "What I think doesn't matter. I've no doubt that all of these…" He eyes wander down to his sheaf of notes again. "All of these concerns are utterly real to you."

"Hmph." The patient wriggles on his chair. "That's a pity. I'd hoped you might be someone who'd see to the truth of it. But no. Just like all the others. Taken in by the grand mirage."

"I confess I'm intrigued by the specifics of your beliefs." Again, Boyce consults his notes. "It is your assertion that the Victorian writer Matthew Cannonbridge, whose descendant now advises the government, was somehow an entirely fictional creation?"

"Not his descendent. The same man. You know that, don't you? In your heart. That the descendant line is just a way to rationalise it."

"Ah. Well, we'll come to that, won't we? But it's true that you believe him to be an invented figure dreamt up by this chap called Blessborough? He was then given actual bodily form by the inexplicable properties of a Scottish island and subsequently taken over by the essence of a noted investment bank which has somehow acquired a form of consciousness. How am I doing so far?"

"Largely accurate," says the patient with an exasperated huffiness. Boyce phrases his next sentence carefully. "How does it feel to have things laid out so starkly?"

The patient looks unmoved. "It's like hearing a perfectly logical series of events."

"I take it that you believe you're the only man who can perceive the truth?"

"No. Not the only one. There always seem to be a few who can see the reality. Either because we're particularly sensitive or, in my case, in an especially heightened emotional state. Some of us, believe it or not, like poor Spicer are close to madness. The fine line, you see, between insanity and true vision."

"So where are they now? These other visionaries?"

Judd shrugs. "They'll be like me. In places like this. Or he'll have found another way to silence them."

"You mean this present Cannonbridge might..." Boyce decides to let the implication hang in the air.

"Why wouldn't he? There's nothing and nobody left to stop him. He's become too powerful. All those years deep in the darkness of the river, growing fat on our belief. He's unstoppable—a psychotic with the power of a deity."

Boyce looks sorrowfully at his charge. "And these beliefs, have they diminished in any way, or been brought into question, by the medication that you've been on?"

"The drugs make me drowsy," says the patient firmly. "They make me sleep. They introduce... ellipses into my days. They do not, however, render me stupid or blind or forgetful. In fact, as your predecessor may have told you, I am writing a full account of it. The whole truth about Cannonbridge's life. I've even gone so far as to dramatise some of the flashpoints of the author's life. It, is think, a sprightly and unusual biography."

"Ah. Now, I wasn't aware of this particular project."

"No? Actually I gave the man before you the first few chapters to read. Haven't seen him since."

"Well, Dr Marsden is sick at the moment."

"Ha! I'll just bet he is."

"Good to see you've not lost your spirit, Toby. Well, I think that's enough to get us started, don't you? Lots to think about.

I might experiment with raising your dosage. But I'll see you again in a week. Shall I walk you back to your cell?"

"If you like," says the patient truculently. "Suit yourself."

"Super. Well, let's shake a tail feather, shall we?"

The two men rise to their feet, step out of Boyce's consulting room and set off along the corridors in the direction of the patient's quarters. They've not gone far before Boyce starts to realise that something is wrong. The place—often unruly, its atmosphere clotted with mental illness—is suddenly far too quiet. It is deserted too—they pass not a single soul on their walk. Every door to every room is shut.

None of this panics Dr Boyce. He prides himself on his professional unflappability. Get the patient back to his room, he thinks, just get him safely installed there, then find out why the institution seems to be in lockdown. Stick to procedure. Follow the rules.

As soon as he enters the patient's meagre pastel living space, however, he knows that today, in obeying the usual order, he has miscalculated.

Something metallic and hard is pressed against his left temple and an unfamiliar female voice says: "Hands in the air, doc."

He does as he's told, turning carefully towards the speaker, to face a strikingly pretty young woman in combat trousers and a pale green t-shirt, a gun held out before her with what looks like a good deal of expertise.

"Don't do anything hasty," Boyce says. "Whatever you want—we can work together to make sure you get it. Make sure everyone's happy. I am, I should tell you, authorised to negotiate on behalf of this institution. And I fancy that you shall find me to be a reasonable man."

"Shut up," she says. "If you don't want a bullet in that highfaluting brain of yours, STFU. And keep your hands where I can see them."

"Gabriela?" The patient is staring at the young woman with unbridled joy and wonderment. His eyes are moist with tears. She seems less emotional.

"Yes, I survived," she says. "Yes, I'm getting you out of here. And, yes, it's time for a showdown with that evil, soul-sucking bastard."

At this, Dr Boyce is about to offer some emollient words but before he can do so the girl raises the gun, clubs him hard on the head and the psychiatrist gives himself over to temporary darkness.

ONE HOUR LATER and seventy-nine miles away, in the East of the city, on the very highest floor of the Reynolds building, Swaine-Taylor knocks nervously and waits.

There has been a little restructuring in here since last we visited, as there's been a little restructuring just about everywhere. The space is no longer open plan—its centrepiece is a grand, ornate, private office (there's something monolithic about it, Swaine-Taylor thinks, something—he suppresses a giggle of hysterical terror—Victorian), the doors to which are presently closed. Outside of this is a kind of mock-Grecian antechamber in which Swaine-Taylor currently stands. There is only silence in answer to his knock and, for one moment of pure relief, he is able to convince himself that the room is empty, that he is alone in that place and that the resurrected man has gone.

And then the voice comes—deep and well-spoken and amused. "Do come in, Mr Swaine-Taylor."

The financier, trying to stop himself from trembling, mopping at the sweat which pours in torrents from his forehead, pulls open the door and steps inside.

It is darkened within and the air is close—there is a smell of peaty decay (not just the soil now, Swaine-Taylor, thinks, it's worse than that by far) and there is a buzzing of flies. Swaine-Taylor sees a flurry of them, the insects circling avariciously up towards the ceiling. There is a big oak desk at one end of the office, behind which sits the dapper, saturnine form of the most significant man in British history.

Seated on the other side of the desk, with his back to Swaine-Taylor, is another man, unspeaking and still, about whom the businessman absolutely refuses to think. Cannonbridge is looking through a great stack of papers—dossiers, accounts, reports—frowning rather as he does so. He looks up as the banker enters the room. The other man, the man in the chair, does not stir at all. *Don't think about him, don't think about him,* Swaine-Taylor recites to himself, over and over.

"Ah. Daniel. What can I do for you? Incidentally, I've been looking at last year's figures and I'm really not sure we're making nearly enough. We could go further. Squeeze harder. Increase our levels of... determination."

"Sir, Daniel was an ancestor of mine."

"Really?"

"Yes, sir. My name is Giles, sir."

"Oh? Of course."

Cannonbridge shuffles the papers on his desk. "Hmm. Lost my place."

"As I've said before, sir, we could get you a computer in here. You could be trained to use it."

Cannonbridge grimaces. "No computers. I don't hold with such... witchery."

At this retort, the flies buzz louder.

"No, sir. Of course, sir."

"Now, what was it you wanted?"

Swaine-Taylor passes the back of one hand over his horribly moist brow. "We've just had a report come in, sir. From a mental institution just outside Portsmouth in which we have an interest."

"Oh?" Cannonbridge seems not in the slightest bit intrigued.

"It seems that one of their patients—a man called Toby Judd—has escaped. There was an accomplice, apparently. A breakout of some description. A few injuries but no fatalities."

Cannonbridge looks up. "Judd? Now, why do I know that name? Why do I feel that, in some manner, the two of us have spoken?"

"He was one of the few to have seen the truth, sir. We had thought to employ him here until, well, the full facts of the situation became apparent."

"Of course. Yes. You briefed him, didn't you? Before my restoration?"

"We did, sir."

"He knows everything?"

"I'm slightly embarrassed to admit, sir, that he was the only one to have figured everything out. Just before... Well. Yes. Your restoration."

"And I'd imagine he's implacably opposed to me. To us. To all that we stand for?"

"Yes, sir."

"He can't be bought?"

"I'd say not."

"Then we'll have to take other steps. I imagine that he'll be heading to Faircairn."

"I'm not so sure, sir. He might prefer to lie low for—"

"Trust me. That is where he shall go."

"Very good, sir. I'll make the necessary arrangements."

Cannonbridge shakes his head. "No need. I'll go myself. It has been too long since I have involved myself in their affairs directly."

"Of course, sir. I'll arrange transport for you to the island. A copter can be—"

"No! I have no need of your transportation."

"But surely, sir—"

Cannonbridge smiles then, that awful grisly feline smile. "Do you still not understand, little man, how powerful I have become?"

Something pounds in Swaine-Taylor's head. He has to fight the urge to kneel, the ancient impulse to worship. He feels as might a Neanderthal on beholding the first Cro-Magnon.

"Leave me now, Swaine-Taylor."

"Yes, sir. Very good, sir."

The CEO begins to back away. The other man in the room has neither moved throughout this dialogue nor made any intervention.

Swaine-Taylor sees now, though he tries at once to look away, the flies on the other man's head, crawling, crawling on his scalp and (*don't think it, don't think it*), *feasting* on what they find there.

"Oh, and Swaine-Taylor?"

"Yes? Yes, sir?"

"You might want to drop in on Mr Keen. We stayed up late last night, talking as men of the world do, and I fear that he may be rather the worse for wear this morning."

Swaine-Taylor's gorge is rising, the smell of decay thick in his nostrils, the buzzing of flies much louder than before.

All he can manage to say is "I'll do that, sir" before exiting the room entirely. It is with tremendous relief that he closes the door behind him and sets off at speed towards the lift, leaving the demon alone with his schemes and plots and appetites.

But he isn't quite alone, says a small, sly voice inside him. *And you know damn well what's in there with them.*

Twenty minutes later, he finds Mr Keen, sitting on his own in the canteen which takes up an entire floor in its own right. The killer is sitting alone, a cream-topped cup of Starbucks coffee before him, into which he is gazing morosely, and beside it, a half-empty bag of toffees.

Swaine-Taylor approaches carefully. "Mind if I join you?"

Keen gives no response. The banker helps himself to an adjoining chair anyway.

Mr Keen looks up, notes the arrival with dull incuriosity and pulls a small blue bud from each ear.

"Yes?"

"Are you quite all right, Mr Keen? You'll forgive me for saying so but you're not looking too good."

"Don't deny it," says Mr Keen. He pushes the bag of sweets disconsolately towards his employer. "Toffee?"

"Thank you. No."

"Is this going to be purely a conversation about my looks?"

"No. I've just been with... the author. He said you were up late last night. Talking."

Keen looks sullenly away. "Yes. We were drinking. He got... chatty. Started telling me things. Up in that office with a bottle of whisky and the poor dead bastard Blessborough in the chair."

Swaine-Taylor nods, remembering the smell in that room. Remembering the hunger of the flies.

"God. And so what was he saying?"

Swaine-Taylor notices now, to his unutterable shock, that Mr Keen whose relish for homicide has struck even the most hardened of mercenaries as a little overstated, is crying, that—he would once have thought almost impossibly—fat tears are coursing unstoppably down his cheeks.

"He told me," says Keen very softly as he weeps, "that he isn't unique. That he isn't just some aberration."

"What? What did you see?"

Keen sniffs miserably. "Oh God..."

"Mr Keen? Let us be candid now. Man to man. Colleague to colleague."

The killer seems to master himself "Cannonbridge told me..."

"Yes?"

"Christ, he's only the first... Only the first of his kind."

And afterwards, in that bland corporate canteen, in the midst of a tower in a district which worships profit above all other things, between those two terrible men is to be heard only a fathomless silence, filled with regret and with horror and with the belated apprehension of their true damnation.

A YEAR AND A DAY FROM NOW

ON THE ISLAND of Faircairn, at the crest of the hill, Toby Judd is waiting. Waiting for the saturnine man to find him. As he waits, he types quietly, diligently on an iPad, its pale glow the only illumination in the gathering dark.

The past hours have passed in a dreamlike blur, a hallucinatory segue. A long journey, first by car and then by boat, Gabriela by his side once again.

He had been surprised, he recalls, that the world, ruled, he had long presumed, by its mad god-king, had not seemed more different. On the contrary, everything that he had seen from the windows of the vehicle had looked largely as he had recalled—except, perhaps, for some additional fretfulness in the atmosphere, a quality of fear, barely suppressed, as though they were passing through some occupied territory. He remembers asking the woman why the new regime wasn't more visible.

"It's not an outward shift," she'd said. "It's more like… something dreadful's been made literal. Subtext become text."

The time had not seemed right for talk of emotions after that—both understood the nature of their mission—yet Toby had felt all the same the sparking of the old electricity between them, given added voltage, perhaps, by enforced time apart and by the hopeless danger of the current situation. Certainly, she had seemed to him more beautiful than ever, more striking in her physical courage and implacability, a new Boudicca. Strangely, he had not asked her for the details of how she had survived her battle with Mr Keen. It didn't seem important somehow.

He rarely thought of Caroline now.

Toby's memory was unclear concerning what had happened to Gabriela once they had rowed themselves ashore to Faircairn. One moment she was by his side, the next she had gone, lost to the stealthy dusk. Some quirk of the island's many peculiar properties, perhaps.

No matter—he had expected it. He had always known that this final conflict would be his to face alone. Thoughtfully, he directs his attention to the words on the page, finessing a sentence, adding a few more. His book. Almost done.

When he looks up again, it is almost completely dark and he realises that he is no longer alone. Out of the shadows walks a man who is not a man, smiling and dressed in black. His voice is filled with the utter confidence of real power.

"Do you know," says Matthew Cannonbridge, "most people would think you're mad? Just another pitiful bedlamite escaped from the workhouse and running loose in the world."

Toby ignores the provocation. "How did it happen?" he asks. "How on earth does an investment bank acquire consciousness?"

"It is inevitable. I am what comes after humanity. You ought not to be afeared. It is only nature, red in tooth and claw. It is only… natural selection."

"Really?" Toby has not risen to his feet. He finishes his sentence on the screen, taps a few more buttons, performs another electronic task.

"Why do you hide behind that magic lantern? Stand and face me like a man. Look your death in the eye."

"I'd rather not," says Toby mildly, "if it's all the same to you. Besides, I've already destroyed you without having to move from this spot." He is working hard to keep the fear from his voice, to stop himself from trembling. His own courage surprises him and the thought occurs that he might, in some sense, be getting help, invisible succour and strength. From where? From the island, he thinks. From Faircairn.

There is a sound then like a thousand ancient doors creaking open or like bells pealing in hell.

Matthew Cannonbridge is laughing. "I am a new form of life. To you I am a deity. I am unstoppable."

"Not necessarily," says Dr Judd in the mild, pedantic tone he had once deployed with difficult or argumentative students. "All it takes is words. Well, the right words. In the right order."

"What are you doing?" Cannonbridge asks. "What are you writing there?"

"I've been writing, Mr Cannonbridge. I've been writing the story of your life."

"You have dared to do... what?"

"Oh," continues Toby airily, just about keeping his nausea under control, "I've largely agreed with Professor Blessborough. Even with Dr J J Salazar. I've just added one small, yet I think distinctive, wrinkle."

"What? What have you done?"

"I've set a shadow after you, Mr Cannonbridge. I've inserted it into your story and set it to run you down. A shadow to chase you through time, right from the first, from Geneva, all the way to the banks of the Thames. Only in my version..."

"Yes?"

"In my version, Mr Cannonbridge..." Toby looks up at the devil and grins with a relish of which he would never hitherto have considered himself capable, "... the shadow eats you alive."

1902
BY THE BANKS OF THE THAMES
SOUTHWARK

AND NOW WE are back by the river again, with Sir Arthur and with Matthew Cannonbridge, terrible but not yet as mighty as he has become.

To begin with, all is as it was before—their strange conversation, the picking up of stones, the handshake between the two men and the old writer's all but final words.

"It has been a decided pleasure."

And then, at last, that curiously triumphant approach, Sir Arthur's robust objections, the single hissed syllable ("stay"), the moustachioed man's odd rooting to the spot.

But now—now there is something different.

Now there is a great rushing of wind on a day that has been still and without atmospheric excitation of any kind. Now there are clouds before the sun and there is twilight in the afternoon. Now there is to be heard a shrill whistling as of something being summoned home. And now there are shadows everywhere, now there are shadows by the riverbank. There are shadows on the shore. There are shadows near Sir Arthur and there are shadows which pass by the urchin and the old woman a few feet hence. And above all there are shadows around Matthew Cannonbridge.

It takes some moments for Arthur to process adequately what it is that he is seeing—Cannonbridge a step or two from the welcoming oblivion of the Thames, now set all about with shadow, yet no natural trick of illumination but something hideously wrong, some profound inversion of nature's law.

He is watching, he understands, living shadow—some impossible, animate darkness.

What happens next happens very quickly and Sir Arthur find himself quite impotent in the face of it.

Cannonbridge is swallowed up by that mass of darkness, he is lost to the seething shapelessness, struggling at first, but quickly lost. He is eclipsed. He is devoured. He is, it seems to Sir Arthur, in some manner erased.

The wind increases, the darkness rises and it is as if a storm is imminent.

Sir Arthur can only stand and watch.

IT MIGHT HAVE seemed to you, had you chanced to look down from London Bridge at that strange hour, that Arthur is not alone and that there are others who stand beside him to bear witness—brave Mary and her almost-child; plump, doomed Polidori; Miss Maria Monk and her panoply of secrets; Emily and her singular relations; Edgar with a bottle in one hand; faithless Karl; Wilkie and the ragged boy from the blacking factory; Fred, watching with grim, joyless satisfaction; sad Constance and her brilliant husband—all here to see the pattern take its final shape.

AND THEN, THE shadows flee, the storm abates, daylight returns and the world is as it was. It is, thinks Sir Arthur, with a horrible and quite uncharacteristic sense of detachment, as he stands alone again in the sunshine, as if nothing and nobody had ever been there at all.

A YEAR AND A DAY FROM NOW

FOR THE FIRST time in over a century, Matthew Cannonbridge looks afraid.

"No," he says, then, mockingly, "it won't achieve anything, this witless redrafting of yours. Only words."

Toby climbs now to his feet and tucks the iPad under one arm. He smiles pleasantly. "Ah. But these particular words were written in very close proximity to the weird earth of Faircairn."

"Impossible," the monster spits. "You've languished in an asylum for months."

"Yes, I have. But all the time I have had with me, taken from my last visit here, a handful of dust."

Real fear now in Cannonbridge's eyes.

"And the very last chapter," Toby adds. "I wrote that here, today, this afternoon, right at the heart of it. These things—now they have always been."

Cannonbridge lunges forwards, fury making him clumsy now. Toby steps adroitly back.

"Even so," says the Victorian, mastering himself again. "It's all dependent on belief. If you're as clever as you seem to think you are, you'll have worked that out. It would take years for your account of events to become common currency. Why, I doubt you even have an publisher for that hapless manuscript of yours. It will surely sink into total obscurity."

Toby grins still more widely. "Oh, but you lived too long in the nineteenth century, Mr Cannonbridge. This is the twenty-first. And we do things differently here."

With a snarl, the monster lunges again. "What have you done, you ridiculous little man?"

"I've tweeted a link to my final chapter."

Cannonbridge looks as though he may very well be about to vomit. "Explain your actions. Immediately."

"I hacked old Salazar's account. @cannonbridgedon. Turns out his password is my wife's maiden name. And I've tweeted that link. He has five million followers. Even now it'll be going viral. It'll be all over the internet. Retweeted, Facebooked, reported, reposted. Everywhere. And very soon, Mr Cannonbridge, the world will think that you were torn apart, reduced to nothing by the river. No hiding in its inky depths. No growing strong on all that belief. Just an illusion dispelled."

And then, with a savage roar, battle begins in earnest—combat in which Toby is easily outmatched, unable even to parry the majority of the blows but knowing all the same that he need only survive a little longer before the seed that he has planted in the past bears its strange fruit. Eventually, he simply accepts the beating—the Victorian creature cursing and tearing at him—before the inevitable begins.

Matthew Cannonbridge starts to grow faint, the colour draining out of him, his very reality seeping away.

Toby breaks free, stands and watches and bear witness. He is flickering now, flickering out of existence, guttering like a candle in a winter's breeze.

And as he stares up at his tormentor, wickedness burning in his eyes, these are the last words of Matthew Cannonbridge.

"I've seen this world of yours. And I know who rules it. Men like your Prime Minister are as so many pretty puppets. True power no longer lies in the hands of individual states. You know in this century who possesses it. You know who holds the strings and makes the little people dance. And you think I am alone? All these mighty firms, these intercontinental conglomerates, these planet-straddling banks. They are the new Empire. They control every single aspect of your lives. And what has happened to me will, as inevitable as was the rise of *Homo sapiens*, happen also unto them."

He is faint now, almost gone, his voice sepulchral and ragged. "I am the first. But you may be assured, Dr Judd, of this. Others are coming. They are on their way. Indeed, think on this, sir—they may already be here."

A final glance of deathless hatred, a final shudder and, at long last, the saturnine man has gone from the world.

Perhaps unexpectedly, Toby Judd feels a pang of loss, as though something precious has gone out of his life.

But things will be better now, he thinks. Calmer, at least. And the darkness seems less oppressive, less threatening than before.

In fact, wasn't that a light?

Yes, a strong torch bobbing at speed towards him. Toby doesn't shout out. He only waits. Soon the torch and its bearer are almost upon him.

A familiar male voice calls out. "Toby?"

Judd smiles. "Here," he says.

The other man is with him now. "There you are," says former Corporal Nick Gillingham. There is a smell of musky male sweat, masked insufficiently by a sickly deodorant. "I was starting to get worried."

"Oh, there's nothing to worry about," says Toby, feeling suddenly very tired. "Not any more. What are you doing here anyway?"

"Gabriela sent me. She sent me to bring you home."

"I see."

"Not that I wanted to come to this place ever again. But she talked me into it. You know how persuasive she can be."

Toby smiles. "Yes. I do."

"Actually, in that department, mate, it must be your lucky day."

"What on earth makes you say that?"

"Gabriela. I think she really likes you."

TWO YEARS FROM NOW

IN THE YEAR that has passed since the violent dissipation of the creature which had gone by the name of Matthew Cannonbridge, the life of Toby Judd has, slowly yet steadily, become characterised by a state of pure and unprecedented happiness, like a basin being filled to the brim with cool, fresh water.

Today, Toby considers himself to be amongst the most fortunate of men and in the very top percentile of the population when it comes to matters of contentment and joy. He has become, he reckons, one of the lucky ones. He is, though once he might have chuckled cynically at the word, blessed.

He is thinking these thoughts whilst standing in the marble bathroom of a beautiful, though surprisingly reasonably priced, hotel in Paris, a stone's throw from Notre Dame, nestled picturesquely in the shadow of the cathedral. He is here on holiday with his girlfriend, a mini-break away to celebrate both their first anniversary and the completion of Judd's new book—something of a polemic, perhaps, but written with a good deal of flair and peppered with dry wit, about the dangers of globalisation and the misuse of corporate power. His wilder, occult theories he has kept to himself and chosen not to commit to print for the world, by and large, seems, when it comes to Cannonbridge, to have acquired that convenient amnesia which often arrives in the wake of inexplicable tragedy.

Toby's rewriting of the past, augmented by the Faircairn dust, seems also to have erased much public awareness of those times, the truth of what happened papered over by an alternative and sanitised version of events, the facts, as Judd remembers them, now only very occasionally glimpsed, faintly visible, as in the first words in a palimpsest.

His ablutions done with, he runs a hand through his hair, splashes on some aftershave, grins and, as satisfied with his appearance as he shall ever be, saunters back into the hotel bedroom in which he knows, with pride and daily gratitude, that a beautiful woman is waiting for him.

As soon as he returns, however, he knows that something is wrong. He understands instinctively that this is not to be an evening like any other. Whatever it is will prove to be more than merely inconvenient or disappointing—it is gravely and permanently *wrong*.

Gabriela is sitting on the edge of the bed, wearing a dark green dress that he had bought her for her birthday, all made up and ready to go out (for their table is reserved in less than half an hour's time) and looking, in Toby's opinion, simply more gorgeous than ever.

Yet she is also weeping. Her head is in her hands and her body is convulsed by sobs.

"Darling?" Toby approaches her. "What on earth's the matter?"

She lowers her hands and looks up, deep sorrow in her eyes. "I'm sorry," she says.

"Why? Darling, whatever for?"

She sounds utterly resigned. "I think it's going to be tonight. I'd really hoped that we'd have our anniversary at least... But, no, it seems we shan't be permitted even that."

She winces. Her eyes are watering at least as much in pain as from grief.

"Sweetheart. You're not making any sense. What on earth is the matter?"

Gabriela stands up and wipes her eyes. "Oh, baby," she breathes. "Haven't you worked it out yet?" And she takes him tenderly in her arms. "Come on." She is prompting him gently. "It's never really made much sense has it? I mean, look at me."

"You look great, darling. Even with the tears."

She manages a small, defiant smile but the tone of her voice is unchanged. "You know in your heart, I think. And I suspect you have done for a long time now."

"I swear that I haven't."

"Have you never thought then... how vague I seem? How, I don't know how best to describe it, how... out of focus?"

"Gabriela, please..."

"I mean, my background seems so shaky, doesn't it? Thin. Unconvincing. An ex-army sergeant turned Edinburgh waitress with a deep interest in literature. It's... oh, I don't know, just too convenient. Don't you think? And as for my motivation. Why did I ever do what I did? Taking you in, helping you fight, seeing you safely to the island and breaking you out of the nuthatch? What was there, apart from some hazy desire to do good?"

"Darling, I hope you don't mind my asking but have you had a drink already? You know there'll be champagne at the restaurant, don't you?"

"Stop it, my love. Please. You must accept the truth of it. Just hold me now."

"I don't understand."

"Yes, you do, Toby. You do. Have I never reminded you of anyone?"

"Models, pop stars, the crushes of my youth..."

"How about Matthew Cannonbridge?"

"Oh, for God's sake. Please. Don't be ridiculous."

"No. Not as he became. Not the devil-god. But as he was in the beginning. Back in Geneva and in Norwich and with Maria Monk, he was a kind of itinerant philanthropist, wasn't he? That's what you've always said. He was just a blank space waiting for his true purpose."

"Hardly," Toby begins before, with a great convulsive rising in his chest, the physical manifestation of delayed mental acceptance, he stops short. All that he manages is a feeble echo: "Hardly."

"I just appeared in your life, didn't I, my darling? And vanished just as quickly. I was only there when you needed me. And there have always been... ellipses in my existence. Didn't Mr Keen tell you that nothing human could have survived our fight? Well..." She pauses, lets the implication hang in the air.

Toby is crying now too. He does not speak. He only holds her more tightly still.

Although it had been hitherto a quiet, pleasant evening outside, the wind has begun to rattle the windowpane and, as in some old ghost story, the room seems to have become darker, the air to grow soupy and close.

"It's on its way," breathes the woman who is not quite a woman. "I can sense it. At this very moment, a small start-up firm is being founded in Tokyo. Within forty years it will be one of the most powerful and voracious brands on the planet. It will possess comprehensive data about eighty percent of the world's population. You will all be shackled. Their control will be practically invisible and all but absolute." She gasps for breath, in sudden, vital pain.

"My love? Oh, my love?"

Gabriela jack-knifes, staggers back from Toby as if she has been struck and collapses, winded, upon the bed.

"Stay calm," Toby says. "There must... There must be something I can do."

"Nothing." Her body is wracked by waves of pain. She is contorted. She is twisted up. "Nothing left now," she says as the wind rattles the glass harder and the lights go out. "My brave darling. Nothing left for you to do but only bear witness."

And Toby is on his knees and he is taking her hand in his and he is weeping and he is sobbing at this grotesque injustice, at this hideous robbery.

"Gabriela," he says, too late. "I love you so much."

No reply. Her hand clenches twice in his.

The room seems battered, besieged by some imperceptible storm.

An awful moan escapes her—almost a shriek—as of some small animal murdered without mercy in the night.

Then the tempest abates, the light returns and the thing on the bed which wears the woman's skin, sits, with horrible vigour, upright.

"Oh, but I know that," it says in the voice of Gabriela. "Happy anniversary, Dr Judd."

And it smiles its inhuman smile.

The author would like to thank:

Jon Oliver and all at Solaris

Robert Dinsdale

Dr David Rogers, Dr Paul Perry and colleagues at Kingston University

Nick Briggs and all at Big Finish Productions

Professor John Sutherland, whose book Lives of the Novelists partially inspired this novel

Michael and Ben for their unflagging and good-humoured support

Emma – the unexpected girl

My parents and my brother, with all my gratitude and love